# COLIN WEEKES
# THE HAND OF FATIMA

SilverWood

Published by SilverWood Books 2012
www.silverwoodbooks.co.uk

Copyright © Colin Weekes 2012

The right of Colin Weekes to be identified as the author of this work
has been asserted by him in accordance with
the Copyright, Designs and Patents Act 1988.

All rights reserved. No part of this publication may be reproduced,
stored in a retrieval system, or transmitted in any form or by any means,
electronic, mechanical, photocopying, recording or otherwise,
without prior permission of the copyright holder.

This is a work of fiction. Names, characters, places and incidents either are
products of the author's imagination or are used fictitiously.
Any resemblance to actual events or locales or persons, living or dead,
is entirely coincidental.

ISBN 978-1-78132-043-3

British Library Cataloguing in Publication Data
A CIP catalogue record for this book is available from the British Library

Set in Sabon by SilverWood Books
Printed on responsibly sourced paper

# THE HAND OF FATIMA

# Chapter 1

It was an insane decision. Wolfe suddenly became aware of his recklessness as the eerie shape of the North Sea oil rig loomed ghost-like through the swirling mist. A gusting wind howled mournfully around the maze of tangled steel, increasing his isolation as he wrestled with the rudder control in the helicopter's descent to the landing pad below. Only the urgency of the situation and the continuing bad weather finally convinced him to attempt a dawn landing. In the remoteness of the skeletal structure below, a stricken oilman was praying for release from pain.

"Looks like a burst appendix," the rig doctor had said. "Must get him to hospital as soon as possible."

Wolfe eased the control clockwise, steering the machine into the screaming gale, approaching the massive steel derrick from the leeward side. A group of workers wearing oilskins and carrying a stretcher appeared. Wolfe flipped the loud hailer above his head and shouted to the gesturing men.

"Clear the landing pad – I don't want to be up here all day."

The rig men retreated hastily as the Sikorsky, bucking

wildly in the storm, continued to descend until it was twenty metres from the platform. A surging gust slammed broadside into the helicopter, pushing it dangerously close to the flaming gas burn-off funnel. A sudden fear gripped Wolfe as he jerked hard on his control levers, sending the machine veering crazily away towards the heaving grey waves, the landing gear clipping the sea. He dragged back on the elevators, lifting the helicopter into a looping turn around the rig as the intercom crackled in his headset.

"This is Piper rig operator. Are you cancelling the landing?"

Wolfe took a long gasping breath, the adrenalin pumping through his body like an electric shock. He thumbed his transmit button.

"Hello, Piper, don't write me off just yet. I shall fly straight in, at landing pad level. When I touch down, load me up quickly. I want to get out of here before it gets any worse."

"Affirmative." The answer grated in his ear. "We're ready!"

Wolfe kept the machine hovering in the gale, holding back until there was a momentary lessening of force, then opened his throttle and surged towards the platform.

"Jesus," cried one of the gaping men. The group dived to the steel decking as the helicopter lifted sharply upwards over the landing pad and bounced to a juddering halt, its rotors rocking furiously.

"Hurry it up," Wolfe yelled above the storm.

More willing hands than necessary carried the suffering oilman to the vibrating machine, lowering the horizontal form behind the pilot.

"Strap him down well," shouted Wolfe, grinning at his tethered passenger.

"Don't worry, Geordie. We are going home now."

The desperately sick man smiled weakly as the machine lifted away from the rig, rising high above the steel superstructure before turning into a westerly course for the mainland. The remaining workers, rain heavy on their faces, stood clutching the metal stanchions watching the Sikorsky vanish into the gloom.

Inside the observation bridge, the chief engineer turned to the rig boss. "I thought for one bloody moment that the lunatic was going to crash into us."

"Yeah! A bit of a shock meeting Jack for the first time, but a handy guy to have around occasionally," the rig boss said.

"Bloody dangerous," the engineer grumbled. "What's his problem then?"

"Dunno. He's a loner, engine failure in Angola. Lost two buddies. Blames himself."

The engineer shaded his eyes as he watched the helicopter gathering height in the distance.

"Nursing his grief is he? Met blokes like him before. Probably got a bloody death wish. Just a matter of time I expect!"

The rig boss nodded, "Maybe you're right, though I don't think the poor guy on the stretcher would agree with you."

Thirty minutes later the Sikorsky cruised into sight of the battered north-east coast, with Wolfe finding better visibility in the light rain. The North Berwick radio mast appeared on the port side and, checking his altimeter, he lowered the machine to eight hundred feet until the small fishing port of Musselburgh showed through the fragmented cloud. Wolfe pushed long blonde hair from his eyes and spoke into the headset requesting clearance for Edinburgh Hospital.

The answering static echoed back. "We have been alerted, Sikorsky Seven. Everything is ready for you."

The old castle perched on the black crag materialised from the mist as Wolfe made a ninety degree starboard turn directly above Princes Street and a long circling descent over the dual carriageway, towards Lauriston Place. The groups of poplars on the hospital perimeter shivered as the helicopter skimmed downwards and landed on the cordoned off ambulance area in front of the stone building. A team of white-coated hospital staff pressed forward, heads held low beneath the threshing rotor blades.

Wolfe uncoupled his safety harness and stretched to revive the circulation in his cramped legs, briefly touching the outstretched hand of the oilman as his passenger was transferred to a wheeled stretcher and hurried away. Wolfe cut the motor and climbed stiffly out of the cockpit.

He leaned against the machine, breathing heavily. The fine drizzle landing on his face was keeping away the weariness but his hands were shaking slightly with relief.

"You look a bit done in, old boy." The remaining doctor smiled reassuringly at him.

"Missed my breakfast this morning," answered Wolfe.

"Follow me," the white-coated man said as he turned and walked towards the main annexe. Wolfe dropped obediently into step behind him until they entered the carpeted reception area.

"One moment," the doctor said, leaving abruptly.

Wolfe sagged into a chair and looked vacantly around at the information posted upon the clinical white walls.

"Take these," the voice said, as the hand proffered a

glass of water and three small pills.

"Wolfe sniffed, "What are they?"

"Only tranquillisers – won't affect your concentration."

Wolfe rose. "No, thanks all the same, Doc. I thought you were offering me a brandy." He turned and walked wearily back through the annexe.

Overlooking the sandy curve of St Brelade's Bay was a rambling colonial-style mansion occupying one of the finest views on the Island of Jersey. It had been the permanent home of George Wolfe for almost fifteen years since the massive financial penalties imposed on him by the Inland Revenue had caused his separation from the mainland. A man in his early fifties with neatly trimmed brown hair and calculating green eyes, he looked at least a decade older than his brother, Jack. The supply of weapons around the world had made George Wolfe a rich man, selling to all countries in conflict and charging extreme prices for delivery.

This cold grey morning he stared dispassionately at the little boats tossing at anchor in the choppy sea beneath his window. For the first time in his varied negotiations a situation had arisen that he was unable to control. The phone jangled incessantly and remained unanswered. A horse and trap clip-clopped beyond the well-tended gardens without raising his interest. He turned to a map on the wall, tracing his finger along the West African coast. Next to the map, a calendar was hanging on the wall. George circled the 6th June 2003. The date his daughter had disappeared. He abruptly thrust his hands deep into his hip pockets, gloomily dwelling on events in that part of the world. A faint beam of sunlight penetrated the wispy clouds outside and the shadows moved fleetingly across the map. The man sighed then turned and opened the large patio window fronting the sea. A number of broad-winged gulls sailed gracefully above, catching the upward currents of air in their silent passage and a solitary bird cruised so close he could have almost reached out and caught it. The strained expression slowly left his face and he smiled. "Of course! Jack!" he breathed, then grabbed for the phone.

Late the following afternoon Jack Wolfe arrived at the small airstrip on Jersey. Catching an overnight train from Edinburgh to Nottingham, he hitched a lift with an old army colleague flying out from the East Midlands Airport. The planes were only half full before the holiday season commenced and the pilot from Dan Air was only too pleased to renew an acquaintance with an old chum. The forty-minute flight was over almost before the memories of the old days returned and Wolfe bade the grey-haired captain a nostalgic farewell, promising to make contact again.

The telephone call from George Wolfe had been terse and disquieting. "Can you get over here, Jack? I can't tell you why on the phone, too involved, but it is a matter of extreme urgency. I need you here now."

It was with mounting apprehension that Jack Wolfe hired the car to drive the few miles to St Brelade's Bay, for there was normally nothing in his brother's character that broached defeat. Jack still remembered a camping holiday they had spent together years before and a tremendous fist fight that had occurred. The elder brother, in his early twenties and with a distinct weight advantage, had severely beaten him and scars of the battle were still faint above his eyebrows. Jack could not recall the reason for the fight but the brutal thrashing he would never forget.

George Wolfe also learned a valuable lesson that day. When your opponent is down, make sure he stays there. The blood-spattered younger brother refused to acknowledge defeat and staggered relentlessly back to his feet until George Wolfe, fear giving way to panic, clubbed him to the ground with an oak staff. It was only the intervention of a game warden that prevented murder being committed that day and the rift between the brothers had never completely healed.

Jack Wolfe drove the vehicle through the wrought iron gates with the obscure family crest and turned into the driveway leading to the house. He pulled a face. George Wolfe had always been the same; the trappings of wealth and identity were important factors in his life. Everything had a price, but for a shrewd man with an indifference to others, he often paid more than good value for his possessions.

The white limestone chippings on the curving drive ground noisily under the wheels as the car scrunched to a halt in front of the pillared entrance. George Wolfe had always enjoyed the early warning system of the loose stones. It gave him time to adjust to visitors and an advantage with his greeting. He met his younger brother at the top of the steps.

"Jack! After all these years – it's good to see you again."

His handshake was firm and the manner affable.

"Hello, you old rat," his brother smiled in return. "You've put on a few pounds since I last saw you."

George Wolfe forced a laugh. "Yes, I wish I were as slim as you," he said, pumping the proffered hand. He placed his arm affectionately around his brother's shoulders as they turned into the house.

"Come inside, Jack. It's beautiful here in summer, but

this is not the best time of year for sight-seeing."

They entered the spacious hallway with the alabaster busts of Roman emperors looking down from Corinthian columns and crossed into a wood-panelled study.

"Reminds me of a museum I visited once," the younger man remarked.

"Just part of my collection, Jack. I couldn't resist buying them."

"Yes, I remember you were a hoarder when we were boys."

"And you spent your time studying martial arts. Where did that get you?" George Wolfe retaliated.

His brother grinned. "In quite a bit of trouble from time to time."

"Yes, I don't need reminding. Are you still a freelance pilot?"

"It's a way of life," the younger man answered.

"You should have married, Jack. You had plenty of chances. It would have settled you down."

Jack Wolfe stared hard at his brother. "As much as I'm enjoying the conversation, just tell me, George, what the hell am I doing here?"

The elder man made a conscious effort to regain his composure, a look of uncertainty on his face. He turned to a well-stocked drinks cabinet at the window. "Is it still brandy?"

Jack nodded, and accepted the glass without thanks, rolling the heavy crystal between his hands. His brother picked up a silver-framed photograph from a desk and studied it intently for a few seconds, before handing it to the younger man. It was a picture of a pretty girl in her teens, with long blonde hair, astride a palomino pony.

"Image of her mother," Jack said.

"In more ways than one. Suzanne has inherited her mother's waywardness."

The younger brother sat down in a leather armchair. This room was the hub of George Wolfe's empire and the various maps on the walls were decorated with flags and lines of troop movements.

"I see you are still pedalling death and destruction," Jack said flatly.

The other man's jaw tightened but he remained silent.

"Sorry, none of my business. Forget I said it. What do you mean about Suzanne inheriting her mother's waywardness?"

"Well, that's part of the reason I asked you here."

George reached into a manila envelope producing another photograph. It was of two men. One was clad in a long classical jelaba of the African people, the other in military uniform. The strong features and the dark hair under the braided cap were undoubtedly that of the leader of the Libyan people, Colonel Muammar Gaddafi.

Jack looked up enquiringly and George answered the question in his brother's eyes. "Yes, I supply arms to Libya and Iraq. If they want to blow the world apart that's their problem. I'm only the salesman."

"A man of scruples," Jack said sarcastically.

The older brother pointed to the robed figure standing beside the Libyan colonel. "This is Achmet Mansoor, the arms buyer for the Gaddafi regime. We had a good business arrangement for some time until Mansoor decided to go it alone. I taught him everything about buying and where to sell the goods. He often stayed here with me, accepting my hospitality and all the time plotting against me."

The younger brother leaned forward, intrigued.

"Well, as you know," continued George, "normally transactions across international borders are always paid for before delivery. Nobody is going to fight a battle on credit, especially if the goods belong to me."

"Prudent!" said Jack.

"Of course, but supplying arms with regular payment made me a soft touch and the Libyan regime had always been totally honest with me. Mansoor used that consideration and ordered a large consignment of small artillery and ground-to-air missiles, which are bloody hard to obtain at any time. I received a banker's draft and authorised the deal. The draft subsequently vanished from my office. By the time I realised what was happening, Mansoor had re-routed the goods and transferred them to a Japanese ship in the Gulf."

"How much did you lose?" enquired the younger man.

"Everything worth having. Mansoor took Suzanne with him."

"Kidnapped?" said Jack incredulously.

"I wish that were the case. She went willingly."

For a full thirty seconds neither man spoke, the circumstances rendering silence. The phone jangled them back to reality. The elder brother took the receiver off its rest and placed it on the table, disconnecting its clamour.

Jack Wolfe had an uneasy feeling and it suggested involvement. "Why am I here, George?" The question was abrupt.

The older man emptied his glass in a gulp. "It's your territory, Jack."

"What is?"

"Africa, the Congo, all that. You speak French and Arabic and you spent seven years in the army. What was your motto? Seek and Destroy. If anyone can find Mansoor, it's you."

"What makes you think I should want to? I have no argument with him and if I did trace Mansoor I am not going to punish him. There are laws against that you know."

"My God, Jack." There was a note of desperation in the older brother's voice. "You are my best hope. I don't want Mansoor. You were always Suzanne's hero. She idolised you. I just want her back. She would never have left with Mansoor if she had known he cheated her father." His lower lip quivered. "Help me out on this. You can name your price and I swear I will never ask you for anything again."

Jack sniffed. "Everything comes down to money with you, doesn't it? I need to think. Leave me in peace for a while."

Exactly an hour later George cautiously opened the door to his study carrying a silver tray and a pot of black coffee. His brother, deep in thought, was staring at the map of the African continent on the panelled wall. George poured out a cup and put it quietly in Jack's hand. The younger man sipped carefully without taking his eyes from the map. "OK George, what leads do we have?"

"You'll do it then?"

"I never said that."

"But you will help – I knew you would never let me down."

"Let's get something straight," the younger man said. "I am not thinking about you. If I can be useful in finding Suzanne it's because of what she meant to me in earlier days."

"As God is my witness I shall make it up to you," George said.

His brother smiled. "I think God understands you have

an integrity problem, but there is something you should know."

George peered anxiously at his brother.

"I'm not the same person I was ten years ago," said Jack. "The truth is I'm an old hack helicopter pilot and regular work cracks me up. I take all the rotten jobs no one else wants because when I am not working I spend my leisure time in solitary confinement looking into a bottle."

George sighed. "You're still my only chance and I do have a definite lead. After Suzanne left, I went through her things and found this." He passed a crumpled telegram form triumphantly to his brother like a man playing a winning card.

"*My darling Danielle*," Jack read aloud. "*Arriving Tangier soon with a friend. Lots to tell you. Suzanne.*" He stared at his older brother. "Who is this Danielle?"

"She is the girl Suzanne roomed with in Lausanne when I sent her to study languages. She's the daughter of a rich old camel drover who made a fortune transporting rugs and brass from the nomads and selling them to Bedouin merchants. It was a most unlikely friendship but Suzanne talked about her a lot. I think we should start in Tangier."

"Hold it a moment," Jack said. "Before I go running to the other side of the world, don't you think it would be a good idea to check passenger lists on flights leaving the mainland?"

"I have already done that. There's no trace of them."

"Then they may still be here."

The elder man scowled. "Oh they have gone all right. Mansoor would not hang around – he is much too clever for that."

"When do you want me to start?"

"Right away if it is possible."

The younger brother sat back in the leather chair. "Do I have time to finish my coffee?" he asked.

Two days later, Boukhalef Airport at Tangier was unexpectedly busy for early morning. Jack Wolfe was surprised to find how little it had changed from the first visit he made as a young soldier on furlough. He recalled with a grin an observation which appeared to clarify the Spartan existence of the desert people. 'The sun rises, the sun sets, you live and then you die.' He shrugged and shouldered his duffel bag as he walked to the arrival gate.

Buttoned inside his old American combat jacket was an envelope containing £10,000 in sterling which his brother had pressed into his hands on his departure from Jersey. "Expenses," said George. "You never know what this is going to cost."

Jack Wolfe agreed. To be without assets in Morocco was a sin for a European.

The customs official scrutinised the worn passport and eyed the traveller coldly. "What is the reason for your visit, Monsieur?"

"Bird watching," said Wolfe.

The officer was about to speak then scowled and pushed the passport back. There were often men like this at Boukhalef; men with a secret purpose of their own. It was nothing to do with him.

The El Minzah Hotel is entered through a cedarwood carved door in the stuccoed wall adjacent to the Kasbah. The old Moorish palace had been skilfully converted and the coolness of the marble interior was an unexpected pleasure after the chaotic drive through the old town. Wolfe had travelled through the night and was tired, but he showered and changed into a fresh shirt. Although it was not yet midday the outside temperature was steadily rising. He wandered down the winding staircase, into the reception hall.

"Can I be of assistance, Monsieur?" The tall concierge clad in flowing white stepped forward.

Wolfe nodded. "Do I look so lost?"

"It is my duty to help, Monsieur. You are alone, with little luggage and a telegram in your hand. You are not in Tangier for pleasure?" There was a faint smile on the face of the concierge.

"You are right," Wolfe answered, looking at the address on the telegram from Suzanne Wolfe. "I need to find Rue Marrakech. Is it far?"

The man bowed from the waist. "Not far, but for someone unfamiliar with the Kasbah, perhaps hard to find. May I enquire the name of the person you wish to contact?"

"Charni," said Wolfe. "Danielle Charni."

"A very respected family in Tangier, Monsieur, and Mademoiselle Danielle is well known to me. Perhaps it would be unwise to wander the Kasbah alone."

Had it not been for the openness of the face before him Wolfe would have imagined a threat, or was there a protective screen around the Charni name? "What do you suggest?" he said bluntly.

"I will have a message delivered to the lady immediately."

"And where shall I find her?"

"Do not worry Monsieur. Tangier is a village – she will find you."

Wolfe decided there seemed little point in arguing and,

thanking the concierge, he left the shaded refuge of the El Minzah. The Grande Socco, the great market 200 metres from the hotel, is the commercial hub of Tangier. At midday it was totally crowded with a mixture of people from all nations. The white linen suits of the Europeans contrasted sharply with the colourful Arab garments and the tall, dark-skinned nomads from the far deserts. Through this melee of pavement vendors and water sellers with bulging goatskins nosed the black taxis, many of them old German Army staff cars still carefully maintained. Busy overhead and resting on every convenient perching place, masses of small sparrows drowned almost all sound with their incessant clamour.

Wolfe selected an outside table at the Café de Paris. For all its grandiose title, it was a small coffee bar with a dozen tables occupied mainly by British and French stalwarts, who had remained when Tangier claimed independence and stayed simply because they had nowhere else to go.

Wolfe ordered cognac and mint tea and sat watching the scene around him. The brandy was relaxing and his eyes became heavy. The strong scent of spices and the chattering sparrows had a hypnotic effect and he found himself dozing in the chair. He was not sure how long he slept, five minutes or fifty. Through twitching eyelids he became aware of a shape in the wicker chair opposite. He sat back, momentarily startled. The woman was in her late twenties, Moroccan, brown-skinned with high cheek bones and long black hair tumbling to her shoulders. She was wearing a blue silk kaftan trimmed with gold and buttoned to the neck. On her forehead was a broad gold circlet, which kept her long hair from falling into the bluest eyes Wolfe had ever seen.

"I am Danielle Charni," she said.

Wolfe stared blankly for a few seconds, and then rose

awkwardly to his feet stammering a greeting. She took his extended hand. The girl was tall, almost level with him. The blue kaftan could not disguise the lissom figure or the shape of her breasts as she sat down.

"How long were you waiting for me?" he asked.

She crossed her legs, the silk robe parting to the knee, oblivious to the admiring glances from around the café. "I am sorry. You looked so tired. I did not have the courage to awaken you." Her voice was precise with a marked French accent.

Wolfe felt a flush mark his cheeks. "I feel foolish. How did you recognise me?"

Her laughter was infectious. "Oh, that was easy. You look exactly like your photograph."

"I'm totally mystified," said Wolfe.

"The photograph Suzanne kept on the dressing table at Lausanne, except in the photograph your eyes are open."

He grinned broadly and relaxed in the chair.

The girl studied his face noting the laughter crinkles cornering his eyes and the faint scars in the eyebrows.

"Why are you looking for me, Jack Wolfe?" she said, speaking his name deliberately.

"This may take some time," he hesitated.

"You have come a long way. I have the time to listen."

Wolfe paused, then launched into a description of the recent events relayed to him by his brother and the subsequent reason for his arrival in Tangier.

"And it was the telegram which brought me here, in the hope that you could lead me to Suzanne."

She had listened without interruption, her face fixed in concentration. "Yes I received the cable from Suzanne, but that was all. She did not arrive."

Wolfe stared back, the doubt at her statement showing in his eyes. Was the girl protecting her old friend? Had he really travelled to Morocco on a fruitless search?

"Oh, but it is true," she protested. "I have not heard anything."

Wolfe felt suddenly drained and picked up his empty cognac glass, peering through it at the table underneath like a fortune teller looking for an answer.

She interrupted his moody silence. "May I offer some advice?"

He looked wearily at her. "If you like."

"Why don't you rest? Tonight we will dine together. I have some ideas which may help."

He nodded in silent agreement and the girl stood up quickly. "The Chameau Rouge this evening. Just inside the Suliman Gate. I shall wait for you." She turned, the long legs moving swiftly and laughed over her shoulder. "Oh yes, my close friends call me Dany."

Jack slept fitfully and was awakened by the muadhin calling the faithful to prayer, the beseeching tones from the temple declaring 'Allah is Good' and willing him back to consciousness. He lay for a while, his finger tracing the pattern on the carved wooden table beside him. The meeting with Danielle Charni had been short but he was looking forward to seeing her again. There was no doubt she was a captivating women and her earnestness in wanting to see him again was flattering. He showered and changed into his only remaining shirt, annoyed at finding a missing collar button.

At the reception he placed the bulk of the £10,000 sterling into a safe deposit box and enquired the way to the Chameau

Rouge (The Red Camel). As usual the concierge was attentive.

"Certainly, Monsieur, through the Suliman Gate. You will find it as you reach the gold market."

Wolfe made his way through the Grande Socco, still commercially busy into the evening hours, cautiously avoiding the sharp-eyed urchins' beseeching pleas for help. "My father is dead, my mother is sick," they said, attracting attention while an accomplice deftly picked pockets without the victim feeling a touch.

The Chameau Rouge was set back inside a walled garden, with early flowering bougainvillea cascading around the arched windows and softly illuminated at the side of the open door by an ornately worked brass lamp. Wolfe peered through the opening and immediately saw Danielle speaking earnestly to a tall Moroccan with the build of an athlete. His hands were resting on her shoulders and they were laughing at a shared intimacy. She pulled his tousled hair affectionately then turned and sat at a corner table. The tall man lit the single candle before sweeping the girl an extravagant bow as he left the restaurant. Wolfe waited a few moments, not wishing to disturb the closeness of the relationship then entered the open door.

"Oh there you are," Danielle sprang to her feet in welcome. She had changed into a startling red kaftan with white lace at the neck and her glistening hair was piled high on her head with two ivory combs holding it in place.

Wolfe found himself staring in admiration, and then took her hand, allowing her to guide him to the corner table. "I hope you don't mind. I have chosen our meal." The scent of jasmine perfumed the curve of her neck.

She poured from a bottle of Muscadet into long-stemmed glasses.

"I understood you were Muslim and did not drink," said Wolfe.

"I am," her blue eyes twinkled mischievously, "but then I am not. Daddy is Moroccan, Mummy is French, which gives me dual nationality. Being French is more fun, don't you think?"

"It would appear so."

She was right about the meal. Seafood brochettes, flamed at the table, with a herb-flavoured couscous and framboise gateau to finish. Wolfe ordered cognac and rocked back in the chair feeling pleased with the evening until, realising the lateness of the hour, he looked around and found they were almost alone in the restaurant. Wolfe was intrigued by the girl and yet the reason for the evening meeting had not been mentioned. He was not ready for the question from Danielle.

"What will you do if you trace Suzanne?"

Wolfe paused, "I don't know. First I have to find her but now the trail is cold I may go back to Britain and start afresh."

Her face clouded. "Perhaps that will not be necessary. Tomorrow you must meet with a friend of mine at the French Embassy. If anyone can help us find Mansoor, he can."

The athletic Moroccan Wolfe had seen earlier appeared at the door and nodded shyly in their direction before taking a seat at the bar. Danielle smiled back and took Wolfe's hand. "It has been a pleasant evening, but now Najib is waiting for me. Until tomorrow?"

"Until tomorrow," echoed Wolfe.

She stood and waved from the doorway, taking the young man's arm.

He dallied another half hour, slowly savouring the

brandy, and then asked for the account.

"There is no bill, Monsieur," the remaining waiter bowed. "It is all taken care of," then he turned away, the request forgotten.

It was close to midnight. Wolfe retraced his steps away from the gold market. The sharp-eyed young pickpockets were still looking for easy prey. Wolfe fumbled in his pocket and produced a handful of small coins. "Here! This will save you the trouble," he said, and flipped the dirham coins into the air before striding briskly away.

Danielle arrived early the following morning and waited patiently at reception until Wolfe appeared down the stairs. She greeted him warmly, then escorted him out into the Rue Pasteur, the main thoroughfare through Tangier with the French Embassy at the crossroads. As they entered the flower gardens at the front of the building a white-uniformed gendarme tapped his helmet with his baton.

"Bonjour, Sergio," she said.

"Bonjour, Danielle. You are expected. Go straight in."

It was a spacious building with a vaulted ceiling and the early morning sun was streaming in from high-level windows.

Major Ravel Boidoin ushered them into a large antechamber with a huge leather-topped desk and hand-woven rugs upon the maple floor. He was a neat muscular man, short, with an engaging smile, a blue suit and matching tie. His kiss to Danielle's cheek was perhaps more than friendly and his firm handclasp to Wolfe gave an impression of toughness.

Boidoin ordered coffee over the wall-mounted intercom and Wolfe felt himself under a guarded scrutiny.

"And how can I be of assistance to you, Monsieur?" the Major asked blandly.

"Mademoiselle Charni told me there was a chance you could help in my search for a certain man," Wolfe answered.

"His name?"

"A Moroccan national and his name is Achmet Mansoor. He has spent much time in Libya and Iran engaged in the arms trade. I have reason to think he may be back in Morocco."

Boidoin's eyes squinted and he tapped the table with the end of his pen. "Achmet Mansoor is known to us. We have a very good espionage system here in Tangier but it is not the same as the old days when we had an international freeport. Now we have only a legation and are guests of the country. Mansoor is on his home ground and we are not aware of any misdemeanours on his part."

"What you mean is you have no proof," Wolfe said.

Boidoin remained inscrutable. He had not been appointed to the diplomatic service for his effusiveness. "We do have a dossier on the man but it would be improper procedure to display its contents without official clearance and a good reason."

"I understand that," said Wolfe, "but by the time that is sorted out the bird may have flown."

Boidoin resumed tapping the table with his pen, then unexpectedly stood and turned to a filing cabinet behind him. He riffled through the contents and produced a grey folder which he threw unopened upon his desk.

"A quaint phrase, Monsieur, the bird may have flown. The English are well known for their comparisons."

Before Wolfe could answer, Boidoin turned to the girl. "Danielle, I have told you how pretty the spring roses are in the rear garden. Would you like to see them?"

"If you wish, Ravel," she answered, puzzled at the request.

"Finish your coffee, Monsieur Wolfe. It is not often I have the chance to walk alone with a pretty girl. We should not be more than five minutes." Boidoin emphasised the time, then took Danielle's arm, walking through the rear door into the garden.

"Thanks, Major," Wolfe said under his breath. "I owe you one."

The folder was packed with newspaper clippings. There were reports of bomb outrages in Istanbul and Namibia and the infamous gun battle at the air terminal in Berlin. From the accompanying reports, it was apparent that Mansoor had been in these locations, sometimes before the events had occurred, and the implication of terrorism was obvious yet unproven.

Engrossed in the folder's contents, Wolfe failed to hear the door open quietly behind him and was suddenly aware of a figure at his shoulder staring at the newspaper cuttings upon the desk. A sallow man in his late twenties with a shaped beard and grey suit was scowling at him.

"I was looking for the major," he said glibly.

"He is in the garden with Mademoiselle Charni. Would you like me to call them?"

"It is of no importance." The man shuffled uncomfortably, then turned and left abruptly.

Danielle and Ravel Boidoin returned and stood speaking noisily outside the French window. Wolfe closed the folder and sat back in his chair as they re-entered.

"There was a young man in a grey suit looking for you," Wolfe said.

Boidoin's eyebrows creased. "Rico Filila – he is on the

embassy staff. Did he say what he wanted?"

"No, he left when I said you were in the garden."

Boidoin sniffed and replaced the folder in the filing cabinet.

Wolfe had the distinct feeling that the major did not have much respect for the sallow Filila.

"I am sorry I was not much help to you, Monsieur," Boidoin extended his hand, "and it is always a pleasure to see you, Danielle."

"You also, Ravel," Danielle said.

Danielle and Wolfe walked in silence until they were in the gardens fronting the embassy.

"What did it say?" said Danielle.

"What did what say?" Wolfe looked blank.

"Don't play games with me, Jack Wolfe," she reprimanded. "It was quite obvious from the smirk on both your silly faces what you were up to."

Wolfe grinned, "Are we so transparent?"

Danielle sighed, "Men can be such fools."

"Well, to answer your question, from a quick look at the folder it appears that Mansoor could be more than just an arms dealer. I think we may be looking for a man engaged in terrorism in a big way."

"How awful." Danielle looked aghast. "And Suzanne is mixed up with him. Is there anything we can do?"

"Not very much I'm afraid. It looks as though the trail is cold before we have even started. I shall have to phone Suzanne's father with the news before I return."

She was silent and stopped to push her nose into a large red rose, cupping the flower in her hand.

"Would you like to see where I live, Jack?"

Wolfe smiled, "Is it far?"

"No, only through the Suliman Gate at the entrance to the Kasbah."

She took his arm and escorted him across the Rue Pasteur into the old market. He felt pleased at the unexpected offer. She propelled him through the crowds, past the Chameau Rouge of the previous evening until they entered a white-walled garden, with a series of stone steps leading up to a carved sandalwood door.

It was surprisingly spacious inside with a heavy oak table and chairs in the centre of the main room. The floor was tiled mosaic with handwoven carpets and a painting of an angry looking old man astride a camel staring down from the chimneypiece.

"Who is that?" asked Wolfe.

"Oh, my grandfather. He gave me the villa for my twenty-first birthday."

"He looks very fierce," said Wolfe.

She laughed, "He could not hurt a fly, but he likes to relive the old days and the adventures he had in the past."

"Are you his favourite?"

Her blue eyes twinkled, "Of course, but I think he would prefer me to be a boy."

She took his hand and led him to a balcony at the end of the chamber – Wolfe was unprepared for the view. He could see across the rooftops of the Kasbah to the coast, with the natural curving bay of Cap Spartel prominent in the distance.

"I will make some coffee," she said, and disappeared leaving Wolfe admiring the scene.

"Do you like my little house?" she shouted from the kitchen.

"It's fabulous," he answered. "Do you live here alone?"

She returned carrying two porcelain cups on a silver tray. "All alone, except for my cat Felix and he only visits when he feels like it."

They sat at the wicker chairs on the balcony, sipping the hot coffee and gazing quietly at the skyline.

Wolfe felt strangely calm. The girl's kaftan rustled as she moved and he looked sideways at the curve of her neck and the shaped eyebrows above the startling blue eyes.

She caught his gaze and looked shyly back. An atmosphere had grown between them and he had to resist the urge to touch her. He sipped at his coffee. Soon he would have to leave Tangier. It would be a pity to break a developing friendship and there was the memory of the tall Moroccan with his hands so affectionately on Danielle's shoulders to consider.

She broke into his thoughts. "Now you must let me prepare dinner – tonight we shall eat *chez moi*. I don't have the opportunity to cook much and you shall be my captive food taster."

Wolfe smiled, "This is becoming a habit, but I can't think of anything I would sooner do."

"Then rest until I am ready. Oh yes, you will find the cognac in the corner bureau."

The day turned only too quickly into night and Wolfe could not remember when he had laughed so much. He was totally at ease. The meal was superb and it was only the lateness of the hour that reluctantly prompted him to make his adieus. She walked with him to the front gate and he took her hand and kissed her gently on both cheeks, denying the temptation to sweep the girl into his arms. She waved cheerfully as he rounded the corner at the Suliman Gate. A chill evening wind invaded his mood.

He paused at a darkened café on the Rue de Far and

ordered coffee to dwell on the events of the day. A small group of locals, their work finished for the day, were noisily drinking *te alla menta* and smoking rolled cigarettes. One jelaba-clad youngster proffered Wolfe a smoke, which he accepted with a smile knowing that everyone smoked the strong kif although it was a banned narcotic. It had been a restful day. Danielle was prominent in his thoughts and the urgency of his trip to Tangier was receding.

He bid the locals goodnight and retraced his steps towards the El Minzah Hotel, realising with annoyance that he had made a couple of wrong turns and was becoming lost. At the same time, the suspicion that four men were following his every move was fast becoming a reality. Wolfe had been in similar situations and knew a mugging when it was imminent. He quickened his step hoping not to aggravate circumstances, yet working out his best method of defence. Wolfe was confident in his ability in an even contest. Army training had made him a powerful adversary, but there was always the unknown strength of an opponent and the ever-present chance of a knife attack to fear... Wolfe resolved to take the initiative.

He did not have long to wait. As he neared a quiet tree-lined avenue a hand was placed on his shoulder, spinning him around. Wolfe ducked under the following punch and chopped an open hand blow to the throat and an upward kick into the groin. His assailant was unconscious before he hit the ground. Wolfe continued turning, landing a back kick to the stomach of the second man, who doubled up in pain. The remaining two men, clearly shocked at the suddenness of the onslaught, were no match for Wolfe who sailed into them, kicking shins and punching groins before they had time to recover.

His assailants stumbled away, and Wolfe, the anger of battle still strong in him, started after them until a man stepped from the shadows in front. His face was vaguely familiar and Wolfe, gasping from exertion, hesitated momentarily to associate the features with a location. The bottle wielded by the man in the grey suit smashed viciously above his ear and the last thing Wolfe remembered was the sound of shouting and figures running, as the blackness closed over him.

The dull throbbing in his head pulled Wolfe back into consciousness. He squinted through narrowed eyes at the battery of lights bright above his head and struggled to rise against the restraining hands pushing him gently back to the hospital bed. Everything in his vision was startling white – the walls – the ceiling – the uniforms of the nurses. He felt a total disorientation and a weakness in his limbs as he allowed a doctor to wash the congealed blood from the side of his face. The athletic young Moroccan he had seen with Danielle in the Chameau Rouge stood looking anxiously down at him.

"Where am I?" croaked Wolfe.

"In safe hands now," answered the man. "We got to you just in time, but it was pure chance that we were nearby. We brought you to the Spanish Hospital and you have ten stitches in your scalp."

Wolfe touched his temple with numb fingers.

"I have sent a message," the man continued. "My sister will be here soon."

"Your sister?" echoed Wolfe, striving to put his thoughts together.

"Danielle!"

"Your sister is Danielle?" Wolfe said stupidly.

"Of course."

Wolfe lay silent, his mind in a turmoil. The affection between the two young people in the restaurant was now clear and he had not imagined the depth of Danielle's feelings towards him. He grinned through the torment in his head as events began to clarify and then he suddenly remembered where he had seen the man who had smashed the bottle against his skull. It was Rico Filila from the French Embassy.

# Chapter 2

The pretty blonde English girl stood on the balcony in the white-washed villa in Marrakech. A few hundred metres away the Arab and African cultures merged in a dazzle of colour at the Jemaa el-Fna square. Suzanne Wolfe was always fascinated by the carpet weavers and the richly-clad storytellers with their intense groups of listeners. She had spent the day exploring the souk before returning, weary but happy, to the villa. It was always hot in the red-walled city, once the Berber capital of Morocco, and she smiled with gratitude as her companion appeared with two glasses of iced orange.

Achmet Mansoor was a tall man, slim with deceiving strength. His dark eyes above a neatly trimmed beard had captivated the girl from their first meeting. He had acquired the villa only recently with the sudden elevation in his fortunes and he enjoyed its quiet security away from his business affairs. She took the glass from him and slipped an arm around his waist.

"I am so happy to be here, Achmet. I just wish the earth would stand still and we could stay here forever."

He smiled down at her and tilted his glass to his lips, "That would be my wish also."

They stood together, listening to the sounds from the market and Mansoor stared across the vast oasis of palm groves to the north. Further along the Atlantic coast stood Tangier and the gateway to Europe. His work was about to begin and soon he must leave this tranquillity. He hated the ways of the infidel. Their western corruption had invaded the Arab world. Although the sun was at its highest, a warning, almost a sixth sense, sent a shiver of apprehension through him.

The following morning Wolfe discharged himself from the Spanish Hospital and Danielle drove him to the El Minzah Hotel. She had stayed at his bedside part of the night, dozing in a chair until he insisted she left.

The staff at the hotel were very gracious and were obviously concerned at his appearance. Coffee arrived almost as soon as he entered his room. He peered at his reflection in the mirror. His left eye was partly closed and an ugly purple bruise stretched from his forehead to his ear, with the jagged ends of stitches protruding through the skin.

Danielle waited patiently in the high-walled gardens until Wolfe returned. He was wearing his old jeans and heavy boots. She looked up enquiringly.

"What now, Jack?"

"A score to settle," he answered coldly.

The girl frowned, "Why should Rico Filila want to attack you? Are you positive it was him?"

"Perfectly sure, and I intend to find out why. After I have phoned Boidoin I shall visit the embassy."

"Do you want me to come with you?"

"Thank you, Dany but I need to be alone for this one."

She opened her mouth in protest, but changed her mind quickly at the hardness of his expression. There was an uncompromising attitude and a stubborn purpose she had not seen before. She nodded agreement. "I will wait for you."

At the embassy Ravel Boidoin received Wolfe in his office. "We have heard about the attack last night and I can only apologise for the incident," the major said, spreading his hands outwards, then indicating a chair.

"One of your staff did a pretty good job with a bottle on me last night," Wolfe growled. "I don't think 'incident' is the right word."

Boidoin looked concerned. "So I can see, but there are three very battered men in the cells this morning. They did not have it all their own way."

Wolfe was surprised. "You have them in custody? And Filila, where is he?"

The major shrugged. "I think the English have a saying – flown the coop – is that correct?"

Wolfe was becoming annoyed. His head was aching and he was not in the mood for flippancy.

He fixed Boidoin with an unblinking stare. "Understand this Major, I intend to find this man and uncover the reason for being on his hit list."

Boidoin leaned forward conspiratorially. "I think I may be able to help you there. We have not been inactive since Filila vanished. He was in such a hurry he left behind his locker keys and personal papers. It appears that Rico Filila and Achmet Mansoor may be related. They were brought up together in a desert region in the Spanish Sahara. Filila's position here at the embassy gave him access to confidential files involving arms trafficking and potential customers throughout the African continent. He must have been a very useful ally in Mansoor's team. Perhaps when he found you in my office and discovered the reason for your being here he decided you were a definite threat and needed to end it once and for all."

Wolfe scowled. "Now that was his first big mistake. I was almost prepared to leave Tangier. Now I have a lead and when I trace Filila I will almost certainly find Mansoor."

Boidoin studied him carefully. "In that case you will need this, Monsieur," he said, and handed Wolfe the manila folder from the filing cabinet.

The grey Mercedes Saloon with Rico Filila at the wheel sped southwards in a cloud of dust. He had not wasted any time leaving Tangier after the attack on Wolfe had failed. The men he had hired were tough, well used to skirmishes in dark alleys but he knew they bore him no allegiance and their tongues would soon wag after a few nights in the grim Kabba prison. The only thing left for Filila to do was to quit Tangier – and quickly.

Hardly pausing to gather any possessions he left a false forwarding address with his landlord and bought a ticket for the coastal train travelling north, making sure he was well observed. Then he seized the opportunity to duck out of the station via a rear entrance and hot-wired the dusty old Mercedes which had been parked at the rear of his apartment and set off, taking a quiet road out of town in the direction of Marrakech.

His usefulness at the embassy was finished but after

years of service to Mansoor he was sure to be welcomed into the business. A good day's travel and he would be safe and virtually untraceable in the old red-walled desert town. It was with a feeling of profound relief that he cleared the diminishing orange groves and saw the long road winding in front of him.

Wolfe was on his knees in Danielle's villa. Spread out on the floor were the contents of the manila folder given to him by Boidoin. Deep in thought, he rearranged the newspaper clippings, frequently cross-checking dates without any comment.

Danielle, mystified by the proceedings, kept quietly busy until finally she said, "What are you trying to do, Jack?"

Without looking up he said, "Trying to find a pattern in this somewhere, or at least a starting point."

"Is this the kind of thing you used to do in the army?"

"Amongst other things." The answer was noncommittal.

The girl remained silent. There was a single-mindedness about him this morning that broached no interference. She knelt at his side wishing she could help. Her closeness and the scent of jasmine twitched his nose.

He smiled apologetically. "I am sorry, I still feel pretty rough."

"Why don't we look for Filila?" she asked. "We do know where he lives."

"The last place Filila will be is at his apartment. My guess is that he left last night but yes, let's check it out. Do you know the Rue Eucalyptus?"

"Of course, it is not too far," she said, jumping to her feet.

They left the newspaper clippings in disarray on the floor and walked briskly through the Kasbah and into the

Place Libertie leading to a small apartment block. Danielle stopped outside a ground floor office and stood checking the names on the occupancy rota outside.

"Is this it?" asked Wolfe.

"Yes, second floor." They entered the shadowed porch and were confronted by an ancient lady cleaner dusting lazily. Danielle spoke in Arabic and Wolfe struggled to follow the conversation. The old lady then scribbled an address and hobbled away into the gloom.

The girl held the crumpled paper up to the light.

"It appears Filila has left but he was foolish enough to leave a forwarding address in Ceuta."

"How do we know it is not false?"

"Because he used the phone in the office to book a train ticket and the old lady heard him."

Wolfe almost laughed, "I bet she did. A cool customer this Filila, but a little too obvious."

She looked disappointed and her blue eyes narrowed.

"Where do you think he has gone?"

"Where would you go when things got tough?"

She thought a moment. "I think I would go home."

"Exactly! And where is home for Rico?"

"In the southern wasteland in the opposite direction to Ceuta," she said excitedly.

"Agreed, now let's find out how he escaped us."

They returned to the villa and Wolfe spread out a large map and resumed his kneeling position on the floor.

"Danielle, can you check on all trains leaving south since yesterday?"

"How about buses?"

"Too slow and unreliable, but you could try the airport for last minute arrivals."

The girl made some rapid phone calls then finally replaced the receiver with a bang, "No luck. All flights are fully booked and there are no trains south for two days."

Wolfe stood up and stretched. "Then he must have used another route. I just can't believe he would stay here in hiding and we know he did not have a car."

"Perhaps he stole one," Danielle said.

"Of course, that's the answer." He took her dark head in his hands and kissed her full on the lips, then released her quickly, surprised at his own impulsiveness.

It did not matter. For a long moment they looked at each other, the girl trembling slightly and then she was in his arms, her mouth eager and warm upon his, and the richness of her body urging against him.

Wolfe walked aimlessly most of the afternoon until the heat of the day diminished and he returned to his hotel. He felt a new reason to stay in Morocco. His whole perspective was unclear. He was strangely happy yet apprehensive and unsure of a direction to follow. He knew he should continue to look for Rico Filila but the last few hours that he had shared with the fascinating Berber girl made the reason for his search appear secondary.

It had been a routine matter to trace a stolen car. The local gendarmerie said three vehicles were missing that week. One was recovered from the sea, burned to a shell. The other was a vintage Volkswagen discovered in an olive grove with nothing of value left inside. The remaining car, still unaccounted for, was a late registration Mercedes Saloon that had been taken from the rear of the Rue Eucalyptus. That had to be the answer and it was the girl who had thought of it. Wolfe pulled a face; he was forgetting his basic training. Always put yourself in the position of the person you are seeking and don't forget the obvious.

He turned on the shower; perhaps he was becoming too old for this kind of thing. The phone rang just as he stepped into the shower.

It was reception. "Mademoiselle Charni is waiting for you in the rose garden, Monsieur."

Wolfe showered and dressed quickly. He found the girl sitting at a table with a large map spread in front of her. "I have almost planned the route," she said cheerfully. "When do think we should leave?"

Wolfe laughed nervously. "Now just hold it a minute, Dany. This is not an excursion. I intend to trace Filila and I don't need witnesses when I find him."

Her blue eyes flashed angrily. "I have been helping you for Suzanne's sake and you are not going to stop me. And another thing, how far do you think you will get in your condition, with your head all stitched up, not fluent in Arabic and not knowing the best route?"

"I can still read a map," Wolfe answered flatly.

"And didn't anyone tell you that desert roads can change overnight with sandstorms and lack of use? I have knowledge of the area and can be more help than you give me credit for."

Wolfe paused. There was no denying the argument but he did not want to involve her in any danger. She noted his indecision and pressed her advantage.

"Be sensible, Jack, you know I am right."

Wolfe leaned back in his chair, "I have always worked alone. A man can move faster that way. You can accompany me until I decide it's time for you to go, is that agreed?" They had reached an impasse but she was relieved at the compromise.

"Agreed," she said, then turned her attention to the map.

# Chapter 3

The flag of convenience hung limply at the masthead of the Liberian cargo carrier as the rusting old ship steamed slowly into the quiet port of Sidi Ifni on the Moroccan coast. The *Sultan Dizah* had taken sixteen days to travel from the Gulf carrying six three-ton boxes which had been transferred in mid-ocean from the Japanese carrier, *Kyoto Maru*. The two captains had only communicated by radio and did not particularly wish to meet again. They were both well paid for their involvement in the transaction, knowing only too well that the innocent looking boxes marked 'Farm Machinery' held something far more sinister than the labels implied.

The *Sultan Dizah* had stood offshore waiting for the tide, as the draught on the tramp steamer was too much for a normal anchorage. Achmet Mansoor had chosen the port well. It was thirty kilometres from Marrakech and was not widely used as the dockside unloading machinery was antiquated and only normally used by local traffic. The arrival of an old cargo ship would arouse little interest, which fitted Mansoor's plans perfectly.

He studied the deliberate docking procedure from his vantage point on the Salin Height overlooking the bay and only descended from his viewing area when the ship was moored at the wharf. In a short while, his cargo would be unloaded, driven inland and sold and with the money he could begin the biggest gamble of his life.

In Libya, three months earlier, he had been made a startling offer. Although frightening in its initial concept, it was financially greater than any rewards Mansoor had every believed possible. It was a simple request. Was it in his power to plant a bomb aboard an airliner? His first reaction of shock and revulsion gave way to greed when he learned the price for the deal and his mind began to work vigorously towards the acceptance of the contract of half a million pounds. Allah had sought to reward him after his years of privation. It was his destiny. It had to be done. Had Mansoor known the identity of the passenger he was to assassinate with all the other innocents, his fear might have cancelled out his greed.

In the dawn hours Danielle Charni arrived at the El Minzah Hotel to pick up Wolfe. She was driving a hired CX Citroen Estate and had spent the previous evening gathering provisions for the journey. She had packed assorted tinned food, rice and bottled water, and covered them with a lightweight tent and awning.

She found Wolfe prepared and waiting. They were soon driving swiftly away from the town with Wolfe pouring over a map whilst Danielle concentrated on the road ahead. They chose a route that skirted the Atlantic coastline, taking them through the orange groves. The early morning sun lifted a gentle mist from the undulating tarmac of the road. Danielle glanced sideways at her companion. He looked better this morning. The bruises around his eyes were not so angry and a night's sleep appeared to have dispensed his caution. They sped past a few solitary wanderers and sometimes a traveller mounted on a plodding donkey, dozing his way to his destination.

"They live where they can," Danielle said, noting Wolfe's interest. "Don't feel sorry for them. They are happy with the simplicity of their lives."

The Citroen cruised steadily onwards into the lightening sky until they reached a crossroads some thirty kilometres later.

Wolfe pointed to the single petrol pump outside the small-stuccoed building. "Stop here. This is what I have been looking for."

"But we have a full tank."

"Yes! But did Rico Filila? If you were driving a stolen car, would you stop to fill the tank or wait until you were on your way?"

She nodded and pulled in front of the building as a turbaned attendant came out. Danielle left the car and engaged the man in earnest conversation before returning jubilantly to the Citroen.

"Your were right, Jack. Filila was here two days ago. The attendant remembers him well as he left without waiting for his change."

She jumped back into the driving seat and drove vigorously away from the petrol station, the Citroen wheels spinning in the dust. Wolfe smiled inwardly at her enthusiasm. Until now he had been making wild guesses but this stroke of luck confirmed his supposition that Filila was somewhere in front. Dany's spirited ability to make people help was becoming invaluable.

He squinted through the morning sunlight at the girl, her hair glossy and pulled back from her face, feeling a tenderness towards her that startled him. She was dressed casually in wide-legged black slacks turned in at the ankle and a white lace blouse buttoned to the neck, with a silver circlet holding back her hair. She drove purposefully for another two hours with Wolfe finding a pleasure in her quiet concentration until they reached the salt gathering pans of the coastal estuary, causing her to blink increasingly against the glare.

"Pull in ahead," he said. "You need to take a break."

She smiled gratefully and pointed to a small party of camels with their owners resting at the roadside.

"I will stop with the arregans."

The Citroen turned off the road and she leapt out as the camel drovers approached. Wolfe, ever cautious, could not understand her! There she was amongst the riders, smiling, touching, hands outstretched in greeting. Then he noticed the striking blue eyes of the men – and the similarity to Danielle's.

"These are some of my people," she laughed. "We are the true Berber, but it is unusual to find them so far north."

Within moments, Wolfe was seated in the drovers' circle nibbling dates and sipping mint tea, listening to the chatter of the party.

"I have difficulty following the conversation," he said to Dany.

"That is because it is the language of the Arregan," her eyes sparkled. "The sound of the camel and some of our words are the same."

"Are you joking?"

"No, I speak the truth. Arabic is the official language

but the descendants of the original people like to preserve our own culture and tongue. It helps us to remember that once the Berber nation ruled proudly in Africa."

The grey-bearded old patriarch, clad in flowing black robes, stood before Wolfe, and took his hands to help him to rise.

"I have told Mohammed of our search for Suzanne and he has something for you," the girl said.

The old man appeared to bless Wolfe then carefully placed a silver amulet on a chain around the younger man's neck.

"It is the hand of Fatima," Danielle nodded. "It will ward off evil spirits and bring you good luck."

Wolfe felt warmth towards the old man and gripped his palm in thanks.

"May I give something in exchange?"

"Only if you want to break the power of the talisman. Just shake his hand and say *Barrakalowfic*."

Wolfe did as he was bidden and the old man beamed.

They had spent too long with the drovers and made their farewells with difficulty as everyone wished to make a speech. Slowly they extricated themselves from the hospitable group and climbed back into the Citroen. Wolfe took the wheel and Danielle sat back, thankful for the rest, as the caravan waved them out of sight.

Wolfe drove in silence for a while, then he asked softly, "Why are you still single, Dany?"

She stared through the windscreen at the wispy cirrus clouding the midday sky. "It is simple. When I went to school in Europe I was too young and when I returned I was too old."

He pulled a face. "Too old, why you're still only a girl."

To you maybe, but Morocco is a man's country and a girl can be married with a family at fourteen. Anyway, I am still looking for a very special person."

"Do you think you will be lucky?"

She pouted mischievously and gently inspected the stitches in his forehead with her index finger. "How can I tell? Perhaps one day."

Sidi Ifni, the Spanish port on the Moroccan coast, was moderately quiet as the old dockside crane unloaded the crated cargo from the rusting *Sultan Dizah*. Achmet Mansoor watched impassively as the goods were lowered and shackled onto the two flat-bed trucks at the wharf side. His plans were progressing smoothly and it was not long before the drivers were receiving instructions for the destination to El Djerib, approximately one hundred and twenty kilometres away at the foothills of the Atlas Mountains. This was a region close to his childhood days, sparsely populated and near to the Western Desert known to wary travellers as the Wastelands. Once the consignment arrived he could be guaranteed of its safety, but always a suspicious man, Mansoor chose not to accompany the convoy.

He watched the trucks lumbering away from the quayside with guarded elation. Within a few short weeks he would be a wealthy man. All the pleasures that money could buy and all doors open to him. His days of servility to his masters would be finished and he could end the clinging indignity of having the young English woman forever at his side, restricting his movements and gazing at him with cow-like adoration in her eyes. Nevertheless, the blonde girl was still an essential tool in his scheme – she was easy to manipulate and would be instrumental in the proposed destruction of the airliner.

Mansoor carefully drove away from Sidi Ifni and stopped in the evening at the seaport of Agadir. Once it had been a busy commercial town but the recent growth of a thriving tourist industry had produced high-rise flats and rapid environmental changes. Mansoor mingled with the crowds on the esplanade, enjoying his anonymity and the relief from pressure before spending an uneventful night at a convenient hotel.

The early morning saw him en route for Marrakech, feeling weary but secretly jubilant. As he entered the city walls he stopped to watch the inevitable snake charmer with his venom-less cobra and the young acrobats entertaining the crowds. He marvelled at their showmanship, adapting the only tools they had at their disposal – youth and enthusiasm.

He was still smiling as he pulled to a halt outside his villa. Parked in front of the iron gate stood a dust-caked Mercedes Saloon and asleep at the wheel was his old companion and informant Rico Filila. Mansoor's feeling of ease vanished abruptly as a dozen questions sprang to his lips. Leaping from his car, he banged urgently on the windscreen, waking the sleeping man instantly.

Rico Filila forced a smile and Mansoor knew immediately something had gone terribly wrong. He yanked open the car door as Filila lurched to his feet stammering an opening.

"I have brought you some information and I thought it best to see you myself."

Mansoor, sensing the fear in his countryman's manner, prepared himself for bad news.

"What is so urgent that you cannot inform me in the usual way?"

Filila struggled to speak but when he began his words came like a flood, recalling the events of the last few days, his meeting with Wolfe and the failed mugging in the Kasbah.

"And as I could be of no further use to you at the embassy, I decided to help out here," he finished lamely.

Mansoor listened in silence but was now trembling with rage. "You are a fool, Rico. You have brought the devil to my door. I know about this man Wolfe: he is the uncle of the girl with me now and has fought as a mercenary soldier many times. A man like that, trained in pursuit, and you lead him here. You are stupid to think he is not following."

Filila smirked. "You do me an injustice. I laid a false trail. By now he will be on his way to Ceuta in the opposite direction."

"And for how long do you think that will delay a man like Wolfe?"

Filila started to bluster, "I don't know why you worry so much, he is only one man and ..."

Mansoor interrupted angrily, "I worry because I have the biggest deal ever on my hands and I don't need to be stopped by this crazy old guerrilla, nor can I afford to lose the girl. She is part of my plans."

"What can we do?" Filila asked timidly.

Mansoor rubbed his chin thoughtfully, "We must find him before he finds us."

"How can we do that?"

"Check out the hotel he stayed at in Tangier. See if he has left and if he was driving and if possible, whether he was travelling south. If that is the case we shall be waiting for him and this time I shall handle the reception committee."

Filila nodded vigorously. "But don't think I am happy with you, Rico," Mansoor snarled. "You have made two serious mistakes. Firstly you underestimated the man. Secondly you did not kill him."

\*

The Citroen with Wolfe at the wheel made good time. Around late afternoon they had driven through the old capital of Rabat and were heading in the direction of Casablanca, still following the Atlantic coast. Wolfe was not unhappy with the distance they had travelled but reasoned that there was nothing to be gained by pressing on through the night.

"We must find somewhere to stay, Dany," he said, looking through the caked windscreen at the gathering cloud bank in front. "Where do you think – Safi or Marrakech?"

She stared at the map spread out on her knees. "Safi will keep us on the coastal route. Marrakech is perhaps too far to go in the darkness and we have the dust roads to negotiate."

"OK then, Safi," he agreed.

Thirty kilometres further on it started to rain. "Damn," said Wolfe.

"I'm delighted," she answered. "We need the rain."

It soon turned into a deluge making driving difficult and causing him to peer myopically through the fogged windscreen. The girl tugged at his shirt and pointed up to the left, as a group of single-storied buildings loomed through the downpour. Wolfe pulled to a halt in front of the brightly painted hotel set back among the date palms and cut his engine. They waited a few moments listening to the rain tattooing on the Citroen roof, then leaped out of the car, making a dash for the hotel together. He slipped on the muddy surface before the steps, flailing his arms to keep his balance, collided with Dany and brought them both to the ground.

She was up before him, her face mud-spattered but laughing as she dragged him to his feet.

Once inside the hotel they were met by a shy young girl who made them both sit before a crackling wood fire to dry their clothes. The rain ceased as suddenly as it had started. Wolfe trudged through the pools to the Citroen and returned with the hand luggage as Danielle booked two adjoining rooms at the rear of the building.

The rural hotel was almost empty, yet the rooms were adequate, sparsely furnished, with handwoven rugs decorating the walls without animals or figures in the design, enforcing the strict Muslim codes of embellishment. Wolfe pushed open his shuttered windows and stood breathing in the moistened air, scented and tranquil after the rain. The faint sound of splashing from the adjoining room and Danielle's soft singing caused him to smile. There was a detached serenity about the evening away from the headlong dash of the early morning and he felt oddly happy, not at all as he would have expected after the day's pursuit.

The shy young girl knocked at his door and informed him that a meal had been prepared and soon Danielle and he were seated on cushions at a low table, sharing a steaming bowl of couscous and warm bread. It had been a long day. Danielle retired early: she had been active since early dawn. Wolfe wished her goodnight and went to his own room, stripping off his shirt and folding his arms behind his head as he laid back on his bed. The night was warm, yet humid. Sleep evaded him and he wished he had a drink. The hours dragged by slowly until he could stand it no longer.

In the next room Danielle awoke, listening for the sound that disturbed her. She waited, straining her ears in the gloom, then rose quietly and pulled on her kaftan. Noiselessly she opened her bedroom door, pausing briefly before gently pushing open the door to Wolfe's room. She stared around. There was no sign of him. She crossed to the open shutters and looked out into the rear garden. If it were not for the sweat glistening on his upper body she wouldn't have seen him. He was standing motionless in the shadows, his back resting against the trunk of a date palm.

She watched him for some time and he did not move. There was a sense of isolation in his manner and she felt unusual compassion at his remoteness. He was a strong yet gentle man but totally unpredictable. She backed away slowly from the shutters, fearing he might see her and become annoyed. There was much she did not understand. Perhaps in time it might become clearer. She went back to her room and lay still in the darkness.

Suzanne Wolfe strolled lazily back from the souk with an armful of fresh aram lilies but quickened her pace when she saw the car parked outside the villa of Achmet Mansoor. She had been lonely away from him and skipped happily through the arched doorway and into the marbled lounge. He stood up as she entered and kissed her lightly on both cheeks, almost paternally but without the affection she had grown to expect.

"Suzanne darling, I should like you to meet a cousin of mine. We lived together as boys and he will be staying with us for a while."

Filila rose stiffly and forced a smile. "Please call me Rico, Mademoiselle."

Although temporarily annoyed she greeted Filila warmly and turned to arrange the lilies in a porcelain vase, hoping the disappointment of not having Mansoor alone was not too obvious.

"Rico and I are both tired and have much to discuss.

Can you cook us something darling?" Mansoor patted her shoulder and nodded towards the dining area.

She almost felt dismissed, but he had returned to her and that was all that mattered. She went into the kitchen as the two men continued to speak in lowered voices.

"I don't understand what you are doing with such a woman," challenged Filila, "and obviously not of our faith."

Mansoor took a long breath and scowled at his kinsman.

"I have an important contract to complete and she is part of the deal. In time I will give you the details of why she is useful to me but first we have to remove the threat of this man Wolfe, before he gets to you my dear Rico."

Filila shivered, "Perhaps this time he will not be so lucky."

"Luck has nothing to do with it. There are only two roads south. I want you to put lookouts on them both. If he is following you he should not take much catching."

"And if we do stop him, Achmet?"

"Then he will find a bullet."

Early the following morning Danielle, armed with a steaming coffee pot and fresh bread, roused Wolfe from sleep. She was wearing her baggy black sheba slacks with a high-buttoned red blouse and jostled him cheerfully into an early start. He groaned, resisting the urge to bury his head beneath the bedcovers. She looked radiant after the events of the previous long day. Wolfe, his eyes heavy-lidded, could only marvel at her activity.

"Danielle," he said unhappily, "morning is not my best time. Too much good humour is bad for me."

She laughed at his weariness and dumped the breakfast tray onto his chest. "Well that may be so, but if you are not ready in twenty minutes I am leaving without you," she said, and vanished through the open door.

The road that morning was almost deserted. The isolated patches of fog, which had previously slowed the progress of the Citroen, had gone. Danielle drove carefully. She wanted to ask about the previous night, and why he had chosen to be alone in the trees, but decided against the question.

The next four hours passed uneventfully. Wolfe spent most of the time deep in thought and the girl was fully occupied with the twisting dust road. She had pushed her dark hair under a wide-brimmed blue baseball cap shading her eyes from the sunlight. She took a deep breath, breaking into his reflections.

"If we find Suzanne, what can we do? Do you think she will leave Mansoor and return with us? She was always headstrong when we roomed together. I still don't think there will be much we can do."

"Perhaps you are right, Dany, but this whole awful business does not feel right. From the information we have pieced together Mansoor prefers to avoid confrontation and always seems to be one step ahead, but I can guess he could be a nasty customer if he were cornered. There are a lot of blank spaces in this puzzle and I have a gut feeling that we are about to find out why."

Wolfe took over the driving, following the deserted route and saying little more to the girl, who appeared to have lost some of her enthusiasm.

The road was aggravatingly tortuous as the Citroen drew nearer to the old city of Marrakech. The sky was a brilliant blue overhead. The spongy vegetation merging into the sandy desert cast little shadow. They stopped at midday and Danielle made mint tea and opened a can of tuna, which they ate with black olives, looking across at the High Atlas Mountains.

An hour later they arrived at a crossroads in the winding road. Twenty metres back from the track stood a battered old Mercedes with its driving door open and on the front seat was a man clad in a jelaba, smoking a cigarette cupped in his hand. At the appearance of the Citroen he threw the cigarette down and, jumping from the car, watched them out of sight. Wolfe continued until he turned a bend then stopped and ran back along the road in time to see the Mercedes hurtling away from the crossroads in a cloud of dust.

He trotted back to the car and a puzzled Danielle.

"What is it, Jack?"

"It looks as though we have been rumbled."

"What does that mean?"

"It means that someone is going to a lot of trouble to find us."

"But why here? We are still 200 kilometres from the real desert. Surely Filila would wait for us in the Wasteland?"

Wolfe reached for the map, "Unless he is not that far away. I think we should find another route. This Filila is not only cunning but I am sure that when we find him, Suzanne will not be far away."

The Citroen ploughed onwards, Wolfe relinquishing the driving to the girl then taking over the wheel in the early evening. Danielle found herself wondering if she had made the right move in accompanying Wolfe on this trip. He appeared detached yet obstinate in the remorseless way he pursued Filila and she was becoming more nervous as time went by.

Almost anticipating her misgivings his mood lifted and

he started to sing quietly, until she started to laugh at his attempt to cheer her.

To the left of the road, high on the bordering cliff, a flash from a mirror or piece of metal silenced Wolfe into a sudden sense of unease as the vehicle cleared the brow of a hill. Swung broadside and completely blocking the road was a Mercedes 190 Saloon with two figures in front. One-man, hands on hips, was directly behind the other who was kneeling, both arms outstretched, and levelling a revolver at the approaching Citroen.

The ambush had been carefully chosen. There was no turning back. Wolfe's immediate reaction was to stand on the brake pedal as he roughly pushed the girl down into the passenger seat moments before the shot exploded his windscreen into splinters. The next few seconds were a blur to Danielle. Wolfe thrust the accelerator hard to the floor and the Citroen leapt forwards like a battering ram.

The kneeling man, realising the danger too late, tried frantically to rise and fire at the same time, but the bullet went into the sky as the heavy vehicle hit him full in the chest. The second man turned to escape but was slammed sideways, somersaulting high into the air before bouncing onto the bonnet of the waiting Mercedes, his head grotesquely twisted beneath him.

Wolfe braked viciously, cut his engine and leapt from the Citroen, ducking low as he ran to the other vehicle. The body sprawled on the road was motionless, face upward, stretched out like a crucifix, the slack mouth gurgling blood and the revolver twenty paces away. The second assassin slid slowly from the bonnet of the car, an almost amazed expression on the purple face, his neck snapped like a rotten branch.

The girl had not moved from the Citroen but sat upright, showered in glass fragments. "Are they dead?" she whispered.

Wolfe nodded brusquely, then turned his attention to her.

"Are you cut?"

"No, I don't think so. My cap stopped most of the splinters but the noise was frightening."

He folded his arms around her and held her close, stroking her neck soothingly, aware of her quivering body.

"I had no choice, Dany. They meant to kill us and we had no way to escape. We were only lucky they were not professional."

She looked astounded. " How can you say that? We nearly died."

He squinted up the road to where the metal had flashed before the ambush.

"Experts would have fired around cover and given themselves a way to retreat. These two briefly wanted us to know our fate. It elevated their strength and that was their mistake. A professional would not have cared less."

He picked up the revolver from the road and doubled back over the brow of the hill. The girl sat down on the sand, staring at the sprawled bodies until Wolfe returned breathing heavily from the exertion.

"Was there anyone else out there, Jack?"

He shook his head. "If there was he did not wait around."

"What do we do now?" she said nervously.

"Find some identification if they have any."

The girl remained on the sand as Wolfe searched the first man. "Nothing, not a thing on him. Let's see if our pistolero friend has anything. Ah, that's better," Wolfe said, as he produced an identity card and an envelope marked Bank of Credit and Commerce Morocco.

"So now we know what our lives are worth, Dany. This is a deposit slip for 100,000 dirham. It's their bad luck they won't be able to spend it."

Danielle shuddered. "I think we are in big trouble, Jack. Do we go to the police?"

Wolfe wiped the sweat from his forehead with his arm. "Not until we try to get Suzanne out of this. Filila must now think we are finished and he may become careless. If we notify the police we may be showing our hand and certainly we won't get far in the Citroen with a smashed windscreen and radiator. Our only choice is to take the other car."

"What do we do with them?" she said indicating the bodies.

Wolfe pointed up the road to where a small defile stood back 300 metres from the highway with some scrub bushes at the entrance.

"That will have to do for now. It may be some time before they are discovered."

He dragged the two bodies into the rear seat of the Citroen and transferred his luggage to the trunk of the Mercedes. It took thirty minutes to conceal the Citroen in the ravine with the sparse vegetation and Wolfe was gasping as he climbed the slope and flopped into the passenger seat of the waiting Mercedes. Danielle at the wheel appeared much calmer now and smiled reassuringly at him.

"I found this in the front compartment," she said, and with a flourish handed him a hire agreement. Wolfe laughed mirthlessly. "I'll be dammed. Rico Filila left us with a forwarding address, possibly the home of Achmet Mansoor – and it's my guess that this time it's genuine."

\*

Early the following morning Achmet Mansoor and Filila left Marrakech for El Djerib, following the route of the flat trucks containing the arms consignment. They hoped to arrive before sunset to supervise the unloading of the goods and had left Suzanne Wolfe alone in the villa, promising to telephone at the first opportunity after completing the transfer. She had spent a solitary day wandering the old town and was committed to a quiet evening with a novel, until a mud-caked Mercedes Saloon halted on the opposite side of the road. She paid it little attention until a vaguely familiar man with a veiled Moroccan girl climbed out and strolled across the road, climbed the steps to the villa and rang the doorbell. Suzanne opened the door cautiously but recoiled with shock as she found herself staring down the muzzle of a revolver held by her Uncle Jack. Before she could speak he dropped a hand over her mouth and pushed her roughly against the wall, listening intently for sounds from the villa.

"Where are they, Suzanne?" he demanded harshly.

Suzanne almost buckled at the knees and her mouth opened in astonishment as the veiled Moroccan girl lowered her yashmak to reveal the concerned face of her long-time friend and confidante, Danielle Charni.

"They are not here," she blurted out. Amazement gave way to anger at the sight of her uncle with his menacing revolver, obviously expecting trouble. "They have gone to Sidi Ifni and I don't know when I will see them again."

Wolfe lowered the revolver and made a cursory inspection of the villa, shaking his head with annoyance as he returned.

Danielle took Suzanne's hands and stood holding them, her startling blue eyes just staring at her friend.

"What on earth is happening?" Suzanne finally challenged. Wolfe pushed the revolver into his waistband. "Not much of a way to greet me after all this time. Things have happened so quickly, Suzanne, I am sure you are not in the full picture. Can we all sit down and I shall try to explain?"

The girl motioned to the living area and sank into a chair, listening in shocked silence as Wolfe narrated the circumstances of his arrival in Morocco. There was no doubting the sincerity of his story but it was totally beyond belief that Achmet Mansoor could be involved in such violence. She knew him too well. It must all be a ghastly mistake. Rico Filila she did not like, but it was too much for her to accept that her lover could be part of any such deeds. There had to be a reason and she thought she knew the answer.

"It would not be the first time my father has fabricated evidence, Jack," she said, "or double-crossed an adversary to get his own way. Do not forget I lived with him – and Achmet is a gentle man who is always badly used. I believe he could retaliate if he was being hounded but the ambush you describe. I can't believe he would know anything of that."

Wolfe sighed in exasperation. "What more can I say? I have told you the facts. If you choose not to believe them I can't imagine the consequences for you."

Danielle nodded agreement. "It is getting late. We must find a hotel. Will you come with us, Suzanne?"

Suzanne shook her head. "I know you have come to help, but not yet. Achmet will contact me soon. If you let me know where you are staying I will speak with you afterwards."

"I can understand that," said Wolfe, rising to his feet, "but you must not betray us or mention this meeting. Is that understood?"

She nodded glumly and Wolfe took her hands, kissing her affectionately on the cheek. The years had changed his niece into a graceful young woman and he could almost feel sympathy for her dilemma and the reason for her troubles.

"Now listen carefully," said Wolfe. "Two men are dead, others are imprisoned in Tangier and we still don't know the reason for any of this. I am asking you to be vigilant and above all trust us, Suzanne."

She mumbled agreement and escorted Danielle and her uncle to the vehicle, unhappily waving them out of sight.

Suzanne Wolfe received two calls that night. One was from Danielle, giving the address of a small hotel behind the Koutoubia Mosque. The other was from Mansoor. At the first sound of his voice all doubts about his integrity disappeared and within seconds she was earnestly retelling the story as Wolfe had described it to her. Mansoor remained silent until Suzanne stopped speaking but his answer was all she had hoped for.

"Suzanne darling, your father hates me because I took his daughter and I do not regret it. I know he never considered me good enough for you and he has invented these tales of terror to enlist help from his brother, an old mercenary soldier who must know every dirty trick in the book."

"But he is my uncle and arrived with my best friend," Suzanne said defensively.

"Of course, it was a clever move, but the man is a killer. He has admitted that to you. Who the unfortunate pair he killed were I have no idea, but if you want to be truly free again and with me, this is what you must do."

The Old Spanish Castle overlooking the port of Tripoli is the headquarters of the Socialist Liberation Bureau. It is the Libyan equivalent of the British Secret Service or the American Federal Bureau of Investigation and has been largely responsible for training terrorists and others in guerrilla warfare throughout many emerging regions of the world. To this organisation Colonel Muammar Gaddafi deferred on decisions of secrecy and policy. In Libya Gaddafi was a legend, admired by many, in contrast to the 'mad dog' image perpetrated by many of his western adversaries. His power rested upon the wealth created from huge oil deposits in the north and improvements in the lifestyle of the Libyan people. For years Gaddafi had pursued a dream, to unite the Arab people and create an empire equal to any in the world. A man with simple faith and high ideals, born into a nomadic life, he grew to maturity in the desert. This Spartan upbringing and dedication made him a hero to his people, but his anti-imperialist stance and a firm belief in the liberation of women, created a backlash by anti-Gaddafi opponents from his own ranks.

High within the castle walls the two directors of the bureau were discussing the downfall of the Libyan leader. Major Riyan Sleyman and Captain Razmet Dhulmet, high-ranking officers in the People's Army, had devised a plan to discredit Gaddafi and seize power. For seven years it had been their sole responsibility to execute acts of terrorism throughout the world and they were thorough in their commitment. Just enough traceable evidence had been left to connect the Libyan regime with many of the outrages committed in the name of the Muslim people, culminating in the disastrous retaliation bombing by the Americans in April 1986. Since then rumours had prevailed and Gaddafi's power had been reduced.

Sleyman and Dhulmet conceived a plan to further

humiliate Gaddafi, hoping for his probable abdication which would leave the way clear for the Socialist Liberation Bureau to seize command. With great care, the conspirators devised a plan to destroy the Moroccan aircraft carrying the Israeli Defence Minister back to Israel after a meeting with the liberal King Hassan of Morocco in Casablanca. The blame would rest on Gaddafi's regime. It was hoped that America would once again punish the Libyan people for their involvement.

The key to the assassination of the Israeli minister rested upon the shoulders of one person, a man with a record of international dealings, in weapons, terrorism and complicity with Gaddafi. His name was Achmet Mansoor.

The hotel behind the Koutoubia Mosque was in a pleasant little street with flower boxes on the windowsills and purple wisteria in full bloom over the entrance porch. Had it not been for the violent happenings of the last few days, Wolfe could almost have enjoyed the relaxed atmosphere of the place. They had booked adjoining rooms and after a delayed supper retired early, dropping immediately into sleep.

The following morning, having not received contact from Suzanne, Danielle decided to stroll as far as the market leaving Wolfe to wait for a call from his niece. At midday Danielle returned to find Wolfe impatiently pacing the floor, his frustration only too obvious.

"I don't like it, Dany. Something has gone wrong. She should have contacted us by now."

"Do you think she has heard from Mansoor?"

He reached for the revolver from the table, spinning the chamber with practised ease.

"Is that really necessary?" she asked.

"I don't have to remind you that we are dealing with vicious men."

"Yes I realise that, but I'm frightened for Suzanne."

"Well I need an edge and this is it," he pushed the revolver into his waistband.

"There is a lot I don't understand about you, Jack," she frowned.

He ignored the reproach. "I'll return shortly," he said.

"Don't leave me here alone, I couldn't stand it. I'm coming with you."

Wolfe paused. "OK but keep out of the way when I tell you to. Understood?"

She gripped the sides of her kaftan and dropped a mock curtsey. "Understood *mon capitain*."

He grinned. The girl was irrepressible but he had a bad feeling about their situation, none the less.

They left the hotel skirting the mosque, through the small copper manufacturing workshops with the youthful faces of the apprentices deftly hammering the yellow metal into patterns, and entered the narrow alleyways with the rich orange- and blue-dyed skeins of lambs' wool hanging from the walls to dry, and approached Mansoor's villa from the rear.

"She is not there," Danielle said positively.

Wolfe peered through the trees. "How can you be so sure?"

"The shutters are open."

"But if she had left she would have closed the shutters for security."

"That would arouse our suspicion that she had left."

"Well perhaps she is still there."

"In the noonday heat, we always close the shutters."

Wolfe stared at the villa. "Dany, I do believe you are right."

"So you think I am still useful?" She invited a compliment.

He took her arm, propelling her quickly towards the stone steps of the villa. "Let's check it out first." The house was deserted and the windows locked, confirming their suspicions. Wolfe swore under his breath.

"Now what do we do?" asked Danielle.

"Try the adjoining villa. See if anyone saw her leave."

Danielle skipped down the steps and engaged the young neighbour in earnest conversation before returning to Wolfe, waiting patiently at the gate.

"As we expected Jack, she left early this morning by taxi, alone with two suitcases. It looks as though we have been wasting our time and she has made her own plans."

Wolfe released his breath angrily. "I should have expected this. She must be infatuated beyond stupidity."

Danielle's eyes met his briefly. "Or maybe she is just a woman in love," she answered quietly.

"Either way she still needs our help and we must find Mansoor because I don't yet know how to explain two bodies in a car hired by us and covered in brushwood. The prospect of a Moroccan gaol does not appeal to me."

The girl shuddered. "Nor me. Where do we start to look now?"

Wolfe squinted thoughtfully. "Do you remember where Suzanne said Mansoor had gone?"

"Sidi Ifni."

"Where is that?"

"It is a port about two hundred kilometres from here on the south-west coast. It used to be part of Morocco, but now it is a small enclave belonging to Spain."

"A port on the Atlantic coast?" Wolfe ran a finger over the row of jagged stitches above his eyebrow. "It makes sense, Dany. My brother told me Mansoor transferred weapons to a cargo carrier in the Gulf. Give or take a couple of days steaming from Suez and into the Med, then the Atlantic coast, the timing is pretty close to where a carrier could be. I would think that is where Mansoor is and if Suzanne wanted a head start it's obvious she has gone to him."

Within an hour the black Mercedes was cruising southwards towards the Atlantic coastline. Wolfe calculated they should arrive after sunset and had taken the wheel for the arduous drive to Sidi Ifni. He was inwardly fuming at his own gullibility in allowing his niece to hoodwink him. He had been within catching distance of Filila and Mansoor and had messed it up, believing Suzanne had listened to reason. Men were easy to work out but he never seemed to have much luck with women. On top of which his head was starting to throb painfully above the bruised eyebrows.

"Are you all right, Jack?" she questioned the scowling man beside her.

"Yes," he growled in reply, without taking his eyes from the road.

"Those stitches should come out. If you want I will do it for you."

Wolfe looked surprised. "Can you manage that?"

"Poof! Of course, we weave beautiful rugs in Morocco. Cutting a few stitches is not a problem." She was teasing him deliberately, trying to lift his low spirits, and in spite of his ill humour he was forced to smile.

"Right, Dany, when we stop again, take them out."

The vehicle moved uneventfully around the suburbs of Agadir and beyond the remote village of Tiznit, until the radiator began to boil over. Wolfe stopped the Mercedes and lifted the bonnet, to find a hose connection leaking badly, which he repaired roughly with an Elastoplast bandage, knowing it was only a temporary measure.

The approaching shadows from the High Atlas Mountains were stealing over the land and he reluctantly gave up any ideas of reaching Sidi Ifni that night. He drove slowly for a few more kilometres until he discovered a small cedar grove with a gushing spring one hundred metres off the dust road and out of sight of travellers. The girl made an impromptu meal with rice and tomatoes as Wolfe once again went to work on the faulty hose. Afterwards they sat drinking mint tea as the darkness drew close.

"Sit on that rock, Jack, or soon I won't be able to see what I am doing," she commanded.

Wolfe obeyed and waited passively as the girl produced tweezers and a fine knife from her purse. Standing above him, she gently snipped away the fine gut protruding from his temple. Her closeness and the rustle of her silken blouse urged him to embrace her and it was with difficulty that he resisted the temptation. He realised this was the first time they had been totally together and he did not want to complicate matters, although he felt an increasing tenderness towards her. She was certainly an unusual woman, serious-minded yet with an ability to accept disasters and pitfalls as an everyday occurrence of life. She finished working on his forehead then bathed his brow with the cooling water from the spring before sitting cross-legged beside him.

"I know so little about you, Dany."

"What is there you need to know?"

"Tell me more of yourself. You are a puzzle to me."

She shrugged. "To myself also. I am unfortunate in being

neither Moroccan nor European. I am too Arab for Europe and too French to be a Berber. Also the men of the African continent are too domineering for my style of life."

"And is there a man in your life?" Wolfe ventured cautiously.

"Oh, of course. My father has more than one thousand camels. It is his belief that one day the oil will all run out and the arregan will once again be the only desert transport which will make him the richest man in the world."

"I didn't mean that," said Wolfe flatly.

"Oh yes, there is Najib my brother. We have always been very close and we own the Chameau Rouge Restaurant that you enjoyed so much."

"You are full of surprises Danielle, but I was not speaking of relatives," Wolfe pushed doggedly on. "I wanted to know if there is a special person in your life."

Her eyes misted and she stared straight ahead. "I was deeply in love once – his name was Ali. He was seven years old and I was six, we had twelve children and..." Wolfe dived at her; she twisted to escape his lunge, before falling helplessly to the ground, squealing with laughter.

That night Danielle slept in the small tent, Wolfe remaining outside under the canvas awning. It had been a warm evening and he was well accustomed to sleeping with only a ground sheet for cover.

Soon the night sky was ablaze with light from the stars, a sight never visible to the town dweller. The stillness of the High Atlas Range could be felt as its awesome vastness towered above them. It was at times like this that Wolfe, embracing the solitude, felt truly at peace. As he slipped gently into slumber, from the dark recesses of his mind the nightmare began. Confused visions of holocaust, battling hand to hand with a shadowy enemy, images of rushing dead faces and his frozen grip upon the helicopter controls as the machine spiralled into the dense jungle below. He cried out in fear, sat up abruptly, his eyes blinking, the sweat clammy on his brow. Danielle was suddenly beside him, her arms cradling his body, as he relaxed with shuddering relief. He lay back, his head on her lap as she held him until his breathing calmed, then lay quietly beside him, her hand in his, staring at the distant brilliance of the night sky.

# Chapter 4

Suzanne Wolfe did not waste any time leaving Marrakech. The phone call from Mansoor and his indignant repudiation of the charges laid against him by Wolfe convinced her to flee. She immediately hired a vehicle to drive her the two hundred kilometres to El Djerib. The taciturn driver she engaged was surprised to learn how far he was to travel but, realising his knowledge of the area was invaluable to the girl, quoted a fee far in excess of his usual charge. Suzanne accepted immediately. There were no definite routes in the wilderness and the thought of being stranded alone in her unhappy frame of mind was more than she could endure. She slumped in the rear seat of the vehicle for the duration of the journey, hardly speaking to the dour man behind the wheel.

The vehicle stopped once, the driver vanishing behind an outcrop of rock for a few minutes before returning to resume the trip without a word. As the first palm trees of El Djerib appeared on the horizon Suzanne's spirits lifted again at the prospect of a reunion with Mansoor.

El Djerib was not much more than an oasis, invaluable

for its underground streams, used mainly by nomads from Algeria en route to the Spanish Sahara. There was a collection of mud-walled huts with corrugated sheet roofs slung unevenly across withered palm branches. Around the five wells were a good number of working camels tethered in separate groups. In the middle distance rose a complicated pattern of Ergs , slow but inexorably moving sand dunes with tips sliding forever downwards creating another dune.

There was no evidence of women at the oasis and Suzanne was relieved to recognise the tall figure of Mansoor, clad in desert jelaba and hood, speaking intently with a group of men. His welcome was affectionate and the obvious concern for her safety convinced her that the choice to follow him was correct. He escorted her to a small white-washed room at the rear of the ramshackle general store that appeared to provide all the necessities of life, the nearest thing to habitation in El Djerib.

The room had only a worn single mattress on a rusting iron frame with a single homespun blanket attempting to cover its austerity. A shuttered window and an oil lamp on a table bleached almost white were the only other furniture available. She grimaced at the Spartan conditions but managed to wash the dust from her face and arms, then changed into a shirt and slacks with a scarf tied at the nape of her neck before venturing out into the store and requesting a mint tea.

Mansoor appeared with Rico Filila and they both joined Suzanne at the table. Filila was friendlier than on his previous meetings but his manner was ingratiating and she had some difficulty in accepting his new attitude without suspicion. Perhaps Achmet had ordered him to be more pleasant? But then it was of no importance. She had not travelled this far to be with Filila. Mansoor placed both his hands on hers and smiled across the table.

"And what do you propose we do with you now, my dear Suzanne?"

"What do you suggest, Achmet?"

His pleasure was apparent. "I would suggest that the courage you showed in the decision to come here can only mean that you have cast aside the old ways and that your future is tied with me forever."

She gulped at the unexpected proposal; she had never totally believed that her life was to be with Mansoor.

"But my uncle and Danielle," she hesitated. "He is unlike other men. I am sure he will not give up following me."

Mansoor shrugged his shoulders. "But here in the wilderness he will be lost like a fly. I have many men working for me: he will be no match for us."

"But I don't want him hurt, Achmet."

"It will not be my choice. In the desert, custom decrees that if we ignore a challenge we show weakness and will lose respect. Would you like me to be a weakling among my people?" He frowned suddenly levelling his eyes upon her.

"No, of course not. I wouldn't want that."

"Then we can only hope that he will not follow us any further."

He smiled again as Filila nodded encouragement.

Suzanne sighed. "There is a lot I don't understand, Achmet. Perhaps I would feel better if I knew more of our plans."

"I agree. The time has come to explain everything in detail. We shall go to the camel stockade and I will show you our complete assets."

Filila stood and led the way to a circular walled enclosure

guarded by two men with rifles. They looked inquiringly at Mansoor who waved them aside, walking through the gateless opening followed by Suzanne and Filila. Piled in neat rows on the sand were assorted cases of light artillery, ground-to-air missiles and ammunition.

Suzanne stopped in amazement, "Achmet, there is enough here to start a war."

"Precisely, and that is what we intend to do."

"My God!"

Fililas's eyes gleamed; he looked highly pleased with the situation.

"But where? How?" she stammered.

Mansoor looked conspiratorially at Filila. "We must tell her everything, Rico."

Filila nodded vigorously – he was enjoying the game. Mansoor had the girl under his control and he was a master at negotiation. He would tell her as much as he needed and omit her part in the scheme.

"Well, this is the way it will be," continued Mansoor. "We have brought the weapons here to El Djerib because it is on the border of four countries. In 1979 Mauritania withdrew its claim to the Spanish Sahara and King Hassan crossed the border to establish sovereignty for Morocco. Then followed the discovery of huge phosphate deposits in the south. The new military rulers of Mauritania want to re-establish their claim to the desert. The only way this can be done is by closing the two hundred kilometre border quickly."

"And this is what the weapons are for?" she asked.

Mansoor's mouth curled. "The military never look for the obvious. They would easily discover vehicles or planes, but these nomad tribes have been journeying the old camel roads legitimately for centuries. The border will be closed under the noses of the Moroccans before they realise what is happening."

Filila was chuckling. "When they find out, it will be too late."

Mansoor took the girl's shoulders in both hands. "I am being paid a large sum of money and I have a task for you. The money needs to be taken to Israel where there are no restrictions on currency and, as a European woman, it will be easier for you to obtain a flight to Jerusalem without suspicion. Could you do this for us, Suzanne?"

The girl blinked away the rising tears. She was being entrusted with the total proceeds of the arms sale and the promise of their future together.

She buried her head on his chest. "I won't ever let you down, Achmet," she whispered.

The old port of Sidi Ifni was only forty kilometres from where Wolfe and Danielle had spent the night. He had coaxed the overheating Mercedes gently to the dockside area to find a garage to replace the worn hose connection. As the vehicle was being repaired Danielle and Wolfe located the harbour master's office on the quayside overlooking the unloading area. They entered the time-worn building and the girl soon engaged an official in Arabic. He laughed suddenly at a shared joke, looking inquisitively at Wolfe as he handed Danielle a clipboard from the wall.

Danielle motioned Wolfe over and they scanned the inventory together. There had been only two arrivals in the port that week. A small fishing trawler with engine trouble was still at anchor and a freighter had docked long enough to unload six containers of farm machinery before leaving on the next tide.

"Ask him what happened to the consignment," said Wolfe.

The official spread his hands and answered in English, "I do not know, Monsieur. We lifted it onto flat wagons and they left immediately. The papers were in order. I cannot tell you anything more."

Wolfe clicked his tongue thoughtfully on his bottom lip, and whispered, "Where do they need farm machinery around here, Dany?"

She shook her head. "There is not a great future in farming the desert."

"Exactly!"

"So you think the boxes contained something else?"

"It's beginning to look that way. A carrier arriving from the Med, clearing off the moment it unloaded its cargo, and the goods vanishing just as quickly, marked farm machinery, miles away from a blade of grass. It looks a bit fishy to me." Wolfe handed the clipboard to the official, thanked him and left the office with the girl on his arm.

"Why were you both laughing at me back there?" he asked.

She fluttered her dark lashes at him. "I was having difficulty getting him to tell me about the arrivals in the port, so I told him you were detained for two days in Casablanca with too much wine and had lost the address for the machinery you were contracted to assemble."

Wolfe laughed. "Thanks a lot. I suppose it was a good excuse."

"Wasn't it? But we still don't know where the stuff went."

Wolfe pulled the battered road map from his pocket. "They did not pass us coming in and the only road good enough to take heavy transport goes the other way."

"But that leads into the desert."

"I know. It's all a bit of a mystery and we could be walking into a hornets' nest."

They arrived at the garage and Wolfe, after inspecting the repair, took the wheel and drove slowly south-west into the approaching desert as the girl sat quietly beside him studying the map.

"I have it, Jack. Stop here."

He obeyed and pulled off the road.

"Here," she stabbed the map with her finger. "El Djerib – the only place left before the mountains. The trucks cannot go beyond that."

"How far?"

"Perhaps thirty kilometres, not much more."

He considered the map thoughtfully then paused before he spoke. "I think you are right, Dany, but now it's time for me to go on alone."

Her blue eyes stared back at him, the anger clearly apparent. "Have you forgotten already that I am Danielle Charni, the daughter of Sarim ebn Charni, the most respected camel master in Algeria? If you really want to rescue Suzanne you will not arrive in a stolen car and alone. We should arrive from the opposite direction, riding camels and dressed as desert travellers."

"I can see the logic in that," he answered. "We would have the element of surprise but where would we find the camels?"

"Here," she prodded the map again. "Hamra, a small oasis probably ten kilometres away. It is the last Berber community before the Sahara. Here we will find all we need."

"Then we shall go further, but I hope my reasons for not wanting you along are clear. I don't want you to get hurt."

Her eyes softened and she touched his arm lightly, "I know, Jack, but let's move on. We still have a long way to go."

Wolfe turned the engine into life and drove into the increasingly barren terrain with the girl silent at his side until she pointed to a group of flat-topped hills entered by a short valley.

"Hamra," she announced briefly, as Wolfe halted under the wild date palms.

The colourfully dressed nomads watched in curiosity as the girl descended from the dust-caked Mercedes. Some greeted her with the traditional touching of their own heart and forehead. Wolfe was surprised to find that many of the travellers were carrying rifles and some of the Berber had a broad knife strapped to the forearm.

Danielle was soon engaged in the boisterous negotiation of camel barter, with much face pulling and shaking of heads from their owners as she ran her hands deftly over the animals before looking inside their mouths.

"They all look alike to me," said Wolfe. "What are you looking in their mouths for?"

"To see how old they are, of course."

"Oh! Of course," he repeated, shaking his head in bewilderment. "Let's take these two, they look sound enough."

"Perhaps, but they are not related. It is better to have mating animals who care for each other and stay together. They have respect for their riders and a good camel master will never split up a family. These two over here will be much better suited to us," she said, throwing a decorated saddle across the male animal. "These are desert arregans." Danielle stroked the neck of the imperious beast. "Tough creatures that can walk seventy kilometres a day without problems and, if we are kind to them, they will adopt us and treat us well."

"You speak as if they are human," he said.

"Better than that. A good camel can save your life and never forget, in the desert they will always stay with the water, so you see we need each other." She threw him a rough spun cloak with a helical pattern at the shoulders. "Try this on," she commanded, pushing his head through the hole in the cape, as his nostrils twitched from the strong animal scent of the garment.

"And this," Danielle said, handing him a close-fitting hat and veil. He put it on and only his eyes were visible. "Perfect!" she nodded approval. "It is the custom for male nobles in the desert never to remove the veil even when eating. It is also the complete disguise." She grinned. "I shall be your dutiful wife and companion. Does that appeal to you?" He nodded agreement. "Then let's eat and continue before darkness."

Wolfe unloaded the Mercedes of all the provisions, pushing the tinned food into the panniers before returning to the girl who was preparing a meal.

"Eat this...," she ordered handing him a plate of potatoes and rice "... and use your fingers. You may as well get used to it."

"Are Berber women always this domineering?" he grumbled.

"Oh yes!" she said. "But some are worse than others."

The desert storm started unexpectedly. The sky was cloudless but the sudden violence of the swirling wind ploughing twisting funnels of sand across the oasis took everyone by surprise. The bellowing camels were dragged into makeshift circles as their drovers struggled to erect their goatskin tents in the centre of the ring. Wolfe, after a futile attempt at helping, secured his animals and propelled Danielle to the security of the Mercedes to escape the full power of the stinging sand.

After an hour the gale subsided as abruptly as it had started and Wolfe had to awaken the girl who had slept immediately he had closed the doors.

"Has it stopped, Jack?"

"Looks like it, but I think we should carry on before anything else happens to delay us."

The camels, grumbling furiously at being disturbed, were awkward to saddle but with persistence the animals were loaded as the camp came slowly back to life.

Wolfe climbed onto the back of the arregan as it rested on the ground, wrapping his legs around the leather pommel. He made the guttural 'kick-kick' sound to make the animal lurch to its feet.

"Bravo!" Danielle said. "You have done this before."

"Couple of times," he answered.

She turned and ran to her own animal, already loaded, and leapt across its back so easily it did not have time to object.

Wolfe smiled approval. "The last time I saw anyone do that was in a circus."

She touched the arregan lightly with her heels and it cantered forwards. "All children can do it, but it is not dignified for ladies and I get so few chances to ride."

"I do not think your kinsmen were overjoyed with the transaction," Wolfe said.

"Oh they were happy enough, they just don't like bartering with a woman." She hefted him an old Lea Enfield rifle, which he caught with practised ease.

"You have used one of these before?" it was almost an accusation.

"Once or twice," he answered, slinging it from his shoulder.

"Not like that," she said. "It is customary to ride with it across the knees when travelling. It is easier to shoot quickly." She flapped her heels at her mount again as the animal raised its head disdainfully and rumbled its farewell to its neighbours before trotting vigorously from the camp, followed by Wolfe.

At the oasis of El Djerib it had taken the whole day to organise and load the camels for the Mansoor caravan. Suzanne Wolfe had watched the proceedings with a detached interest, fascinated with the burdens transported by the animals and hardly believing that twelve tons of armoury could so easily be concealed by handwoven carpets. It was early evening before the caravan commenced its measured departure, skirting the slow-moving dunes at the southern end of the oasis and continuing steadily onto the level plateau beyond.

Mansoor, standing close to Suzanne, remained silent, watching the last animal into the distance.

"Why are they all walking abreast of each other?" the girl asked.

Mansoor looked surprised. "Oh, I see. You watch the American movies. Would you like to be eating the dust of sixty camels when there is the complete width of the desert to walk in?"

"No! Of course, I never thought of that."

"There are many things I must teach you, Suzanne and, as we will soon be following, I shall tie up the loose ends here and follow at a safe distance."

"Why must we do that?"

"Just a precaution. Filila is leading the caravan but if we were apprehended we would have no connection with the arms."

"Is there any chance of that?"

"Very remote. The borders of desert countries are not definite and wilderness travellers have no passports like Europeans. The African continent has no fences." He turned and walked back towards the ramshackle store as she thrust her hands deep into her pockets, dropping into step beside him. "When do we get the money, Achmet?"

He faltered in mid-step as his mind raced. "When the weapons have been delivered to the Sahari army platoons along the boundaries," he answered.

"Who is paying?" she pursued.

"The new leader of the Mauritanian government and as soon as we receive the money this is where you must play your part. You will be carrying more than half a million in sterling and must do so without attracting attention to yourself. Once the plane lands in Israel I shall join you and together we can start a new life."

She put her arm trustingly through his, letting her head brush his shoulder, relaxing in the joy of his complete faith in her.

Wolfe and Danielle rode steadily through the long night. The sky was partly screened by fitful cloud and the ground temperature was moderately lower. A cooling breeze flickered against the girl's face and she twisted in the saddle to see the hooded menacing shape of Wolfe following silently behind. She was about to speak to reassure herself that it was really him, when her mount became agitated, its nostrils dilating and its pace quickening as Wolfe rode alongside her.

"What is making them so nervous?" he asked.

"They can smell water, which means we can't be far away, but we cannot approach an oasis at dawn. It was always a good time to attack from the light of the dawn and would not be considered good manners for an early arrival."

"So we wait, like honest men," said Wolfe, dismounting and leading the animals towards a scrubby outcrop.

Danielle slumped wearily down, her back to the unyielding sandstone and dozed until the first silver fingers of sunlight lightened the early day. Wolfe prepared coffee on a small fire made with scraps of brushwood and handed a tin mug to Danielle, staring into the distance as his eyes became accustomed to the increasing light.

The shadowed buildings of El Djerib could be plainly seen approximately one kilometre away. Wolfe opened his saddlebags and dragged out his worn army binoculars, scanning the village for movement.

Still weary from the night's activity Danielle remained cross-legged on the sand. "Can you see anything, Jack?"

"Not too much at this distance, apart from two very large flat-bed trucks beside an enclosure at the outskirts of the village."

She jumped up excitedly taking the binoculars from him. "Let me see, you are right, they are parked beside the camel paddock. Until now I was not even sure we were going in the right direction."

Wolfe sniffed and mumbled, "Neither was I."

"I think Suzanne is not far away, Jack, and if Mansoor is here he will not be without men."

Wolfe scanned the distance. "Then it's time we found out, Dany," he said, throwing the remains of his coffee on the smouldering fire.

"You must ride first now as a good wife will always travel behind."

"It is the custom," they said in unison, and the girl laughed at his teasing.

The oasis was almost deserted, the camel compound empty and only a small group of travellers were at the wells. Wolfe dismounted, leading the animals towards the only visible store to find a solitary workman repairing the makeshift verandah with planking from large packing cases. Clearly marked on several pieces were the stencilled words 'Farm Machinery'. The girl tugged at Wolfe's sleeve.

"I see it," he said quietly. "Ask if we can rest here."

Danielle entered the store, and then reappeared shortly, beckoning Wolfe over.

"We have the use of the only rear room which was occupied until yesterday by a young blonde English girl."

"Where is she now?"

"She left in the late evening, a couple of hours after a caravan took the old camel trail towards the Atlantic coast."

"Then she was with someone?"

"The man who organised the caravan. It has to be Mansoor."

Wolfe's eyes squinted above the veil. "Then we are only hours behind. We shall have to press on."

She shook her head vigorously. "No, Jack. The animals cannot work night and day. If we force them and they collapse we are in serious trouble."

Wolfe pondered, "You are right. The camels will travel faster if they are fresh."

He took the animals' bridles and led them to an enclosure, giving the thirsty arregans their fill of the fresh water, before returning to the store.

The girl stumbled on the veranda as he approached. Wolfe thrust out his hand to support her.

"You must be exhausted, Dany, sleep for a while and then we will review the situation."

She yawned apologetically. "One thing is baffling me, Jack. If weapons have been driven all this distance out here, why are they being taken back in almost the same direction, towards the coast and by camel?"

"Yes, it's mystifying. I have a feeling they will not reach the coast and the only way we are going to find out is to keep their dust in sight until they give the game away."

She nodded agreement. "And if they do spot us we are only nomads following the established border road."

"Perhaps there is something in what you say, Dany. Maybe it has to do with the border."

She stood swaying on the veranda, the blue eyes blinking with fatigue as he took her hand and led her to the sparsely furnished chamber at the rear of the store. She flopped gratefully upon the old mattress and was asleep in seconds.

The caravan of Mansoor, with Rico Filila at the front, made steady progress along the camel road, the hired drovers singing quietly to their laden animals to coax the most truculent beasts onwards. They made forty kilometres that day and with the arrival of dusk had already met with one platoon of waiting Sahari soldiers and off-loaded one third of the consignment of arms. The Sahari, camped in a rocky depression and wearing jelaba over their uniforms, looked just like any other group of nomads. Rico Filila was beginning to feel that the contract was proceeding as planned.

Captain Kuchak, the platoon officer, with raised tribal tattoos grained beneath his eyes, soon formed an uneasy liaison with Filila, believing him to be a person of authority and was proud of his selection to play such an important part in the proposed coup.

Filila flattered the man's vanity over a shared pipe of kif and prompted questions of the Sahari strategy.

"I am in complete control," Kuchak said, looking pleased, "and in radio contact with our other detachments placed along the border. Within three days from now, when all the weapons have been unloaded, at my signal we shall close the line of demarcation. Shortly afterwards our armoured transport will arrive to reinforce our positions, providing of course that you have accomplished your deliveries on schedule."

It was almost a question to Filila who was nervously aware that he had heard nothing from the men hired to deal with Jack Wolfe but he drew deeply from the pipe of aromatic kif and answered unhesitatingly.

"We have a good organisation and are happy to be of service to the new military rulers of Mauritania."

Kuchak nodded assent, blowing the mild narcotic smoke through his teeth.

"Then we shall both be happy together."

Shortly after daybreak the following morning the campsite was a scene of scrambling activity. The Sahari soldiers were busily engaged in the degreasing and assembly of the new armoury and were firing the weapons to test them.

The increasingly restless camels, stamping and grumbling, were making it difficult for Filila's drovers to load their arregans. Until the previous night, no one had known the exact nature of their contract and now they urgently wished to leave the area.

Into this scene of confusion trotted the two camels of Mansoor and Suzanne Wolfe to be greeted by the woeful Filila, his hands spread sorrowfully wide.

"I could hear gun shots miles away," Mansoor shouted at Filila.

"Well, what can I do? I am not in charge here."

"Then who is?"

Filila indicated the robed figure of Kuchak standing hands on hips watching the newcomers. Mansoor heeled his mount over to the captain and stared contemptuously downwards.

"This is supposed to be a secret operation. You could be heard in Marrakech."

"Who do you think you are to tell me my business?" retorted Kuchak angrily. "What I choose to do with my commandos does not concern you."

Mansoor recoiled. "I want to see the remainder of the weapons delivered safely, without warning half the country of our plans."

"We are an army now. If you can't stand the heat, then run for the shade," Kuchak mocked.

The Sahari platoon cheered and loosed a fusillade of shots skyward.

Mansoor wheeled his mount around confronting Filila. "Let's get out of here before this lunatic gets us all involved."

Filila jumped to obey, urging the drovers to load up more speedily until the caravan hastily moved from the campsite through a gauntlet of jeering soldiers. Filila grabbed the bridle of Suzanne's mount, leading her away from the depression, leaving the tall, mounted figure of Mansoor glowering at the Sahari captain. A hush fell over the watching soldiers as they waited expectantly to see what Kuchak would do. For a few long moments the two men glared in silence, then Mansoor released his breath, wheeled his mount around and set off after the departing caravan. Suzanne Wolfe, the relief visible on her face, smiled as Mansoor, still shaking with anger, rode alongside her.

"I was worried when we left you back there, Achmet."

"The power has sent them all crazy," he scowled.

"Our best chance is to deliver the rest of the arms as quickly as possible before we become involved. If the Moroccan border patrols discover us before the weapons are delivered, nowhere will be safe for us. How far to the next platoon?" he asked Filila.

"About forty kilometres."

"Good, let's see if we can be there before midday."

Filila shouted orders to the drovers who flicked their leader sticks at the camels' flanks, urging the obedient arregans into a faster pace for a few lurching steps before the shrewd animals resumed their measured tread.

It was almost noon when Danielle awoke, her eyes focusing on the rusting corrugated sheets above her as she lay collecting her thoughts. That early morning had seen her reeling with fatigue but a few short hours of rest had soon restored her energy. She swung open the bedroom door to find Wolfe sat alone on the veranda, deep in thought. She crept up behind him and dropped her hands over his eyes.

"Guess who?" she said.

"Give me a clue. I don't know too many people around here."

She laughed and pulled his hair, "I could eat a horse."

"Sorry I can't oblige. Will you settle for some couscous?"

"Anything, so long as it's quick."

She was still eating as Wolfe returned from the camel compound, leading the already loaded animals.

Soon after, they rode away from the oasis heading out towards the old camel road.

"How do you feel now?" he asked.

"Much better, although last night was an ordeal."

"It could get worse."

"I know that," she answered grimly.

The sun was high and at its fiercest. Wolfe accepted the usefulness of the veiled headdress as the arregans trotted along the indefinite camel road. The ancient route was a well-trodden impression, about five hundred metres wide, and Wolfe knew it could be strayed from easily but the disdainful arregan strode the uncertain course without urging.

"They are following the spoor," said Danielle.

"Then we don't need a guide?"

"Not when we already have two."

They stopped twice, walking with the animals and not meeting any other travellers. The vegetation was almost gone and the terrain increasingly barren as the early evening drew close. They had not spoken much, the conditions of travelling using their complete energy.

On the gentle wind came a staccato crackling sound.

"Did you hear that?" the girl asked.

He nodded. "Gunfire and not more than a few kilometres away."

"Who do you think it could be, Jack?"

Wolfe reined his mount to a halt. "It will soon be sunset and that will be our best time to find out. We don't want to wander into an armed group without knowing who they are."

"I agree," Danielle said, heeling her animal towards the cover of the dunes at the side of the old trail.

Wolfe dismounted awkwardly, his limbs aching from the unaccustomed exertion of swaying for hours on an animal's back. They watered their mounts from the goatskin carriers slung across the saddle horn.

"Don't give them too much," the girl admonished. "They will drink us dry if you let them."

As the first stars emerged they were back on the trail, walking the arregans now with hooves muffled with strips of cloth torn from Wolfe's jeleba. The animals had complained bitterly but Danielle persevered and they moved quietly towards the sound of gunfire. Within three kilometres the flicker of campfires burning in a short valley could clearly be seen.

"Hang on to this while I have a look around," Wolfe said, handing his bridle rein to the girl.

Before she had time to answer he vanished into the gloom, leaving her standing motionless in the centre of the old trail. She peered around, suddenly conscious of her vulnerability, before leading the arregans to cover at the side of the trail, making them crouch to avoid being visible on the sky line.

Wolfe ran, rapidly crossing the ground towards the fires, dropping flat and wriggling his way forwards to the edge of the depression, as a sudden surge of laughter caught his ears. He was unprepared for the sight in front of him. There was not a sign of the caravan he had been trailing but a contingent of about eighty men were squatting in orderly lines listening intently to a uniformed soldier.

Wolfe strained to hear but could only make out a few words in Arabic until the officer picked up a carbine from the organised piles of weapons and, shouting a slogan, shook the weapon in the air. The assembled company echoed the battle cry before breaking ranks and returning to the campfires.

A shadowed figure behind Wolfe surprised him. Clad in a jeleba and carrying a rifle the man was walking straight towards him.

Escape seemed impossible. Wolfe cursed inwardly for not spotting the sentry but rose slowly and started to walk down the slope into the depression. The man behind him spoke and Wolfe grunted unintelligibly in return without turning around. For a moment the soldier stared after Wolfe then resumed his patrol of the perimeter as Wolfe entered the camp carefully avoiding the fires.

Most of the men were cloaked but wearing boots under their jeleba with evidence of uniforms at the neck. Wolfe strolled casually around the boundary of the camp, noting the number of camels tethered on a continuous line and the suspicious boxes under the tarpaulin covers. The tall uniformed figure he had seen speaking was suddenly before him. Wolfe, his nerves taut, slowly turned towards a small table containing a barrel and ladle and scooped up a measure of water and drank it noisily. The soldier waited until Wolfe handed him the ladle, wiping his face on his sleeve at the same time. The man accepted the ladle without thanks as Wolfe turned and wandered nonchalantly away from the fires, his hands clasped behind his back until he was clear of the perimeter before dropping low and doubling back up the trail to where he had left the girl.

Danielle was not where he had left her but the increasing starlight displayed a rocky escarpment to the side of the trail and he circled it, approaching from the rear to discover the girl kneeling and peering into the gloom towards the camp. She jumped in surprise as he appeared over her.

"My god, Jack, you are like a phantom."

"Sorry, Dany, it's my job."

"Did you find out anything?"

"Yes. Mansoor has beaten us again. He has left a consignment of weapons and carried on. There is a company of heavily-armed soldiers down there, and they are certainly not Moroccan!"

She put her hand to her mouth. "Then it must mean the same old fight. They are reclaiming the border. That means many people will be killed and almost always the innocent ones."

"I think you are right, Dany. I have seen enough territorial disputes to recognise a boundary war."

"And Mansoor is supplying the goods."

He nodded. "I don't think Suzanne has the faintest idea of the mess she is in."

"Then we keep following?"

"If we don't, her chances are pretty slim."

Danielle was silent, her hand gently stroking the flank of her crouching animal. "Morocco is my home, Jack and I have a duty to my country. I could never forgive myself if I did not warn the authorities of the developments here."

He fingered his forehead gingerly. "And I have a contract to get Suzanne back and it's become a personal issue with me now, Dany."

"Then we must try to follow Mansoor tonight as it seems

we are always one step behind, even if it means burdening the camels," she said.

Wolfe rose to his feet. "I have to agree, but only for Suzanne's sake. I don't need to be involved in any more battles that don't concern me."

"Then let's move," she said, coaxing her resting dromedary to its feet.

They led the animals until they were half an hour away from the army camp and had rejoined the old camel trail, then they remounted.

The sturdy arregans trotted quickly through the early night, side by side as if they were aware of the urgency of the situation. Wolfe was inclined to slacken the pace but the girl disagreed.

"Let them have their way, Jack. They will let us know when it's time to slow down."

Weariness overcame Wolfe in the middle of the night. He looked across at the girl, her head bent to her breast, and was about to speak until he realised she was asleep, rolling easily with the flowing motion of the animal beneath her. With an effort he forced himself awake, searching ahead for any sign of the caravan. The muffled sound of the camels' feet and a slight breeze was the only noise in the barren surroundings and, after an hour, he felt himself dozing fitfully, until he almost fell from the saddle, just retrieving his balance with difficulty. There was a stifled chuckle beside him; she reined to a halt pointing to the lightening sky.

"I thought you were asleep," he said.

"We must walk for a while," she answered, dismounting slowly.

The low grumbling of a disturbed camel was suddenly

carried on the wind. Wolfe and the girl slipped to the ground, listening intently.

"Looks as though we may have caught up, Dany. Travelling through the night has probably paid off."

"Don't leave me here, Jack. If we leave the animals and put the water skins on the ground they will not stray, but I want to come with you."

"All right, but do as I do," he answered, leading the arregans to safety at the side of the trail.

They moved carefully at the perimeter of the worn route selecting cover and pausing before carrying on towards the coughing of tethered animals.

The shape of a man standing motionless was evident on the skyline.

"Is that a sentry?" she whispered.

"Yes, and where there is one, they must have something worth guarding," Wolfe answered, moving towards the solitary man. Within a few metres he could see the area clearly. Approximately sixty camels were present, with half that number of men in attendance around a flickering fire in the centre of the group.

Danielle pulled at his cloak. "It that Suzanne curled up by the fire with the blanket over her? See the blonde hair in the firelight. Now what can we do?" she said, her eyes searching his face.

"I must have one last try at convincing Suzanne of the trouble she is in. Perhaps she already knows that now, but if I can't, she is on her own."

"What about the sentry?"

"Leave him to me," said Wolfe, moving in the direction of the guard.

The man was standing mute, until Wolfe picked up a

pebble and lobbed it over the guard's head. As the stone glanced off a rock, the sentry turned and Wolfe, covering the ground quickly, rose to the man's left and struck a vicious knuckled blow above his ear. The guard collapsed and Wolfe caught him, lowering him quietly to the ground.

The girl appeared beside him.

"What next?"

"Just stand here on the skyline with your back to the camp as if you're the lookout and take this fellow's carbine. If he comes round, smack him with it."

"He looks dead to me."

"Not yet, but he's going to have an awful headache when he wakes."

Danielle stood, occupying the sentry's last position with the carbine slung on her shoulder.

Wolfe ducked towards the camp, and aware of the increasing dawn, eased his way into the encampment. At that precise moment Suzanne threw off the blanket and stood up, stretched and made her way stiffly to the edge of the site. Wolfe, seizing his opportunity, quickly covered the ground and confronted the girl. As she looked questioningly at him, he pulled aside his veil and her look changed to amazement.

Wolfe put a warning finger to his lips. "Suzanne, please listen. I don't have much time. You have no idea what you are doing and this may be your last chance to es…"

"Achmet," she wailed.

For a moment there was total silence, then pandemonium as the camp came to life in a scene of confusion.

Suzanne fled and Wolfe dived to the ground as a bullet ricocheted from a rock beside him. The camels were bucking wildly to escape and the drovers ran everywhere in an attempt to restrain them. A burst of machine carbine fire exploded into the dawn sky from the bogus sentry on the skyline, causing a check in the proceedings and enabling Wolfe to gain the safety of the rocks and run wildly away from the camp towards Danielle.

A fusillade of bullets whirred around his head and he felt a tug at his shoulder almost knocking him over. He carried on grimly until he could see Danielle hurtling across the camel route to where they had left the animals. She leaped behind an embankment as Wolfe furiously chased after her. The machine carbine appeared over the top pointing directly at Wolfe.

"Don't shoot. It's me," he yelled in panic, clearing the low bank and almost colliding with her.

"I can see that," she shouted, and fired a burst at the men following, checking them in their pursuit, before they doubled back to the rocks on the opposite side.

Wolfe and the girl lay gasping for breath until he reached over and touched her arm. "Good thinking, Dany. If you hadn't fired when I was in the camp I would never have made it back."

"But what happened?" she panted.

"Well, I started to remonstrate with Suzanne until she yelled for Mansoor and then all hell broke loose and I was lucky to get away in one piece."

A bullet ploughed into the rocky bank in front of them.

"No time to worry about that now, they are getting our range. Our only chance to slow them down is to get ahead. I can't fight an ambush from the rear."

He picked up the machine carbine. "When I draw their attention, Dany, I want you to take the animals and circle around in front of them. They don't know our strength so they will be cautious. This will give you a bit of time but don't hang about. When I have drawn them away, I shall double back into their camp. We need some more ammunition."

She stared at him incredulously.

"You're going back into their camp?"

He winced at the dull pain throbbing in his shoulder.

"It's the last place they will expect me. They think we will be running, so that's our advantage. Always do the opposite. It confuses the enemy."

"It's confusing me!" said Danielle.

"Right. When I say move, you go."

He checked the machine carbine. There were only a few rounds left.

He pulled the old Lea Enfield rifle from the camel saddle and slipped off the safety catch, studying the shadows gathering across the trail before taking deliberate aim and firing. There was a violent curse and a body pitched to the ground, kicking furiously.

"Right! Move it," he shouted to the girl.

She leapt to her feet and ran, dragging the reins of the trotting arregans. Wolfe kept up a rapid fire at the shadows.

"That should keep their heads down," he said, as he watched the tall figure of Danielle leap into the saddle of her animal and canter away from the escarpment towing the other camel.

The firing from the opposite side was increasing but spasmodically. It was obvious they had not located Wolfe shooting around cover.

He almost laughed. "Just like old times," he muttered, backing away from the protection of the rocks and carrying both weapons further down the trail out of direct fire. It was now fully light and he loosed off some shots from various positions, zig-zagging low and shouting orders to himself, before stopping for breath behind a scrubby bush. He sensed the danger before he saw it, spinning around as he emptied the carbine at the hooded figure before the downward stroke of the knife sliced across his forearm. The man fell on top of him, temporarily knocking Wolfe off balance as he struggled to dislodge the body.

There was movement – and figures ran towards him as he lay motionless among the sandstone. Two men, bending low, searched beyond his hiding place. Wolfe snaked his way along the ground before turning and heading back towards Mansoor's camp. The camels were milling around but only under the surveillance of one guard. Another, his back to Wolfe, was standing beside the heaped armoury, straining to follow the events on the dust road.

Wolfe, crouching low, wasted no time and only rose from cover when he reached the man guarding the weapons. The man half turned as Wolfe clubbed him to the ground with the butt of the Lea Enfield. The camel guard spun around, his face twisted in fear and shaking visibly as he fumbled with the rifle dangling from his shoulder. Wolfe brought his machine carbine level, realising it was only a boy, no more than sixteen years of age.

"Move quickly and you die," snarled Wolfe at the terrified youth.

The boy's hands jerked upwards as Wolfe advanced towards him relieving him of his weapon.

"Thank you," Wolfe smiled. "My carbine is empty, but next time I may not be bluffing."

Before the youngster could respond, Wolfe swept his feet from beneath him, pulled the boy's hands behind his back and bound his ankles and wrists with one loop from the youngster's belt before swiftly gagging him. The boy lay motionless, hardly believing his luck, his eyes fixed wildly on his unconscious comrade.

Wolfe cut the camels' lines, scattering the animals but knowing they would not go far from the water before turning his attention to the arsenal, removing firing pins and as many parts as he could before throwing them in the campfire.

There were sounds of men returning a few hundred metres away. Wolfe hastily heaved some boxes of ammunition and grenades into the fire before grabbing the hapless youngster and dragging him behind an outcrop. There was only time to grab some carbine refills and a few boxes of ammunition before staggering awkwardly from the camp, running in the direction taken by Danielle.

The girl had ridden headlong from the skirmish for ten minutes before pulling the straining animals to a halt. She was waiting patiently at the side of the trail. Wolfe had told her to go, and she had seen enough of his decisions to know that the violence in his nature could erupt without warning when under threat. She sat listening to the sporadic bursts of gunfire in the distance until an explosion lit the morning sky, followed by another and the whining of bullets.

Wolfe plodded into sight weighed down with a heavy load. He made straight for her before collapsing heavily to the ground.

"Get this stuff off me, Dany," he gasped. "I feel like a bloody racehorse."

She dragged at the carbine boxes, taking hasty stock of the weapons.

Another violent explosion ballooned crimson into the sky.

"What was that?" she asked.

"It looks like my brother's bank account just went into the red," Wolfe said.

She pulled a face, shaking her head sideways.

"They're not going to be very pleased with us, Jack."

He shrugged. "Well, I'm not finished with them yet. I still owe Rico Filila and Mansoor, if I can ever find out what he really looks like."

"You mean to carry on then?"

"It's not over by a long way, Dany. We have only travelled one third of the border. Mansoor must be expected further along the camel route by other companies of soldiers, but now that we have depleted his armoury no doubt he won't be so welcome. It amazes me why he didn't just sell the stuff and not get involved with deliveries."

The girl lifted Wolfe's forearm, grimacing at the slashed wrist welling blood. "Perhaps he got a better price: greed can make fools out of men."

"You are probably right, but now I am in front of them and their next rendezvous and that gives me the edge."

There was a single-mindedness in his manner and Danielle looked uncertainly at him.

He answered the unspoken question in her face. "Yes, Dany, the time has come for us to part company. Without you I would never have found them, but now I know my enemy and I don't want you in the firing line any longer."

She was silent at the unexpected change in his attitude, her blue eyes hardening and her mouth set grimly.

"But I can still be very useful, Jack," she remonstrated.

He put his hands on her shoulders.

"More than you know, Dany, but I fight dirty. Hit and run is my speciality and if I am worrying about you I could easily lose my advantage. I hope you can understand that."

She nodded slowly. "What do you want me to do?"

"Something equally as important that you are more capable of than me. You must alert the authorities at Sidi Ifni of the trouble. It will mean taking a direct route across the Wasteland but you will be on the Moroccan side and away from any fighting."

"And what will you do?"

"What I am good at – harrying the opposition. I calculate two or three days at the most before the soldiers waiting for the arms delivery will come looking for it, by which time you will have alerted the cavalry."

She smiled nervously, indicating the spreading bloodstains on his shoulder and wrist. "Let me look at that."

He shrugged off his jeleba and shirt, wincing with the effort.

The bullet had run a deep crease across his left shoulder and blood was running freely down to his slashed forearm.

"God, what a mess," the girl said.

"Looks worse than it is, Dany," he said, crossing to his camel and fishing out a bottle of whisky. Taking a gulp he poured a liberal amount over his wounds, almost dancing with the pain.

Suspended on his chest the hand of Fatima glistened in the morning light.

"Forgotten about that. It really does keep off the evil spirits."

Her bottom lip trembled and her blue eyes misted over.

"Now stop that, Dany and wrap these cuts up or I will be leaving a red trail everywhere I go."

With shaking hands she ripped bandages from his shirt and tied the wounds securely.

"I could not bear it if I were never to see you again, Jack."

"Don't worry," he answered. "I'm a born survivor and you already know my feelings for you."

She stared at him, the blue eyes clearing. "Do you really mean that?"

"The next time you see this," he said, fingering the silver amulet, "I shall be putting it around your neck." There was a silence between them until Wolfe said gently, "But this is not quite the time to be standing on the skyline discussing our future, Dany."

"You are right," she said, throwing her arms around him, forgetting his wounds.

"Ouch!" Wolfe grimaced.

"Oh, but it's only a little cut you said."

Her mood had changed dramatically. "When shall I leave?"

"The sooner the better. I need to plan a little strategy before Mansoor's men get back on the prowl for me."

She swung easily into the saddle of her arregan and Wolfe handed her a carbine. "I don't think you will need this but stay watchful. I am thinking about you."

"*Merci.*" She gave a salute, wheeling her mount around. "But I think you are a bit crazy, Jack Wolfe."

He watched her go with mixed feelings. She turned only once to wave and disappeared into the distance. He felt relieved to be totally alone.

The camp of Mansoor was in chaos. The animals frantically ran away from the exploding ammunition and the cursing drovers pursued them, adding to the confusion as Mansoor returned to his campsite almost speechless with rage. Five of his men were finished, either dead or crippled, and the normally ordered atmosphere of a caravan had been replaced by shock and fear. Rico Filila loped back into the scene of disaster confronting Mansoor standing with the trembling Suzanne Wolfe.

"We have found two fresh sets of prints, Achmet. If it is Wolfe, he must have another with him."

Mansoor exploded into anger. "Two men only and leaving us in total panic. I can't believe it."

Filila cowered under the onslaught. "But we know of this man. He is trained in espionage. It could have been much worse. I think we were lucky to have…"

Mansoor cut him short. "He is a devil and I still blame you, Rico for bringing him after us."

"But we were unprepared. How were we to know he could find his way out here?"

"Because it is his business," shouted Mansoor, turning towards Suzanne. "And he must be working with someone who knows the desert. Do you think he still has the girl with him?"

She shook her head in disbelief. "No, Achmet, it can't be true."

"But you said yourself that they followed you to Marrakech. Who else could Wolfe enlist so quickly to do his dirty work?"

The simple logic of his statement showed on her face and she quivered uncontrollably as a lone runner stumbled into the camp approaching Filila.

"We have followed the tracks but they have split up. An unladen camel has gone north across the Wasteland."

"And the other?" said Mansoor.

"The tracks doubled back and then we lost them among the rocks."

Mansoor cursed. "So it looks as though the girl has gone

directly for help and Wolfe is waiting in ambush somewhere in front of us."

Filila gulped. "What shall we do?"

"We must catch the girl."

Suzanne squirmed beside him.

"And when you have her, bring her back here," Mansoor added hastily. "We can use her to bargain with Wolfe. Take three men," he ordered Filila, "and follow the girl. I will split the caravan into two groups and continue on both sides of the trail one hour apart. He can't be waiting for us in two places at the same time."

Filila jumped to obey, organising the men before mounting and wheeling his camel in pursuit.

"Rico!" shouted Mansoor, running after Filila and out of earshot of Suzanne. "When you catch her, don't bring her back."

Wolfe pulled apart the boxed ammunition, loading the machine carbine and filling the spare magazines. His camel nudged him in the back like a playful dog, prompting Wolfe to sponge its muzzle with water from the spare canteen.

An hour elapsed and he filled his bulging pockets with spare bullets while watching the trail through his binoculars until he could see two parties leave Mansoor's campsite. He patted the animal's neck affectionately. Danielle had chosen the young animal well. It held its head high despite being ridden through the night, and it still looked physically strong.

"I hope you are up to this old girl. I think they intend to make us work hard."

The animal nodded vigorously, causing Wolfe to laugh aloud. "I'll be dammed if you don't understand every word I say."

He loaded the patient arregan, leaving the rock cover, and set a course parallel to the nearest group of drovers. It was only when he was within firing range that he noticed a small dust cloud to the north. Pulling the animal to a halt he stood to his full height on the camel's saddle and trained his binoculars on a group of four mounted men disappearing into the distance.

"Good God, they're following Danielle."

He dropped into the saddle, twitching his leader stick at the animal's flank. "Change of plan Lady. We must stop them before they catch Dany."

The arregan set off at a fast pace, causing Wolfe to rein back slightly.

"Steady old girl, don't run out of steam too soon. We have a long day ahead of us."

The morning sun was causing a mild heat haze to appear from the earth and an intermittent shimmering obscured Wolfe's sight of the riders he was following. He reasoned that if he could not see them clearly and he was a smaller target the chances of them noticing him would be greatly reduced, but he had to make good progress before being observed.

After keeping a steady trotting pace for an hour he was pleased to find the distance had shortened to four hundred metres without him being seen. He hung on grimly, willing the quartet in front not to check behind.

His opportunity arose as the riders laboured up a slight incline. Once they had vanished over the top, Wolfe put his camel to a gallop urging the game animal upwards to the ridge, before leaping from the saddle and slamming a magazine into the old Lea Enfield. The distance from the riders was three hundred metres. He knew it would have to be a lucky shot to be any good.

He wiped the perspiration from his eyes, levelling his rifle at the furthest man before releasing his breath and squeezing the trigger. The group carried onwards until the sound caused them to wheel about. Wolfe slammed another round into the chamber and took aim at the same target, until the rider slumped in the saddle and fell to the sand.

Wolfe fired at another drover who clutched his shoulder, pulling his camel violently down with him for cover. The two remaining men put their mounts to the whip, setting off at a gallop as Wolfe furiously pumped shots after them without any apparent effect. He ran frantically back and remounted, twisting the animal's head and kicking the arregan forwards.

The startled beast stumbled away, pitching him out of the saddle. He landed awkwardly on his injured shoulder, the jarring shock making him yelp with pain. He lay dazed, feeling the open wound coursing blood. The camel stood motionless, its fetlock raised and its head down.

"Sorry old girl, that was stupid. I was told to look after you," he said, putting his arm round the arregan's neck, and pulling himself upwards.

The two remaining riders were now well out of firing distance. Wolfe shook his head ruefully.

"Well I made a mess of that old girl. I can only hope that Dany can out run them."

The arregan nuzzled him gently and Wolfe, apologetic for his rough handling, was very aware of the strengthening bond between himself and the patient animal in the desert emptiness.

"I know," he said. "All we can do now is to get back and cause some mayhem."

He retraced his steps southwards, walking with the animal until it ceased to limp, then mounted carefully.

"In your own time Lady."

The arregan snorted and, lifting its head, sloped into a steady gait back towards the old camel trail.

In low-level areas of the Sahara plains noise can carry for miles and Danielle could clearly hear the sharp sounds of gunfire in the distance. She knew Wolfe was thinking of her safety when he sent her away, but it was a challenge to cross the Wastelands alone, away from any established control. He must have faith in her ability and she resolved not to let him down, but the thought of him fighting single-handed made her bite her lip with concern.

It was late morning when she saw the two riders who were following her, their pale shadows shimmering above the sand in the mirage heat. She understood the threat immediately and dismounted, throwing off all excess weight from her animal and retaining only a goatskin water carrier and some dates before checking the carbine and continuing steadily on her way.

The arregan was coaxed into a brisk walking pace and Danielle knew that if she did not panic, she could stay ahead without difficulty. Sidi Ifni was two days away and if Moroccan troops were alerted, Jack Wolfe would not be alone too long.

After an hour the distance between her and her pursuers was closing rapidly and soon she could see the men kicking their mounts furiously. She purposely kept to the same steady pace, estimating the decreasing distance carefully before heeling the arregan into a gentle canter and pulling steadily away.

When she looked around her pursuers had stopped, their animals completely winded by the urgent demands made on them. The game played on throughout the day. Danielle often walking with her animal and then remounting, as the riders appeared closer. She was almost cheerful with the cat and mouse game, knowing only too well the consequences if she were caught.

A flirting breeze rippled her hair and she again slipped from the saddle, shouldering her carbine and walking ahead of the camel, which trailed by a guide rein. The arregan stopped suddenly, the halter tightening as Danielle stumbled forwards, her hands outstretched to break the fall. The ground was soft and her arms vanished to the shoulders, her face plunging into the morass. She had walked into a sandpool: a sickening fear seized her as she thrashed violently to escape the frightening hold that gripped her.

The girl was no stranger to the desert and had heard many tales of caravans lost to sandpools, but she had never encountered this particular peril herself. The arregan stood almost motionless, pawing the ground as Danielle sunk deeper, the fine powdery dust closing around her. She tried not to panic and found she was still holding the bridle rein. She pulled with all her strength and her body moved slightly upwards as she yelled at her animal, causing it to jerk falteringly backwards, dragging the kicking girl clear of the morass and onto firmer ground. She sprawled gasping for breath as the agitated camel see-sawed to a crouching position beside her, braying its relief. It was quite obvious to the girl that there could be other sandpools and she decided to put her faith in the animal with its keen sense of danger.

Looking back at her pursuers she saw that they had

used the time to gain valuable ground but their camels were almost at a walking pace. Mounting quickly she urged the dromedary to its feet and, carefully avoiding the area of her almost fatal disaster, trotted away parallel to the sandpool. The nimble-footed animal frequently stopped, testing the ground and making small detours, causing the distance between Daniel and her puzzled pursuers to steadily decrease.

She thought she would have to stand and fight so she unslung the carbine from her shoulder. Just then her mount broke into a lively canter away from the men. They were thrashing their camels unmercifully now, the winded animals no more than five minutes behind. Danielle, looking over her shoulder, was fascinated by the drama that was now unfolding.

The leading camel had stopped abruptly, pitching its rider forwards to the ground. Regaining his feet he started to strike the animal around the head with his leader stick before overbalancing and falling backwards. Without a sound and the briefest waving of his arms he vanished abruptly into the morass.

The remaining rider was at a dead stop and the girl could clearly see the bearded face of Rico Filila, the full horror of the quicksand reflected on his face. Danielle dismounted, took careful aim and fired a burst at the ground in front of the man, puffing up the dust, the sound, echoing back from around the rocky landscape. Filila did not move, he was at her mercy. She had already tasted the fear of the sandpool and now Filila was caught, petrified, and unable to help himself in his moment of terror.

Danielle hung the carbine on her saddle pommel. Filila was not going anywhere. He was too fearful to test the wilderness any further. She remounted and her animal trotted slowly north, leaving Filila stranded and alone.

In the Libyan Intelligence Service in Tripoli Major Riyan Sleyman stood at a high window, hands clasped behind his back and deep in thought, oblivious to the activity in the sunlit harbour below. Ten days from now the Israeli Defence Minister would be boarding a plane at Casablanca for the flight to Jerusalem. It was a normal scheduled flight but the minister was travelling under an assumed name for security reasons. The explosive device would be detonated shortly after take off. Riyan Sleyman had envied the power of Colonel Gaddafi for years and he was relying on Achmet Mansoor to end that power for good.

Mansoor was using an English woman to carry the explosives aboard the plane, and there would be just enough fabricated evidence to connect Muammar Gaddafi to the outrage. It was Riyan Sleyman's belief that this would unleash the might of the Israeli Army. This could only force Colonel Gaddafi into further discredit and reduce his power, leaving the way for Major Riyan Sleyman to seize authority.

The Libyan Intelligence Service, with Sleyman and Dhulmet already in command of the huge oil revenues, had negotiated to pay Mansoor half a million pounds for his part in the conspiracy. The money would not go undetected for long, but by the time the embezzlement was discovered Colonel Muammar Gaddafi would not be the undisputed leader of the Libyan people.

His accomplice, Captain Dhulmet, entered the office disturbing Riyan Sleyman's thoughts. Dhulmet had a cautious attitude to his superior officer and an awesome respect for a man who would conspire to challenge the power of Colonel Muammar Gaddafi.

"Are you still worried?" Dhulmet queried.

Sleyman drew a nervous breath. "There is nothing to worry about. Achmet Mansoor openly supplies arms to the Gaddafi regime. There is nothing to connect us to him and we shall ourselves denounce Mansoor as the tool of Gaddafi by giving him the money in advance."

Dhulmet shuffled apprehensively. "But if something were to go wrong and we lost the money, how would we explain its disappearance?"

Sleyman turned to smile at Dhulmet. "Why are you so cautious? It is a small price to pay for a country, don't you agree?"

Dhulmet nodded vigorous approval. "And how do we pay the money to the Moroccan?"

"That will be your task. I shall leave you to make all arrangements with Mansoor for delivery in Casablanca one week from now and it needs to be a matter of public record. This way our illustrious colonel will not be able to deny anything and we will not be implicated."

# Chapter 5

Wolfe reasoned that a caravan of dromedaries wishing to stay together could only travel at the pace of the slowest animal. It meant that to prepare an ambush he would have to try to be in two places at the same time since Mansoor had divided his party. This also worked two ways. If you split your force, you halve your strength. Wolfe had the advantage of surprise and speed. If he picked his areas carefully and used natural cover, his adversary would have a hard time in finding him. The old rules of hit and run applied very strongly with a smaller force.

It was late afternoon when he saw the first detachment of drovers, strung out in a line, contrary to practice, and using only flat land in the belief that they would be difficult to surprise. He urged his mount forward, searching for a good position until he reached an undulating series of sand hills with the western side in shadow. He dismounted, watching the slow-moving procession approach to within five hundred metres, before riding purposefully into full view of the group.

The oncoming party slowed and regrouped, anticipating

some form of attack, forming a circle with the crouching camels in the open area beyond the sand hills. It was all Wolfe had hoped for. They were waiting for a reprisal. He stroked his arregan's neck before turning back into the shadows of the low hills.

"Divided we fall, the rule book says, Lady. They obviously haven't read it. That should keep them quiet till dusk and give us as a chance to slow down the other lot if we can find them." The animal bawled. It knew its rider was pleased and trotted briskly into the shadows of the high dunes parallel to the old camel route. The terrain away from the established sand road was both rocky and difficult to manoeuvre, without any sign of the other party. Wolfe had an uneasy feeling; he was being watched, and it made his body tingle with apprehension.

He was soon convinced that he was too far ahead of the other group and decided to make a long sweep to higher ground on the other side of the pass in the hope of finding them. The shadows were lengthening and the sun had lost some of its urgent heat. The arregan adopted a plodding gait as they rounded a rock plateau and without warning stumbled into the camp of Mansoor.

The drovers, completely unprepared for the sight of the lone rider, were thrown off guard, obviously believing they were far ahead of Wolfe, who used the brief moment to spur his mount to a gallop firing his carbine indiscriminately without picking a target into the middle of the camp. He only checked his wild charge at the sight of Suzanne Wolfe, standing transfixed, before he was out of the campsite and storming away into a narrow defile.

The pursuit was immediate. Wolfe, crouching low, could hear shouted obscenities as he reached the end of the cutting, leaping from his animal and dropping to the ground, with the old Lea Enfield rifle ready in a firing position. His pursuers, not waiting to mount their animals, ran madly into the defile and Wolfe, shooting around cover and working the bolt action on his weapon like a pump handle, kept up a rapid fire at the leading men, dropping them to the ground as they appeared, before jumping to his feet and leaping onto his waiting camel, kicking its flanks urgently to escape.

Achmet Mansoor struggled hard to control the exasperation surging through him. His plan of dividing his force had not worked and his rage was apparent to the rapidly depleting ranks. The sudden shock of Wolfe riding into the centre of the camp, alone and firing everywhere, convinced him that the Englishman was totally mad.

The mercenary crew Mansoor had assembled for the drive were scattered and the impromptu attack had knocked all of the fight out of the remaining drovers. He knew it would not be long before there would be trouble in his own ranks. The men, although hardy, were not soldiers and had not expected to fight their way along the border trails. The man stalking them was a demon with the luck of the devil and the once orderly caravan had been reduced to a shambles, and now the consignment was not only undelivered but incomplete. The burning resentment of his thwarted plans was replaced with an overwhelming desire to destroy this assassin.

Suzanne Wolfe clung speechless to his arm and he almost wished he had never met her, but she still had her part to play in the attack on the airliner. It was not over yet. He took her shoulders in his hands.

"Suzanne, your uncle is a barbarian and I am sure he meant to destroy us all, yourself included. We have not harmed him in any way and only conduct our business as your father has done for years. I'm sure Wolfe has a personal vendetta against us. I think the only thing for us is to return to the Sahari platoons along the trail and enlist their help. My contract was to supply, not to fight my way to the coast. We must leave the caravan together and get help."

The girl searched his face. "When can we leave, Achmet?"

"Now whilst we have a chance."

"Saddle two camels," he shouted to a drover, "and the rest of you, take up defensive positions."

The men rushed to obey, grateful for an authoritive voice, quickly saddling two animals and leading them to Mansoor. He hoisted the girl roughly onto her standing camel and they trotted away, back to the trail, leaving the weakened caravan to their own recovery.

After she had left Rico Filila stranded to his own salvation, Danielle proceeded methodically across the Wasteland towards Hamra with a careful urgency. She needed to alert the military with as much haste as possible but had no desire to encounter another desert hazard like the sandpool.

Although the daughter of a camel master, this was the first time she had been alone in the Wasteland of the Atlas plateau. She stroked the gentle animal below her, grateful for the companionship in the awesome silence. Left to its own choice the plodding gait of the arregan often slowed to a halt and Danielle, recalling the songs of the drovers to coax their mounts, began to sing the parts she could remember. The haughty beast would promptly resume its rolling stride, wandering steadily onwards and detouring around the obstacles in its path.

The girl was losing track of time. The rolling movement

of the beast and the vigorous activity from the previous night added to her increasing weariness until she found herself spasmodically jerking to stay awake. The evening warmth held not the slightest breeze; the landscape hazy to all sides was almost without feature.

She awoke with a profound sense of unease. The arregan was standing rigid, its head down and silent. She searched the sandy emptiness of the arid landscape, the reason for her isolation unclear. The animal lifted its head and snorted. The girl stretched awkwardly in the saddle, changing her position to scan the horizon. There was only a wisp of cloud in the far distance and it slowly dawned on her that she could be completely lost.

She felt like yelling out loud but the only creature to hear would be her companion. She had heard the desert could drive a person mad, like confinement in a prison. The only answer was to continue. She still had a long way to ride. The girl heeled the animal forward and they continued at an ambling pace until the warmth left the day and the first stars showed bright in the twilight.

She stopped and scanned the evening sky. The Great Bear was faintly to her left and the North Star perhaps thirty degrees away from her proposed direction. It had been easy to wander away but if she had carried on this bearing there was no doubt she would have rambled into the trackless void of the Sahara Desert.

She dismounted stiffly and untied the goatskin water carrier. To her dismay she found it half empty from a leaking seam. She sponged her animal's nozzle with the wet hide and licked the remaining moisture from her fingers. It was not sensible to travel the darkened hours across unknown territory but the absence of water and the insecurity of her whereabouts gave her no choice. Her thoughts drifted to Jack Wolfe. She had made a commitment to him and it gave her a calmness to know he was relying on her to finish the task he had given her. Her animal was game and had already proved its ability to sense danger.

She walked a good distance, ever fearful of soft ground and holding tight to the bridle rein, and then mounted again singing gently to the animal. She carried on alternatively riding and walking through the long night until the dryness in her throat caused her to stop. She had a vision of riding in a circle and a jumble of mixed emotions caused her to believe she was looking down at the reflection of herself wandering forever the timeless land. The grey fingers of early dawn appeared and she swayed drunkenly in the saddle, dehydrated and unable to swallow.

The sky was spinning and she looked blankly at the upturned faces and beckoning hands unable to comprehend the sudden babble of voices, as she fell into the arms outstretched towards her with a flush of relief and realised she had finally reached Hamra and her Berber kinsmen.

The company of Sahari soldiers Achmet Mansoor had so recently quarrelled with were silent at his return with the English girl. They entered the campsite watched cautiously from all sides until they confronted the belligerent captain. He scowled apprehensively, knowing there had to be an exceptional reason for the return of the Moroccan arms dealer, but was soon appalled at the description of events following the departure of Mansoor's caravan.

"You are telling me that one man is holding back our control of the border?" he shouted in disbelief.

Mansoor nodded grimly. "He is not an ordinary man.

He has the devil's luck and when we have had him cornered he vanishes without trace."

The captain sneered, "He may be a devil to a bunch of herdsmen, let's see what he can do against trained soldiers."

"Yes! I would like to see that," said Mansoor.

There was an irony in his answer that made the captain hesitate.

"Why is this man so opposed to you?"

Mansoor nodded towards Suzanne, "He is after the girl."

The soldier stared in surprise. "Then give him the damned woman."

Mansoor glared back. "I choose to keep her – she is useful to me."

The captain shrugged abruptly. "Do as you wish. I shall make him an example to others who may want to challenge our authority."

He turned away giving orders for the breaking of camp and within minutes all were saddled and heading out along the trail towards the coast with the captain leading. Mansoor and the girl watched the departing camels over the skyline.

The girl was mystified at the attitude of Mansoor. "What is it you find so funny, Achmet?"

He spat into the sand after the disappearing soldiers. "I have sent a desperado to catch a shadow. Perhaps they will finish each other."

She was troubled, remaining quiet.

"I know he is your kin," he said touching her hand, "but he did not think of that when he charged into our camp firing everywhere. I swear he meant to kill you, but one thing I am sure of – he will not be able to follow us any further. Now we can get back to Casablanca without being hunted.

Our money is there and the sooner you are in Jerusalem the sooner our new life will begin."

She listened, the doubt creasing her forehead.

"This will soon be a memory, Suzanne," he continued soothingly. "Nothing great was achieved without effort."

She released her breath in a shudder.

"I know you are right, Achmet. So much has happened, I am not sure of anything anymore."

He pulled her close, cradling her head to his chest.

"Let me do the worrying 'Little One'. We are together and that is all that matters to me."

Danielle was unaware of how she came to be in the framed goatskin tent. She surfaced from the relenting fatigue to find herself on a bed of piled woollen rugs with two elderly Berber women in attendance, having her face washed gently, and the other rubbing the life back into her numbed hands. At the raised tent flap a group of young anxious faces peered in inquisitively, until they were gestured fussily away.

"Is this Hamra?" Danielle questioned feebly.

The woman smiled, supporting her and raising her head to drink from an earthenware cup. The water was cool and it spilled down the front of her kaftan.

"Yes, this is Hamra," one of her nurses answered, "and what you were doing alone in the desert without water is puzzling us all. Another day and you would not be bothered where you were."

Danielle relaxed back on the woven carpets, piecing together the events of the last few days.

"My name is Danielle Charni and it is very important that I speak with your headman immediately."

The old women exchanged glances before one hurried

out, returning soon with a tall, blue-eyed patriarch with a grey beard.

He bowed respectfully. "My name is Mohammed Isteil. I remember you from some days ago. Your were here with an Englishman, buying camels."

"Yes, I am Danielle Charni and I need your help urgently."

"The name of Charni is well known to me," answered the gaunt wayfarer. "If you are needing help, you have only to ask."

The girl told the old man all she could of the problems on the border and her journey across the Wasteland.

He listened impassively until she finished.

"Always there are men desiring greatness and it is often gained with the blood of innocents. All land should be free to everyone without boundaries or fences. We have enjoyed the freedom of the wild places since time began, although our home is now Morocco. Rest with us," he continued patting her hand. "I will send my two sons to Sidi Ifni at once They will alert the militia there."

Danielle struggled to her feet.

"I must go with them. Without me it will be difficult to say where the Saharis are."

"It would be better if you rested," answered the patriarch. "You are not yet strong enough to travel."

"That may be true, Mohammed, but I have much to tell and I cannot be much use here."

The old man inclined his head. "So be it. We shall travel at sunrise."

Danielle felt herself slipping back into drowsiness, gladly submitting to sleep, unaware of the silent departure of the headman leaving the tent.

\*

The following dawn Danielle awoke to find the old Berber women fussing her into wakefulness. There was a carafe of ground coffee steaming at her side with some fresh rice cakes. She demolished the food rapidly before rinsing her face from a water pitcher, and left the cool sanctuary of the skin tent.

The old headman was saddling Danielle's dromedary as she stepped into the dawn light.

He inclined his head in greeting.

"*Bonjour, Mademoiselle.*" He spoke in French although his natural tongue was Arabic.

"*Bonjour,* Mohammed," she repeated. "Are we ready to begin?"

"Indeed, I shall accompany you, together with my two sons and as time is important, I suggest we commence as soon as you are able."

"I am ready now, Mohammed," she grinned at the two young men smiling shyly back at her. "And please call me Dany – all my friends do."

The younger of the men handed Danielle the bridle rein, while the other cupped his hands to lift her to the saddle. She swung upwards, thanking him graciously, just resisting the urge to leap frog on the patient animal, yet noticing the pleasure in the man's face.

The complete camp came out to wave good-bye. They all knew now the problems on the border and good wishes rang in her ears as the quartet of riders trotted northwards out of the oasis towards the seaport of Sidi Ifni.

At midday, they stopped to rest the animals and Danielle spoke at length of the events leading up to her arrival at Hamra. The old Berber headman nodded agreement, before introducing his sons into the conversation. The two young men appeared to be more interested in the girl's life in Tangier and the time she had spent in university than the problems on the Moroccan border. She also found them an interesting pair. They had travelled the Silk Road to Samarkand and she found a common bond in their storytelling.

Almost reluctantly they remounted, cantering away along the now clearly defined dust road, the old man singing to his animal and Danielle joining with the young men in the parts she could remember.

Towards evening the sparse vegetation gave way to small-cultivated plots and the group were soon within sight of the outskirts of the town. At the first houses the older man enquired the whereabouts of the local gendarmerie and was directed to a white-stuccoed building standing alone at the crossroads near the fruit market. The little troupe dismounted, leaving the youngest son with the camels as Danielle and the two men entered the low white-washed building.

Inside the sparse room were two uniformed officers engrossed in the heaped literature spread out on the desk before them. They glanced up inquiringly as the dust-covered trio entered. The grey-bearded Berber bowed from the waist as the policemen rose to their feet.

"I am Mohammed Isteil, this is my elder son Abdul and this is Mademoiselle Danielle Charni," he said in the time-honoured custom of Berber introduction.

The officers returned the greeting, looking curiously at the girl as she stepped forward.

The events of the last few days crowded into Danielle's brain and she found it difficult to know where to begin, but when she started to speak, the words overflowed each other.

One of the officers smilingly interrupted her. "Would you like a chair, Mademoiselle?"

She nodded gratefully, aware that all eyes were on her. The older Mohammed stood behind the chair and placed his hand reassuringly on her shoulder.

"The young lady has been under great stress and has overcome many problems to be here to speak with you now."

"Please continue," said one of the men.

She breathed deeply and started again, speaking at length of Wolfe and the assault on the border by the Saharis. The policemen listened intently until she finished speaking.

There was a silence in the office, the only movement was from one of the policeman, rocking backwards on the rear legs of his seat, arms folded across his chest – he stood up pointing towards a map on the white-washed wall.

"Can you show us Mademoiselle where this action is taking place?"

She stood looking at the map for some time before answering.

"About here." She indicated an area midway on the old camel route.

The two uniformed men exchanged glances, and then one spoke.

"I do not doubt your sincerity Mademoiselle but the distance involved is about one hundred and fifty kilometres from Hamra and you say it took only two days. That kind of progress across such terrain is hardly believable. Perhaps you have made a mistake?" he looked questioningly at the girl.

The gaunt old Berber levelled his blue eyes on the gendarme.

"There is no mistake. Mademoiselle Charni is the

daughter of Sarim Ibn Charni, the caravaneer. She rode alone through the night and across the wilderness to reach Hamra, before collapsing from exhaustion. It was only the will of Allah that saved her from perishing without trace."

The officer visibly flushed from the headman's chastisement.

"Forgive me Mademoiselle, I had no idea. Please accept my apologies. I was only trying to ascertain the precise location of the trouble."

His associate picked up the phone speaking volubly for some minutes. She relaxed completely for the first time that day; the old headman patted her shoulder, looking down affectionately at her.

"Yes, yes, here in front of me now," the policeman said into the receiver. "Would you mind having a few words with the colonel, Mademoiselle?" he said passing the phone to the girl.

She answered countless questions barked at her from the Moroccan soldier before he asked to speak to the policeman again. After some moments the officer placed the phone back on its cradle turning to the Berber headman.

"Monsieur, it would be an honour if your party could remain as our guests tonight."

Danielle, pleasantly surprised, was about to agree until she felt the old man's hand tighten on her shoulder.

"You mean we cannot leave?" he questioned.

The officer opened his palms apologetically.

"You would do us a service if we could question you further. Anything you may have missed could have great bearing on future events with the military."

"What do you think, Danielle?" the old man asked her.

"We have come this far, Mohammed. Perhaps we need

to rest, and a few days won't do us any harm."

The old man shrugged. "So be it."

"It is agreed then. I will arrange accommodation and tonight you shall be our guests."

Danielle smiled. "I would settle for a hot bath."

Everyone laughed; the tension suddenly eased and the policeman escorted them to an enclosure for their camels at the rear of the Alhambra Hotel. The young men were delighted at the unexpected luxury and even the older Mohammed managed a grin. After feeding the animals the girl plunged into a steaming bath and lay dreaming in a mountain of lavender scented bubbles. She could hardly believe she was here, after the harsh conditions of the desert. If she only knew what had happened to Wolfe, or if it were possible to contact him, she would have felt relieved. Whatever the outcome, she promised herself that she would renew her relationship with the desert nomads and try to cultivate the heritage that she had been born into.

The urgent knocking on her bedroom door disturbed her thoughts. It was the younger son of the headman entreating her to come to dinner prepared in their honour.

"Yes, I'm coming right away," she shouted, sinking lower into the luxury of the hot foam.

Wolfe had chosen his concealment for the night with care. There were many hiding places in the rocks at the side of the desert trail but he chose to avoid these areas, finding a slight depression with little cover but good all round vision. This gave him the advantage of not being surprised and an enemy rarely searched where there was little camouflage. He coaxed his animal to the ground, leaving it saddled, and drank sparingly, feeding his arregan the ripening dates. His shoulder wound was throbbing furiously and he redressed it awkwardly, but there appeared to be no sign of infection.

He had an approximate idea of the ground occupied by his opponents and positioned himself near the rim of the depression with a clear view over the trail. It was impossible to say how long he could continue with these guerrilla tactics against a larger force. He needed sleep desperately, but to be caught unawares on open ground would be a fatal mistake. Adopting an old army trick of squatting cross-legged on the ground, he managed to doze fitfully but as he relaxed completely, he fell forwards, waking himself again. This was not the most satisfactory method of resting but it kept him alert to imminent danger. His periodic search of the skyline revealed nothing. His dromedary, usually a good warning system, snored peacefully beside him, but the nagging fear of reprisal was always there.

The moon rose pale above him, the same vision that Danielle would be seeing if she were still safe. He tried not to worry about her but it was impossible not to. She was an intelligent woman and with good luck should make it safely across the Wasteland, if she used the water sparingly. He wished he had abandoned this pointless vendetta and accompanied her to Hamra. His niece had made her choice. Maybe his interference was making things worse. It was too late for recriminations. He had chosen to stay and that was the end of it.

It was a long night. He lapsed in and out of sleep, the memories of earlier days and other battlegrounds uppermost in his mind. It was only when the luminous sky softened and the stars lost their brilliance that he woke properly, watching the earth take on recognisable shapes. Very slowly the first troupe of mounted men came into focus. They were riding in a long column, unlike the orthodox habits of caravaneers.

Wolfe had not expected this. They were obviously military but from which side? He studied the approaching group through his binoculars, hoping to make an appraisal of their numbers. Soon they were in good view and stopped, retaining ranks. Wolfe recognised them as the company of Sahari soldiers that he had already encountered. If they had left their holding position to come this far west, it could only be for one reason. They were looking for him. The sensible thing would be to remain in hiding until an opportunity arose for withdrawal. The odds were stacked against him now. There would be no more 'hit and run' against an armed force.

Wolfe heard the low whine of the aircraft engine long before it was visible. It approached from the Atlantic coast, flying at a thousand feet, a single-engined Cessna with Moroccan markings on its wing tips. He realised with relief that it was possibly an airforce reconnaissance plane. Did it mean that Danielle had made it to Sidi Ifni already? It was hard to believe but unless it was a routine surveillance plane the evidence was there above him. It swooped low over the Saharis still clad in their disguise. The assembled company waved cheerfully at the Cessna just like a normal group of travellers.

"Damn," Wolfe said aloud. "I hope he doesn't fall for it."

The light aircraft climbed away into the distance, leaving Wolfe fuming with annoyance. He had missed his chance and there was nothing he could do about it.

Some minutes later he heard the sound of the light engine again and the Cessna reappeared, flying into a low spiral above the assembled Saharis. They waved back but

Wolfe, unsure of the situation, could not wait for another chance. Cocking his machine carbine he fired into the sky until his magazine was empty before banging in another clip and repeating the manoeuvre. The plane veered away from the trail, gaining height before circling warily around to where Wolfe stood in the depression, his arms stretched out in a crucifix position. The plane swept not more than three hundred feet above him and as Wolfe turned, it see-sawed its wings in recognition.

Wolfe almost cheered and turned too late as his camel, startled by the noise, raced away from him in the direction of the Sahari forces. He shouted and broke into a run after the animal, knowing full well that his chances of catching it were decreasing whilst the possibility of capture was increasing, the nearer he got to the camp. After a few yards of pursuit he dropped to the ground, cursing his own foolishness. He should have expected it. The laden dromedary trotted steadily towards the soldiers, who were shading their eyes in the direction of the approaching camel.

Wolfe watched in dismay as his animal was caught by the waiting men. He wriggled forwards towards a cluster of scattered sandstone rocks, groaning with annoyance as he saw a trio of soldiers urging their mounts in his direction. His only remaining tools were his knife and binoculars and he wasn't going to take on armed men. He scratched frantically with cupped hands at the soft sand, trying desperately to create some cover before the men reached him. It would hardly be sufficient but he flopped face downward into the shallow indentation, piling the sand around him as best he could.

He lay silent, shoulders exposed, shielding his face among the low boulders, waiting for the inevitable discovery. The men explored each rocky outcrop and Wolfe almost stopped breathing as a rider approached, stopping within a few metres of him. The man was almost above him, searching the horizon, his face screwed up against the early sun. The camel snickered, lowering its head towards Wolfe. It wanted to investigate. Its rider flicked the animal's shoulders with his leader stick, urging it forward past the motionless man, missing him by an arm's length.

Wolfe lay for an indefinite time, not daring to turn his head until he heard the shouts of the Sahari soldiers growing fainter. The heat from the sun was increasingly painfully on his back when the riders finally returned to their company. It was then that the two parties of Mansoor drovers appeared around the bend in the trail and joined the waiting soldiers. There was a hasty reorganisation of the loaded animals before the complete party moved away, the soldiers forming an armed cordon around the caravan.

Wolfe watched the departure through his binoculars. He had been lucky to avoid detection and had a fair idea of his fate if he had been caught. The armed men had discarded their jeleba and were now wearing full uniform, obviously sure they had been apprehended by the Moroccan spotter plane. The charade was over and they needed to move quickly.

There was not much of a choice left. Wolfe could shadow the caravan on foot with the chance of possible capture and just hope to regain a mount, or wait on the main camel route in the hope of a friendly group of nomads assisting him. As he lay thinking about it, his first option trotted away up the old trail, leaving him contemplating his next move. It would be senseless to wait for help. He had not yet seen any other wayfarers on the journey. Without provisions and most of all water, the longest he could last in this heat would be a few days and yet the alternative did not give him much choice.

There was nothing for it but to take the shortest route back to Hamra. That meant heading in the direction taken by Danielle, across the Wastelands. He checked the time, lining up the hand on his watch with the sun, giving him an approximate course, then he picked out a low feature on the horizon to walk towards. With a final look at the dust cloud from the caravan disappearing into the heat haze, he turned and strode north into the wilderness.

At mid morning the following day Danielle and her Berber companions were taking coffee in the marbled lounge at the Alhambra Hotel when two army vehicles and a police car pulled to a halt outside. A full colonel in the Moroccan Army leapt out accompanied by a captain and the two police officers Danielle had met the previous day. They were shown to the waiting quartet and patiently observed the formal introductions of the Berber headman before the colonel took a seat, motioning his entourage to gather around.

"We have much to discuss Mademoiselle and the management of the hotel say we will not be disturbed." The girl nodded, pouring some more coffee and handing it to the colonel.

"Help yourselves gentlemen. This could take some time," she said.

"I know that Mademoiselle Charni, but we need more specific information and we need to check thoroughly before we run off half ready."

Danielle frowned. "At this time, my good companion Jack Wolfe is in a lot of trouble and every minute you delay may cost him dearly. I don't know how long he can last out or even if he is still alive, outnumbered and without..." She choked on her words.

The colonel raised his hand, his face relaxing as he looked into the troubled blue eyes of the girl before him.

"Then perhaps it would interest you to know that just after dawn this morning a reconnaissance plane from our airforce made a sortie along the old border route. He was unable to find any trace of troop movement's corroborating your story, although there were many travellers, which is unusual at this time of year. Eventually when the pilot decided he was wasting his time and was about to return, he was fired on by a single man with an automatic weapon. On investigation he found the caravan he was checking out was indeed an armed patrol of Mauritanian commandos, thus confirming your story. This can only have been your compatriot, but to disclose his position to the enemy like that was suicidal."

The girl jumped to her feet. "But at the time he was safe."

"At that time, yes, although he must be heavily outnumbered."

The older Mohammed rose, taking her hand gently.

"What are you going to do, Colonel?" he asked.

The soldier sipped at his coffee. "We have already sent a battalion of infantry towards the border. If things go as planned we could be there by dawn tomorrow, always a good time to attack."

Danielle buried her face in her hands. "But that may be too late."

"Danielle," the officer spoke her name gently, "you have been of great service to us and I know that your thoughts are with your friend out in the desert, but from the little information given to me about Monsieur Wolfe it is my guess that he is very capable of looking out for himself."

"But there are so many of them."

"A situation we are about to remedy young lady, but I would tell you from my own experience that some men are born survivors, a law unto themselves when alone, and that is the order of their lives. They prefer it that way."

Danielle sat down abruptly.

"Now tell me more of this Mansoor. He has to be found and punished."

"All I know of him is that he is with the drovers delivering the weapons along the border. He knows the area well and is always out of the way when transactions are taking place."

"He sounds a very slippery customer, Mademoiselle."

"Yes, we have found this to our cost."

For almost an hour the girl was questioned until the colonel, finally satisfied, rolled up his maps.

"I think I have all I need. Is there anything else you want to tell us, Danielle?"

She took a deep breath. "I did not tell you about the ambush. Two men fired on us as we drove over a hill near the High Atlas before any of this really started. It all happened so quickly that we just collided with the men shooting at us, and afterwards we put the bodies in our car and left it because we were so close to rescuing Suzanne. We had every intention of going to the police but never got the chance," she finished apprehensively.

The colonel looked sideways at the policemen.

"We have found the car and two men. It was a mystery to us how they got there, but we do know their identities. They were known villains with long records. I don't think this needs to go much further. If Mademoiselle Charni will give us a statement to this effect, our inquiry can be closed quietly on the matter."

The colonel extended his hand to her.

"I must make a full report to my war office, Mademoiselle. I have no doubt they would like to convey their appreciation to you for your resourcefulness."

Danielle flushed. "I would not have made it without help." She nodded towards Mohammed and his two sons.

"Of course!" the soldier gripped the headman's hand. "You are a true patriot, Mohammed Isteil." The old man bowed without emotion.

"And now we must go," the colonel said. "I wish you all good fortune," then he turned and strode out of the lounge followed by his staff.

# Chapter 6

Achmet Mansoor had no time to loose. He had already forfeited valuable days in running skirmishes with Wolfe and he still had to take delivery of his fee and make all preparations for the assault on the Israeli airliner. He urged the two camels onward, the sense of urgency conveying itself to Suzanne Wolfe. She was a willing fool and as soon as she was gone he would be able to disappear to any haven where a rich man would be welcome. Without a convoy and nothing to slow them down they made good time, speaking briefly to each other until the palmed oasis of El Djerib finally appeared on the horizon.

After a brief halt, Mansoor bought the only available transport. It was an old American Second World War jeep, much faster than a camel but a bumpy ride. The route to Sidi Ifni was not more than half a day and as dusk approached he switched on his headlights to find they were not working. Further movement after dark was not safe and he pulled into a flat area at the side of the road to rest for the night. They were both weary and slept almost immediately on the unyielding ground.

Mansoor stirred uncomfortably after midnight, the squealing of metal in the distance and the low hum of motors waking him sharply. He knew immediately the sound of half tracked vehicles and watched unseen from his vantage point as the column of light militia drove by. This was unexpected. A force of Moroccan infantry was out here, for which there had to be a good reason. Perhaps his instincts had been right again. If there was to be any fighting he did not want to be anywhere near it.

The concern in Suzanne Wolfe's face was apparent and he tried to calm her fears with poor results. She was annoying him to exasperation and it was with relief that he saw the faint low outline of Agadir in the distance.

Loneliness was no stranger to Jack Wolfe. He had learned to accept it without emotion as one of the penalties of his trade, but the awesome barrenness of the surrounding landscape conveyed a feeling of deep isolation as he trudged purposely north. A swirling wind had arisen making visibility difficult and he squinted painfully against the fine dust particles stinging his eyes. It became increasingly hard to focus on any distinct feature ahead, but not to do so could result in the problem of walking around in a circle. He knew that dust storms could last days, but the absence of any shelter made it impractical to stop. He carried doggedly on until the sheer pressure of the gale forced him to his knees. Covering his face with his veiled headdress he rested until there was a lessening in the surging sandstorm, allowing him to continue.

This action was repeated often in the hours that followed, walking and resting until the wind suddenly died away. He slumped exhausted to the ground, wiping the congealed dust from his face, pushing the thirst from his mind. There was still good daylight yet it was impossible to calculate how far he had travelled, although the chances were that it was probably less than he thought. It was easier to pick out an object on the horizon now, which made the direction easier to follow but he was unprepared for the sight of some scrubby bushes in a short depression in the scorched sand. Where there were plants there was moisture and he urgently needed water now.

He almost ran towards the welcoming greenery, flopping to the ground where the shrubs were thickest and resting before picking a wind-flattened stone to use as a shovel. After an hour of methodical digging with the sand running remorselessly back into his excavation he almost gave up. The action was only weakening him and yet the sand had changed colour. There was no doubting that it was moist. He renewed his efforts, holding back the sand with stones until a trickle of muddy water formed at the bottom of the hollow.

Resisting the urge to bury his face in it he continued digging around the newly-formed puddle, savouring the moment when he could drink. The weariness made his limbs ache and his head was spinning in the heat. He lay prostrate, scooping the brackish water to his mouth before plunging his face into the pool. The water was sweet. At some previous time this spot could have been a small oasis, long forgotten.

Wolfe sat on his haunches. There was cover here. He cut some branches in bivouac fashion from the bushes, then placed foliage over it to give him some respite from the sun. Within seconds he was asleep. When he awoke it was evening. The air was cooler and there was a small darting movement at his water hole. A furry desert rodent was eyeing him cautiously, before edging slowly to the water hole and drinking greedily without taking its eyes away from his. Wolfe smiled. He was not completely alone; if an animal could survive here, so could he. Conditions were the same for both of them.

He decided to move on, now that the heat of the day was lessening. If only he had a goatskin he could have carried water. There were his binoculars of course. He carefully prised off the eyepiece and filled the space with water, then pressed the eyepiece back on again. Considering the deprivations he had recently encountered Wolfe felt remarkably well. It was the first time in days that he had given way to deep sleep and the future did not seem so daunting now. He took a long drink from his well before abandoning it to his small companion, and then strode off into the deepening shadows.

He walked some miles before the night closed in. The stars appeared, faintly at first, then resumed their steady brilliance, lighting the earth into eerie shapes. He plodded steadily onwards, stopping briefly and reasonably satisfied with his progress. He tried to ration his meagre water supply but found sometime after midnight that it was gone. He dozed for a short time, and then continued, marking an object on the horizon and walking towards it.

He knew his direction was good but could only guess at the distance. Somewhere to his front, the shadows moved. He dropped to the ground searching for the silhouette ahead as he reached for his binoculars only to find them fogged and useless. The shadows moved again. The night can play tricks on a man but he had not imagined it. He waited. The outline of a camel with a hooded rider wandered aimlessly towards him.

Wolfe could not afford to be cautious. This was enemy territory and surprise was the only advantage he had. He crouched low, waiting until the approaching dromedary was a short distance away, then sprung at the mounted man apparently asleep in the saddle. The force of his onslaught was so great it almost knocked the camel to the ground, and the rider screamed in fear as Wolfe fell on top of him. Wolfe was up first, spinning the man round by his shoulder and was confronted by the terrified face of Rico Filila. Wolfe pulled out his knife and held it to the throat of the trembling Moroccan.

"Caught you at last," Wolfe snarled.

Filila stared back, hypnotised by the blade glittering in the light.

"Now, answer me one question," said Wolfe, "and if I think you are lying..." he made a sweeping gesture across Filila's jugular with his knife. "What happened to the girl you were chasing?"

The Moroccan gasped. "She led us into a trap, then escaped. She nearly killed us all."

"What kind of trap?"

"Shifting sand. She lured us into a sandpool and within seconds it was all over."

Wolfe smiled grimly. "And then?"

"Then she rode off leaving me alone in the middle of it. I don't know why she didn't finish me off. She had the gun."

"Is that what you would have done?" said Wolfe.

Filila shuddered again.

"No, no, I didn't mean that."

"But you tried to kill her, didn't you?" Wolfe shouted, pushing the blade against the Moroccan's throat.

"No, I swear, I was only obeying orders. We only wanted

to hold her until it was too late for her to contact anyone."

"You expect me to believe that," Wolfe said. "Four armed men sent to delay a single girl."

"It is true," Filila yelped desperately. "I am not your enemy. I only work for Achmet Mansoor."

"Then you should pick your employers with more care," said Wolfe, his grip relaxing on the man's shoulder.

Filila was finished as a threat. Wolfe felt almost guilty for terrorising the man but was not finished with him yet.

"Do you have water on the camel?"

"Yes, yes, and food too."

Wolfe stood, dragging the man up with him.

"Move quickly and you are a dead man. Understand?"

Filila nodded urgently as Wolfe went to the dromedary and lifted off the saddlebags. There were two full goatskin water bottles and some tinned fruit. He drank deeply then opened a tin of peaches with his knife. Filila lowered himself slowly to the ground and sat cross-legged, watching Wolfe carefully. He knew the man before him was violent and any false move would be the end.

"Where are Mansoor and my niece?"

"They are with the caravan."

"I shall ask you just once again," Wolfe scowled. "Your future will be decided by your answer."

The Moroccan trembled, the piercing grey eyes seemed to look into his soul and the fear of death almost froze his lips.

"They must have returned to Casablanca," he croaked.

Wolfe was mystified. Why Casablanca and not Marrakech?

The man was too frightened to lie, but his gaze was fixed to the ground in front of him. The point of Wolfe's knife drew blood at Filila's throat.

"You are lying to me?"

"No, no, I swear it, I will tell you everything I know."

"Then begin, and if it does not sound true..." The knife went a little deeper.

The Moroccan gulped. "They have to go to Casablanca to put the bomb on the plane."

Wolfe was astonished.

"Go on," he said.

"Achmet is using the girl to take the bomb onto the plane. She does not know she is carrying it."

"But cases are always searched before boarding."

"Not in the luggage compartment. They are never searched. No one expects a bomb in the baggage area if the passengers are on the same plane. Hand luggage is only searched for weapons."

Wolfe was silent, searching the man's face.

"Which plane will it be?"

"I don't know," Filila cried out, as the knife pressure increased. "As Allah is my witness, I don't know."

Wolfe felt a momentary compassion for the terrified man. It was obvious he knew nothing more. He sheathed his knife slowly. "Cover your neck before you bleed to death."

The Moroccan released his breath in a shuddering gasp, unable to believe that his ordeal was over, but remained very cautious as the Englishman stood and contemplated him.

"Well, Rico you have a problem," said Wolfe. "I have never executed anyone in cold blood before but you don't have a camel and I haven't the time to take you with me. I think you will have to find your own way out of it."

Filila was awestruck. "If you leave me out here I am finished."

Wolfe nodded then divided the provisions from the

saddlebags equally, leaving one goatskin of water on the arregan.

"They say that solitude is good for the soul, Rico. If you start now you should be in Hamra in about three days."

He swung up into the saddle, wheeling the animal to the north and trotted steadily away.

"So long, Rico. The walk should do you good."

There was a general feeling of anti-climax in the Alhambra Hotel after the Moroccan colonel and his staff departed. Now that the army was on alert a feeling of relief replaced the anxiety Danielle had felt but she still had nagging doubts about the safety and whereabouts of Jack Wolfe. It seemed that the infantry colonel had more faith in his survival tactics than she had, but the odds were stacked against him and if he were not such a stubborn character he would have left the border area with her, instead of remaining to continue his vendetta.

The little group sat in the gardens and discussed the probable outcome of future events, knowing that it was now out of their hands. After coffee there was a lull in the conversation and some meaningful glances were exchanged between the headman and his two sons, before the younger men rose and walked out through the ornamental iron gates into the quiet road behind.

Danielle looked puzzled. "What is happening, Mohammed, something mysterious going on?"

The old man looked tenderly at the girl. "They are both young," the headman continued, "without experience in the ways of women. In our world they are leaders of men. All they know of life is travel and commerce, and we do have a home at Ceuta as our permanent residence." The old man's eyes twinkled. "It is my pleasure to ask if you will share our home as the wife of one of them."

Danielle's mouth dropped open and it was some seconds before she answered. "Mohammed, I had no idea, I thought we were just good friends."

"More than that I hope, my boys have great respect for your courage and education. A union with the daughter of Sarim Charni and a son of Mohammed Isteil would be of great advantage to both our families. The small problem of course is the choosing, as they are both enamoured with you. I know this is a surprise," the old man continued. "You have a western culture, but my sons are quick to learn and realise that with your help they can improve their status, but the overriding feeling is of an *affair de coeur*."

The girl clasped her hands together. "What can I say? A month ago things were much different – now I am not sure of anything."

The old headman nodded wisely. "You have a fondness for the Englishman?"

"I must confess I have."

"But perhaps your affection is like the Mistral. When it blows it is only from one direction. Does he have the same feeling for you?"

Danielle made a wry face.

"I can't be sure. We only met a short time ago and parted so quickly. I am told the English are not demonstrative like us and yet when we were together..."

Mohammed nodded. "Then I shall tell my sons you are unsure at this time, but they have much to offer and are quite wealthy young men in their own right."

The girl took the headman's hands in hers. "Mohammed, I am honoured by your proposal and if I was to favour one of the boys I could not decide who it would be."

"Then you will forgive me for being so direct and perhaps it is not totally out of the question."

"No, of course not, but it is not the right time, Mohammed."

There was a silence between them as they sat listening to the birds in the thorn bushes. The younger men returned and squatted cross-legged on the grass before the headman. Danielle kissed them both on their cheeks, as they looked inquiringly at their father.

"All is not lost yet my boys, we just may need a little more time," he said, a twinkle showing in his eyes.

Wolfe rode steadily into the early light of dawn, then dismounted and dozed for a while with his back pressed tight against the snoring arregan. He awoke with the sunlight in his eyes. A trio of turbaned riders passed within two hundred metres, waving a greeting to the man on the ground. Wolfe acknowledged them and remounted his animal, groaning from the stiffness in his limbs.

A few kilometres further on, he came across a well-trodden path leading to the west and continued until the sun was at its zenith before walking beside the resolute dromedary. The travellers were increasing now, some eyeing him suspiciously, but mostly a nodded greeting was enough. Late afternoon he saw the cloud of dust on the low horizon, followed by the arrival of a Land Rover with police markings. Wolfe waited until the vehicle closed in, before pulling his mount to a halt and lowering his veil.

A uniformed officer leapt out. "Are you the Englishman Wolfe?"

He scowled an answer. "What's the trouble?"

The policeman laughed, placing his hands on his hips. "No trouble, Monsieur. We are here to welcome you."

Wolfe relaxed. "Sorry, haven't had much sleep lately. How did you know where to find me?"

"We didn't. There are patrols everywhere looking for Achmet Mansoor."

"Then you know what is happening on the border. And Danielle Charni – she reached the authorities safely?"

The officer nodded. "A very tenacious young lady. Such women are rare."

"I know that," answered Wolfe thoughtfully, "but why are you not searching the border for Mansoor?"

"Because we have information that he bought a vehicle in El Djerib two days ago, travelling with a blonde woman companion. We have road blocks all the way to Sidi Ifni, but he has somehow managed to avoid them."

Wolfe groaned, "I believe they nicknamed him the chameleon."

"Perhaps, but we will catch him and his accomplice and when we do," he patted the pistol at his hip.

Wolfe frowned. "The girl is my niece."

"And the penalty for treason is death Monsieur. We do not make the law and I am only a servant of my country."

Wolfe was too weary to be drawn into a political argument.

"Do you know where Mademoiselle Charni is?" he asked.

"Of course. She is at the Alhambra Hotel in Sidi Ifni. Would you like us to take you there?"

"Sure would," said Wolfe gratefully. "What shall we do with the camel?"

"Camels are not like dogs, Monsieur Wolfe. Just leave

her and when ready she will find her way into town. Our animals are very intelligent you know."

Wolfe grinned and climbed into the rear seat of the vehicle. "That I have found to be very true."

It was a bumpy ride. Wolfe, in spite of the journey, nodded off and slept with confused visions of approaching civilisation as the Land Rover turned into the relative smoothness of a tarmac road. Within minutes they were in the suburbs of Sidi Ifni and had stopped outside the Moorish façade of the Alhambra Hotel.

"Please convey our respects to the Mademoiselle," the officer said as Wolfe clambered from the vehicle. "I hope we meet again Monsieur."

Wolfe took the outstretched hand and shook it warmly. "Look forward to it."

The white-robed concierge looked gravely at the dishevelled man before him, noting the blood-stained shoulder and the obvious fatigue.

"Mademoiselle Charni," Wolfe said brusquely.

The man changed, beaming and indicating the gardens at the rear of the hotel. Wolfe peered through the shaded window at the little group sat at the iron table, glimpsing Danielle's dark hair piled high on her head. He was suddenly conscious of his bedraggled appearance and wished he had cleaned himself up first. He loosened his jeleba at the neck and unclipped the silver amulet from around his neck.

"Please give her this."

"A pleasure, Monsieur. Is there a message?"

"No, I shall wait."

The concierge placed the amulet on a silver plate and walked solemnly out to the group, then presented the amulet to the girl with a little bow before turning and walking respectfully away. Danielle held the chain like a pendulum, her eyes fixed on the silver hand of Fatima in bewilderment. She looked searchingly towards the partly screened windows then ran impulsively towards the dark shape waiting in the shadows. Wolfe met her on the top step, her arms flying around his neck as he spun her in a circle, her hair tumbling into his eyes and the scent of jasmine strong in his nostrils.

"Oh, Jack, I knew it could only be you."

He held her for a long time and then, putting his fingers into the girl's hair, gently pulled back her head, kissing her full on the lips. She stretched up on tiptoes, her arms never leaving him.

Danielle's companions remaining at the table were clearly surprised. The headman shrugged his shoulders resignedly and his sons shuffled uncomfortably. The concierge stood, patiently smiling near the door.

Wolfe laughed. "I'm sorry, I'm in such a mess."

Her eyes glistened. "Jack, how did you get here?"

He shrugged but did not release her. "Had to walk most of the way until I met Rico Filila. He loaned me his camel."

"I left him behind in the Wasteland when he tried to follow me." The girl's hand went to her mouth. "What did you do with him, Jack?"

"Don't worry, Dany, he decided to walk back. We won't have any problems from him again. Sooner or later the police will pick him up."

Danielle disentangled herself and took Wolfe over to the Berber caravaneers, now standing waiting.

"Forgive me, Mohammed, may I present Jack Wolfe?"

The three men bowed courteously and introduced themselves. "I have heard much of your exploits from

Danielle, Monsieur Wolfe," the headman said.

The girl grinned, taking Wolfe's hand. "Without Mohammed and his sons I would probably still be wandering in the Wasteland."

"I thank you for that, but please call me Jack!"

The younger son frowned. "I would not have sent Danielle alone to find help. The desert is always changing and treacherous. I think it was foolish because she could easily have been lost forever."

The girl's grip tightened on Wolfe's hand as she felt his body stiffen but the headman spoke first.

"That is not a thing to say to a friend," he chastised.

"I am sure there was a good reason why Jack sent Danielle away."

Wolfe saw the resentment on the young man's face and his obvious enrapture with the girl and relaxed, understanding why the protectiveness had spilled over.

The youngster flushed. "I am sorry, Dany. Do you forgive me?"

She reached out and ruffled his hair. "Of course. Friends should not have to apologise to each other."

Wolfe decided to let it pass as the weariness overcame him. He swayed on his feet, Danielle looking sharply at him, noticing the half closed eyes and exhaustion apparent in his body.

"Sit down, Jack, you look awful."

He slumped silently into a chair and the elder Mohammed nodded thoughtfully to his sons. "We will leave you together, Danielle. I think Monsieur Jack needs some peace at this time."

She touched his forearm gratefully. "Thank you, Mohammed."

The concierge hovered in the background. "Shall I prepare another room, Mademoiselle?"

She nodded absently. "The quietest one you have."

He turned on his heels abruptly. "It shall be done."

Wolfe did not remember much after that, only the girl leading him to his bed along the tiled corridors. She unlaced his boots and pulled them off as he surrendered to the creeping weariness and the softness of his pillow. She watched him for a few seconds then placed the silver hand of Fatima on the bedside table before letting herself quietly out of the room.

# Chapter 7

The coastal town of Agadir was crowded with sun-seeking holidaymakers at this early part of the season, but Achmet Mansoor found this to his advantage as he cruised the perimeter of the old town, searching systematically for a middle-class hotel. The Chella at the centre of the Rue Philippe served his purpose well and he booked a double room on the first floor with a view of the main entrance. Suzanne immediately flopped on the bed and Mansoor, leaving the sleeping girl, ventured out into the old town.

An hour later, with his hair trimmed short and his beard neatly sculptured, he bought some lightweight holiday clothing and returned to the hotel. The girl was only half awake when he entered the room causing her to jerk in amazement at his transformation.

"Achmet, you startled me. I did not recognise you with your hair cut. You look so different."

He smiled back at her. "That is the reaction I was hoping for Suzanne. We have to face the fact that the police may be looking for us now. I did not intend to become involved in a border dispute but now the authorities possibly want us,

I think it is sensible if we both change our appearance."

He handed her a parcel. "I bought you these clothes in the market. They should fit but perhaps they are not what you are used to."

She pulled away the wrappings, holding the garments to her for his approval.

"There is something else you must do," Mansoor continued. "The police will be looking for a long-haired blonde girl. You must cut it short, Suzanne."

The girl looked horrified. "But I've always had my hair this length."

"Precisely, I have to change your appearance from a long-haired woman in a kaftan to a short-haired European girl on holiday. There are hundreds of women just like that walking around Agadir."

She stared speechlessly at him.

"You know I am right," he pressed on. "We are only a few days from the end of all this. We don't want to be caught on the last lap and your hair will grow again."

The girl sighed resignedly. "I suppose you are right, Achmet. How do you think I should style my hair?"

He stifled the feeling of irritability. "Like all the pretty girls of your age."

"When shall I do it?"

He smiled persuasively. "Now! Before you change your mind."

"Then help me," she turned to the dressing table, "my scissors are very small."

He nodded and picking up the scissors cut the blonde hair two inches from the crown. The girl watched in dismay until it was roughly the same length all over before turning her head to the mirror.

Almost an hour later a curly-haired blonde girl in shorts and shirt with a dark young man in attendance left the Hotel Chella and were soon mingling with the holidaymakers on the esplanade.

Wolfe slept deeply for the rest of the day and through the following night. He awoke to the sound of street vendors and the scent of early flowering hibiscus from the bushes outside his room. He lay for some time, his body still aching as he watched the sunlight brightening the shadowed date palms through the window. The luxury of his inactivity did not last for long.

The bedroom door opened very slowly and a glossy head wearing an American baseball cap poked around the door jamb. Wolfe clamped his eyes shut and breathed deeply.

"It won't work," she said, approaching his bedside. "I saw your eyelids twitch."

He grinned upwards and pulled her down to him. She wriggled away laughing. "Enough of that, you look like a toad."

Wolfe sat up. "It's been said, if you kiss a toad it could turn into a prince."

"Not until he has had a shower."

He looked in the mirror and at the reflection of his sweat-stained face and rubbed his stubbled chin thoughtfully. "I see what you mean. I could eat an arregan."

"Not on the menu," she answered breezily. "Will you settle for a plateful of croissants?"

"Sure, and Dany can you find me a razor and a bandage for my arm?"

She fished in her pockets, producing some packages, which she waggled under his nose.

"You think of everything, don't you?" he said.

She smiled and left him alone in his room. Wolfe felt physically strong but a feeling of apprehension lingered as he tidied himself up. He went down to breakfast and the girl, interpreting his thoughts, remained quiet.

"Where are your Berber friends this morning, Dany?"

"They had much to do and left yesterday evening. They asked me to give you their respects and apologise for not saying goodbye."

"Well, that's a shame," said Wolfe, the humour flickering in his eyes, "because I think the younger Mohammed had a bit more than brotherly love for you."

She nodded. "He's a nice boy, I was quite fond of him."

Wolfe stretched out in his chair and nipped the bridge of his nose absentmindedly. "Our problems are not over yet."

"Tell me all of it, Jack."

"I don't know where to start." His fingers drummed on the table. "Suzanne is putting explosives on a plane from Casablanca."

Her mouth dropped open in amazement. "Oh my God. When? How can this be possible?"

"You know as much as me. Rico Filila made a dead man's confession with my knife at his throat. I know he wasn't lying."

The girl's hand went to her mouth. "You didn't kill him, Jack?"

"No! I left him to walk home, but he thought he'd had it, and he told me everything."

"Then Suzanne must have gone completely mad."

"I'm afraid that's the awful part about it. She doesn't know. When she leaves Casablanca, the bomb will be in the luggage compartment. You can be sure that Mansoor will not be travelling with her."

"What kind of a man is he?" she said. "Does he have any feelings?"

"Oh yes, but not for people. Money and power are drugs to some men. Once hooked it's impossible to stop."

"Then we must alert the airport authorities at Casablanca."

He nodded. "That's the obvious answer, but if Suzanne is caught I don't think we will ever see her again. I figure we have a few days to find them and then we will have to tell the police all we know."

The girl shuddered. "Suzanne is my best friend but we can't allow her to go through with this. Everyone could be killed and what is so special about this particular plane anyway?"

Wolfe bit his bottom lip. "That's what we have to find out, but I am learning a bit more about Mansoor every day. He has an irritating habit of dodging the action and doubling back on his tracks, but he is always quite close. I would confidently say he is not in Casablanca at this time, but somewhere within striking distance."

Danielle sighed. "If we only knew what he looked like. Where do we start to find him?"

"Well, I know where he is not. Marrakech is where the police are waiting and the nearest place to Casablanca where a man can get lost is probably Rabat. That is closest and it is my guess amongst the resorts along the coast."

"It's a lot of ground to hide in," Danielle said.

"I know, but we do have one advantage. Mansoor is not aware that Filila has confessed about the attempted bombing and he will not be expecting a reception committee. Perhaps he even thinks we are both stretched out in the wilderness."

She pulled a face. "We nearly were. I was thinking about you, Jack, wondering if I would ever see you again, and I just kept going."

"Yes! You make me very proud and I love you truly."

She flushed suddenly beneath her tanned complexion, and then whipping off her baseball cap placed it over her face with only the blue eyes showing. "Do you mean that, Jack?"

He reached out and took the cap gently from her.

"You know I do."

The Boeing left Tripoli at 08.15 precisely. In the VIP section, wearing a sober grey suit, Captain Razmet Dhulmet of the Socialist Liberation Bureau stared grimly from the small starboard window. The sealed diplomatic case clamped to his wrist by steel handcuffs chaffed at his skin but the half a million high-denomination currency weighed lighter than he expected.

It was only a matter of hours before he could deliver the money to Achmet Mansoor at a time not yet specified by the Moroccan arms dealer but Dhulmet knew the transaction was imminent. Dhulmet's commander, Major Sleyman, had summoned him at short notice to make the delivery to Mansoor, but the wily Moroccan had only given Sleyman the address of the hotel where he wanted Dhulmet to stay.

On the same plane but unknown to Dhulmet were two officers of the Liberation Bureau Investigation Group armed with telescopic camera and recording equipment. This was to be used to record the handing over of the money to Mansoor, thus implicating Colonel Muammar Gaddafi and his unwitting emissary Razmet Dhulmet. Riyan Sleyman had devised the entire assassination attempt but had carefully avoided contact with the accomplices. In the event of anything going wrong, he could denounce the perpetrators as traitors and wriggle out of trouble.

Mid morning Captain Dhulmet walked through the Casablanca Airport terminal and boarded a taxi for the city. The driver took a route around the old town, through the Muslim centre in the old port and into the wide streets of the office and commercial centre, finally arriving at the residential quarter and Dhulmet's hotel. It was cool in the marbled interior and he deposited his valise in the large hotel safe before mounting the spiral staircase to his first floor room overlooking the Medina. He had a bad feeling about all this. The room number had already been allocated and he was not in control of the situation.

Dhulmet stood at the balcony watching the road below. He did not like Casablanca. He felt vulnerable and the waiting make him nervous.

Early the following morning, Wolfe and Danielle left Sidi Ifni taking the coastal road to Casablanca in a rented Volvo. The previous evening had been spent anticipating the probable movements of Achmet Mansoor but Wolfe knew his chances of tracing the Moroccan were slim. Until the actual time that Mansoor surfaced at the airport and showed his hand, there were a thousand places he could hide. Wolfe accepted he might have only one chance to stop the man before he vanished again.

Danielle drove steadily, saying little to Wolfe who was searching the map spread upon his knees for some clue to the whereabouts of Mansoor. The sun was at its highest and the car's cooling system was inadequate, making the journey uncomfortably warm until they finally reached the rebuilt town of Agadir. The old port had been virtually destroyed by the violent earthquakes of 1960 in which 20,000 people had lost their lives, but the town planners had rapidly constructed a new resort to the south, closer to the fine sandy beaches. The girl slowed the vehicle as they neared the sea frontage, enjoying the fresh breezes from the coast. Wolfe pointed towards the assortment of restaurants and clothing bazaars lining the esplanade.

"Looks like a good place to eat, Dany."

She nodded agreement. "Good idea, I'm starving."

They parked the Volvo under a group of shaded date palms a hundred metres from the beach, and strolled into the Sportive Bar. Wolfe had been unusually quiet that morning and Danielle guessed his silence was due partly to the problems at the moment and made no attempt to lighten his demeanour. It was only after a couple of large cognacs that his manner eased and he began to look inquiringly around. They ate a light meal and sat under the awning in the shade, watching the tourists, before walking the length of the esplanade. The girl picked a peony from a flower box, placing it deftly in her hair, which made Wolfe smile.

"Suits you, Dany, but I think we should carry on now."

She took his arm as they walked back to the Volvo, the pleasure of the day and each other's company making them both feel good. It was almost with regret that the girl drove away from the shaded palms and took the road for Casablanca along the coast.

Some ten minutes later a battered American jeep pulled into the space recently vacated by the Volvo and a pretty blonde girl in shorts and T-shirt leapt out and walked hand in hand into the Sportive Bar with her bearded companion.

\*

The Volvo cruised into the Casablanca medina in the early evening. Danielle drove carefully, noting the recently improved market area which still retained the Portuguese and Moorish character of the buildings. She lost her way on several occasions but eventually found the Rue Janitas at the suburban end of the market. She stopped at the entrance to a walled courtyard covered in purple vines.

Danielle, who appeared unable to pass a telephone without using it, contacted a cousin who insisted that she should stay with Wolfe at her villa. They were greeted ecstatically by a tall woman in her mid-thirties in a cream kaftan with the unmistakable blue eyes of the Charni family. Wolfe felt immediately at ease and soon they were seated at a long table with the assembled family of almost a dozen eating a hot meal amid the chatter of youngsters eager to speak to Danielle. After supper the group retired to the flower-scented garden and listened in almost total silence as Danielle recounted the hectic tales of the last few weeks.

The evening stars appeared with the coolness of the shadows, the young family retiring early. The tall cousin, Nabila, showed Wolfe to a small-whitewashed bedchamber at the rear of the villa. Unusually for a Muslim household, there was a crucifix above the bed head. Then with a mischievous twinkle in her eye she led Danielle away to share a room with her eldest daughter.

The room was quiet, yet Wolfe could not sleep, his mind a confusion of the possibilities before him. After a while he rose and walked silently back into the lawned garden, surprised to find Danielle and Nabila in deep conversation. "Couldn't you sleep either?" the tall Nabila asked.

Wolfe shook his head. "Too much to think about. Things always appear worse at night."

"I'll make us a hot drink," she said, disappearing into the kitchen, leaving Wolfe alone with Danielle.

She turned her head, scrutinising his face. "You look worried, Jack."

He sat under the swinging awning, nodding agreement. "You're right. I hoped it would be routine to find Suzanne but as time goes by the chances grow slimmer and there is always the possibility that she is not the only threat to the airline. Perhaps Mansoor had another device rigged up somewhere as a decoy. We both know he plays a very deep game."

"Do you think we should inform airport security now?"

"I can't see that we have much choice. They have got to be alerted and it looks like being a busy time for you and I because we are the only two people who know what Suzanne looks like."

"But the number of people travelling will be enormous."

"I agree, but there is no other way."

Nabila returned with three cups of steaming herb tea and Danielle sipped the hot liquid slowly. "What do you think will happen to Suzanne if she is arrested?"

"Who knows, but if we prove Mansoor intended she was to be blown up with the plane, I believe she could lead us to him."

"What a terrible thing to happen to Suzanne. When she was with me at school she was such a fabulous person, and now her world could end in chaos."

Wolfe sipped his tea. "I agree, but it amazes me the power men have over women."

Nabila placed her cup on the table with a thud. "I agree – just look at the size of my family," she said cheerfully.

For a moment they looked at each other, before Danielle and Wolfe spluttered into helpless laughter.

The telephone shrilled monotonously in the darkened bedchamber of the Azad Hotel. Razmet Dhulmet lay, momentarily bewildered by the strident noise and the strange surroundings before reaching for the phone.

"Allo, yes," he croaked into the receiver.

"Allo," the answer came back. "It's Achmet Mansoor."

Dhulmet rubbed his eyes and looked at the dial of his watch, luminous in the gloom. "Do you know what time it is?"

"Where are you?"

"Downstairs in the lobby, waiting for you."

Dhulmet levered himself stiffly from the bed. "Give me ten minutes and I will be with you."

"Make sure you come alone."

"What do you mean? I am alone."

There was a pause before Mansoor spoke. "Now don't tell me you know nothing about the two men who arrived on the same plane and are in Room 137 directly below you."

Dhulmet's face creased in anger. "Then you know something I don't."

"Do you take me for a complete fool?" Mansoor responded. "You have been watched from the moment you boarded the plane. I know your every move, including your pretence of travelling alone. Do you think I don't have an organisation?"

Dhulmet started to bluster until Mansoor cut him short. "In ten minutes and if I feel nervous you can kiss our deal goodbye."

The phone clicked in Dhulmet's ear.

The captain dressed, his mind in turmoil. Was Mansoor bluffing or had Riyan Sleyman really sent an armed guard to protect his investment, or perhaps Sleyman may not have trusted him with such a large amount of currency? Whatever the reason Dhulmet felt ambushed and was in a highly agitated mood when the elevator stopped at the ground floor. Apart from the night porter dozing at the door the only other person was a tall bearded man in holiday clothing waiting for the elevator to arrive. Dhulmet looked around the lobby as the bearded man stepped into the elevator.

"Dhulmet!" The bearded man in the elevator beckoned the captain towards him.

The Libyan officer stepped quickly back into the elevator as the doors closed behind him.

"Mansoor?" he questioned the bearded man.

The Moroccan nodded curtly but remained silent until the elevator stopped at its highest limit. Mansoor and Dhulmet walked out onto the balconied roof garden. It was almost without light and the clouded moon gave an eerie luminosity to the ornamental terraces.

Dhulmet was weary and becoming short tempered. "Is all this sneaking around in the middle of the night completely necessary?"

Mansoor shook his head disdainfully. "You would prefer we met at police headquarters?"

The sarcasm in his voice promoted Dhulmet to fury, "I am a captain in the Libyan Army," he shouted, "and I will not be spoken to like this. I could make life very unpleasant for you."

The chill in the voice of Mansoor made his back tingle. "Secrecy and concealment have kept me alive for many years. Do exactly as I say or you may be facing a Libyan firing squad."

Dhulmet sat down heavily on the stone terrace. "I don't like to be treated like a fool."

"Then don't behave stupidly, because you are expendable."

The fragility of his position dawned upon Dhulmet.

"What do you want me to do?" he asked plaintively.

"Follow orders. I believe the valise you put in the hotel safe contains the money?"

"Yes, but how did you know?"

Mansoor interrupted. "And you did not realise that two of your people were shadowing you?"

"No, I was not aware of it."

"Then I suggest you find out what their game is. I need to know."

"When do you want the money?" said Dhulmet.

"It is safe where it is. I will let you know when the transfer is to take place. Until then do not leave the hotel until I say. Do you understand?"

Dhulmet nodded vigorously. Mansoor almost smiled. The man before him was now totally obedient.

"Now, go back to your room and wait for me to contact you."

The captain turned and strode into the elevator.

Mansoor raised a finger. "Never forget, my people are watching."

Dhulmet breathed deeply as the elevator slowed to the first floor almost opposite his room. The door swung back and he found himself confronted by two alert looking men in grey suits. "Where is he?" one of them demanded.

"What do you mean?" responded Dhulmet.

The other man pushed Dhulmet roughly back into the elevator.

"Don't fool with us. We are from the Liberation Bureau like yourself and we need to contact Mansoor."

"Then it is correct. I was followed from Tripoli?"

"It was for your own good. If you had known, you could have given the game away."

"I left him in the roof garden, he gave me orders and they did not include anyone else."

"We shall see," the first man said.

Moments later the door swung open to the roof garden. The moon showed suddenly, brightening the terraces as the grey-suited men searched the balconies before returning mystified to Dhulmet.

"He is not here," one of them said. "If you are lying you could be in big trouble."

"I told you, I left him in the garden."

"Well, how did he get past us? There is only one way down," the man said.

In spite of the unexpectedness of it all and the early morning, Dhulmet found himself smiling at the annoyance on the faces of the two officials of his bureau.

"Don't ask me," he said. "You are the detectives – you figure it out."

Suzanne Wolfe remained in Agadir when Mansoor made an early evening departure to Casablanca in the battered old jeep. It was an inconspicuous vehicle and he took the coastal route through Safi, avoiding the walled city of Marrakech and arriving in the bustling tourist area before midnight. Although the girl wished to accompany him, Mansoor had insisted she remained, emphasising the danger of his negotiations. He was glad to be alone and urgently needed to prepare the ground for the delivery of the Semtex explosive and detonator that Suzanne would carry aboard the same plane as the Israeli defence minister.

Mansoor parked the vehicle behind the domed mosque and walked the cobbled alleyway to the end. He turned left and waited, his back pressed against the wall, then after a few moments retraced his steps, searching the faces of the few people he encountered in the street. Satisfied at not being followed, he knocked heavily at the sandalwood door of number thirteen. An upper panel slid back immediately and a pair of bushy-browed eyes confronted Mansoor.

Without a word the panel was replaced and the door swung inwards allowing the Moroccan to step inside.

The rich fragrance of orchids and leather met his nostrils and the unusual scene of opulence lit from the crystal chandeliers hanging from the oak-beamed ceiling caused him to blink with the sudden light. Mansoor had been here before yet was always surprised at the air of respectability fronting the clandestine operations at the rear of the building. The stocky man who ushered Mansoor through the door bowed, turned on his heels and beckoned the arms dealer to follow, walking softly down a long corridor covered in wall tapestries. He opened an iron grille under a high archway and the dark outline of a short man in a jeleba and turban appeared. Achmet Mansoor was always cautious in the presence of Adnan Khalifa. The deep penetrating stare of the man broached no nonsense but Khalifa bowed, touching his heart and forehead with a flourish.

"A great pleasure to see you again, Achmet."

"And you also, Adnan," Mansoor replied.

Khalifa turned to his retainer. "Coffee for my guest."

The servant hurried away as the turbaned Moroccan indicated a circle of deep leather cushions in various colours and sank into them. Mansoor followed suit as Khalifa spoke.

"It is some time since I have seen you. Has life been good to you, Achmet?"

Mansoor spread his hands. "We are what we are. We do not choose our fathers, but the sun shines for us all."

Khalifa laughed. "Always a wise proverb."

The servant returned with the coffee on a silver tray, with two porcelain cups and a salver of chocolate mints.

Khalifa waited until the coffee was poured. "There is another and more satisfying proverb," he indicated his retainer with a brief nod. "Be cruel to your dog and he will always obey you." If the servant heard he showed no emotion, but Khalifa was quick to notice the smile in Mansoor's eyes.

"We are alike, you and I," Khalifa said. "You like the feeling of power, Achmet?"

"I like the feeling of money."

"We cannot have one without the other and is that the reason you seek the help of Adnan Khalifa?" The turbaned man's mouth smiled but there was no humour in his question.

Mansoor sipped the bitter coffee thoughtfully. "You still have the Czechoslovak explosive?"

"The Semtex, but of course, a most useful tool."

"Then tell me the price of this."

Khalifa, looked offended. "The price, why ask the price when I have the only market in town?"

"I just need to know."

"Then the price will be fifty thousand pounds sterling, in cash."

It was Mansoor's turn to be annoyed. "That is much

more than I expected to pay."

Khalifa sighed. "My dear Achmet, it is not the Semtex which is expensive. It is the knowledge of its construction and the high cost of silence."

Mansoor stared back at the unrelenting Khalifa. The man had him in a stranglehold and he was applying pressure. He tried not to look angry. "When can it be ready?"

The turban inclined forward. "In three days it will be ready."

"Then it is a contract?"

"It is a contract," Khalifa confirmed.

Mansoor rose from the cushions. "I thank you for your hospitality, Adnan. If you will excuse me I have another appointment."

"At this hour of the morning? She must be truly beautiful."

Mansoor bowed at the door. "Perhaps Adnan, perhaps not. I also know the high cost of silence."

# Chapter 8

Raschid Hirasch stood at the window of the commercial area of Casablanca Airport with a clear view of the runways. The call from police headquarters had been disturbing and unclear to the airport chief and, with a sense of apprehension, he ushered Danielle and Wolfe into the command centre. The greetings were brief and introductions to the security staff were also cautious.

"Perhaps you had better begin, Monsieur," his said, his voice rising gently.

Wolfe stared briefly out of the window and turned to confront a dozen pair of eyes studying him intently. He took a deep breath, "Well, it's just guesswork and may all be for nothing."

Hirasch's eyes narrowed. "Monsieur Wolfe, just tell us all you know and let me do the job I am paid for."

Wolfe flushed at the reprimand and his back stiffened, until a soft hand entered his. He looked directly at Danielle and she nodded. He relaxed and answered the question.

"Tell you all we know? OK. How you handle it is up

to your department, yet we came to help and can make an identification."

Hirasch's eyes softened. "You are jumping ahead, please, start at the beginning."

The only sound in the command centre for the next twenty minutes was the voice of Jack Wolfe, who held his listeners' attention without interruption.

"And that's why we are here," he finished feebly.

Silence governed the room. Hirasch stared at the floor then lifted his eyes, a slow smile spreading across his face.

"Thank you, Jack." Hirasch had used Wolfe's name for the first time.

"Do you believe all this?" The voice behind Hirasch belonged to a uniformed officer with ranking stars on his jacket.

"Do you think anyone could make it up, and for what purpose?" said Hirasch

"Some kind of diversion," the officer answered.

"Possible, but not reasonable."

The airport controller cupped his hands.

"We have little choice in the matter but must be vigilant without being obvious and we do have an advantage." He paused.

"All assistance must be given to Jack and Danielle. Without their identification and testimony we could be facing a disaster." He paused again.

"And we don't need any heavy-footed gendarmes in our security operation."

Hirasch took a key from a ring in his pocket and turned to a steel cabinet built into the wall behind him. "You will need a weapon Mr Wolfe. I am sure you are familiar with these," he said, indicating the neat rows of handguns.

Wolfe selected a Smith and Wesson 32 calibre revolver, spinning the chamber effortlessly. "Do you have a shoulder holster for this? I would prefer concealment to confrontation."

Hirasch nodded. "A good choice, Monsieur, and a prudent attitude to adopt. Let's hope you will not have to use force."

Wolfe's shoulders twitched, "We are dealing with a dangerous man here."

"I know that," Hirasch said, the strain now showing. "You must do as you think fit. My concern is primarily with the passengers but I don't want to stop Mansoor at any cost."

Wolfe looked puzzled. "I am unclear at this moment what you want me for. You say you will back me up and in the next breath you say that you don't want me to stop Mansoor if it causes too much trouble."

"What I was trying to avoid saying is that I don't want a private vendetta endangering other lives, Monsieur Wolfe."

Danielle spoke quickly, breaking the conflict as the two men stared at each other. "But we still don't know what Mansoor looks like and you said yourself that he never seems to be around at the conclusion of his plots."

"Well, if that is the case," Hirasch said, "I shall have to rely on you to stop the girl as you are the only two who know her. We have to be thorough in our searches, especially in the cargo hold, and cannot exclude the possibility of more than one bomb."

"I don't understand who will benefit from bombing innocent people," said the girl. "It is not as if a ransom has been demanded."

"That is the problem," Hirasch scowled. "An attack like

this could be a reprisal or just a warning. Who knows the mind of a terrorist?"

Wolfe looked blankly through the window, his mind racing. "I don't agree. Someone is paying Mansoor. He is not an idealist, works only for gain, not principles. I believe there is a good reason and the attack will be a specific target. He may not even know why, or care."

"And Operation Socrates? What is that?" Danielle said, pointing to the airport model on the table before them.

"Full red alert, Mademoiselle. Electronic screening and information passed to security on the public address system," Hirasch said.

"How can that work?" enquired Danielle.

"We warn all our people immediately without alerting the public. For example, will Monsieur Socrates travelling to Gibraltar on flight ALA 37 please contact the information desk."

Wolfe laughed, "So Monsieur Socrates is the suspect and the flight number is his destination?"

"Correct," Hirasch said.

Wolfe allowed himself to relax. "Looks like most of the obvious angles are covered."

"Let's hope so Monsieur Wolfe. That was just routine. Now we must look for the unseen and the untried."

In the late afternoon, Razmet Dhulmet stood on the hotel verandah, hands resting on the iron balcony over-looking the rooftops of Casablanca. The Azad Hotel was not centrally placed and the inactivity of the area was boring him. A muffled knocking disturbed him and he warily opened the door to be confronted by a diminutive young porter carrying a bowl of fruit.

"Compliments of the management, Monsieur."

"Put it over there." Dhulmet flipped a coin to the youngster and the lad picked it expertly from the air and bowed himself from the room. Dhulmet ripped open the white envelope accompanying the fruit bowl. There was a single line written on the paper enclosed. 'Be in your room tonight with the money.'

The captain's first reaction was to contact the Libyan officers prowling the reception area beneath him, constantly analysing everyone who entered the Azad Hotel. Then he had doubts. Why should he? He had not received instructions from Riyan Sleyman in Libya to negotiate with these men and if they were genuine they had already shown incompetence at being unable to catch Mansoor earlier in the roof garden. The Moroccan arms dealer was also a more fearsome adversary than the officers of the Arab Liberation Bureau and Dhulmet had been sent to negotiate solely with him. He tore the letter into small pieces, and then tossed it from the balcony like confetti into the wind. He turned and made his way to the elevator, opening the door cautiously as it stopped at the ground floor. The lobby was empty except for hotel staff and Dhulmet withdrew the briefcase from the safe.

"Where are you taking the money?" The Libyan officer appeared at his shoulder.

"To my room for safe-keeping."

The officer frowned. "I hope you are not keeping anything from us. If you have heard from Mansoor it is your duty to tell us."

Dhulmet hesitated and the answer showed on his face.

"We have been sent to gather proof of Gaddafi's connection with Mansoor and to implicate him," the officer said.

"But this will involve me," Dhulmet protested.

"It will not matter after our colonel has been removed from power."

Dhulmet squirmed inwardly. His own life appeared forfeit, whatever the consequences.

"Mansoor is coming for the money tonight," he said flatly.

"At what time?"

"I don't know. He said to have the money ready tonight."

The Libyan officer allowed himself to smile. "Then we shall be prepared for him."

The time dragged slowly that evening. Razmet Dhulmet stayed in his room with the two Libyans, who said little to each other, engrossed in the playing cards before them. In the annex, a video camera had been carefully concealed to give a view of the complete room.

It was close to midnight and the card players were becoming agitated. One threw his cards on the table in annoyance. "He is not coming," he said.

Dhulmet flinched. "Don't know why, perhaps he suspects something?"

"Why do you say that?" one of the officers asked.

"Have you given the game away?"

The phone shrilled, cutting short Dhulmet's rising anger and the three men looked blankly at each other until the captain reached for the phone.

"Don't scare him off," one of the men hissed a warning.

Dhulmet put the receiver to his ear.

"You have the money?" Mansoor queried.

"Yes, it is still in the briefcase."

"You have company also I believe?"

Dhulmet paused.

"There is no need to speak further. Throw the money out of the window," Mansoor commanded.

"Repeat that," the captain said.

"Throw the briefcase from the window."

Dhulmet laid the phone on its side, picked up the briefcase and walked to the balcony. Beneath his first floor window was an open-backed Ford truck with a solitary man standing in the rear beckoning upwards. The captain looked up the deserted road, and then casually lobbed the briefcase into the arms waiting below. The man caught it awkwardly then banged the top of the cab, sending the driver speeding into the night.

"What the hell are you doing?" snarled one of the officers.

Dhulmet turned and smiled. "Obeying orders."

The Liberation officer grabbed the phone, listening to the continuous buzz of the disengaged tone before he banged it back onto its stand, cursing Dhulmet.

Twenty minutes later the Ford truck pulled to a halt on the quiet outskirts of the town. Mansoor leapt out carrying the briefcase, motioning his companions to stay in the vehicle before he entered a crumbling arched façade in the wall of the old town. At the front door in the darkened alleyway he fumbled with a key and went inside the shuttered room. The oil lamp spluttered slowly into flame as he placed it on a wooden table with the briefcase before going to the corner of the room and pushing aside a well-worn horsehair couch.

Kneeling down Mansoor removed some floorboards revealing a compartment in the floor. He extracted a leather roll with a curved knife and a small calibre pistol and silencer, which he pushed into the waistband of his jeans. He turned to the briefcase and slid back the catches deliberately, opening the lid an inch before peering inside. It did not appear to have any devices attached and Mansoor sat down on the table as the case fully opened, displaying its contents. The neat rows of banknotes pressed tightly together made him catch his breath. He extricated a slim bundle, thumbing the high-denomination notes on the table, and then went outside to where his two companions sat smoking a kif in the cab of the truck. He beckoned them inside and they followed, blinking nervously in the half-light from the oil lamp. Mansoor indicated the bundles of notes on the table and they jostled each other in their eagerness to count it. The money was divided hurriedly and, turning towards Mansoor, their elation died as they found the pistol aimed at them.

The arms dealer fired into the chest of the first man, hurtling him back into the wall, the money flying from his grasp, a surprised expression still fixed on his face. His companion stood rigid, the fear making him proffer the money towards Mansoor. The arms dealer took deliberate aim, shooting the man in the head. Mansoor waited. The silenced pistol had made surprisingly little sound in the confined atmosphere of the room, yet he still listened for sounds of movement in the old building. It remained quiet.

Mansoor pulled the bodies to the side of the room, shielding them with the old couch, then collected the money scattered around the floor. He left the room after extinguishing the oil lamp, hastily locking the door on his departure. He climbed into the cab of the Ford truck and drove steadily away, checking once for pursuit in the rear view mirror. The streets were abandoned and Mansoor breathed with relief as he swung the wagon east towards Agadir and Suzanne Wolfe, the briefcase hard on the seat beside him.

# Chapter 9

The airport of Casablanca was cool inside the terminal buildings. Jack Wolfe positioned himself near the runway entrances with a clear view of the embarking passengers at passport control. There was no definite pattern in his surveillance. The twenty-four-hour day would be split between himself and the girl as they felt the need.

He could see Danielle from his vantage point. She was sampling the assorted perfumes in the airport shop and he smiled at her ability to disengage herself from the problems confronting them. She looked up and waggled her fingers at him as she tapped the scent behind her ears. Wolfe shook his head reprovingly but he pulled her a face before returning to his scrutiny of the passengers. Raschid Hirasch appeared regularly and the airport controller's eyes always asked the same question. Wolfe invariably shrugged and the controller would stroll wordlessly away.

The ordered routine of the international airport appeared normal, but all the exits were covered by sharp-eyed men, looking patiently over the tops of newspapers, or reclining on cushioned benches, with countless cups of cold coffee.

Wolfe was sure everything possible was being done without attracting attention; the security personnel were thorough in their searches.

There was little time for relaxation with the constant stream of travellers, yet the day passed quickly, the increased vigilance netting a cocaine smuggler and two men armed with revolvers in separate incidents. The airport controller was pleased at the success of his tactics, yet still apprehensive over the capture of Suzanne Wolfe. The appearance of a group of nuns all dressed in similar habits jangled the alarm signals in Wolfe's brain, subjecting them to an intensive search under the watchful eye of Danielle.

The day gave way to night allowing Wolfe to grab some sleep on the makeshift bed in the ambulance section, leaving the girl solely in attendance at passport control.

Two hours before dawn Achmet Mansoor drove into the car park of the Chella Hotel in Agadir. He hid the revolver under his seat and entered the lobby unobserved with the laden briefcase. He dialled Suzanne's room from reception and a sleepy voice answered him.

"It's me, darling," he said.

"Achmet, where are you?"

"Downstairs in the lobby. I didn't want to startle you."

She was happily waiting for him, a silken gown pulled around her shoulders. The warmth of her welcome surprised him. With difficulty he pulled himself from her arms and threw the briefcase onto the bed.

She eyed it suspiciously, "What do you have there?"

"Take a look," he said, sliding the catches and snapping open the lid.

The girl stood transfixed, staring at the neat bundles of

notes, her hand tightening upon his.

"My God," she said. "What is all that?"

"That is our future, Suzanne. The payment from the arms sales on the border," Mansoor lied. "Now it is up to you to take it to Israel."

She looked up at his face. "It will last us the rest of our lives."

He gathered her into his arms. "There is more to come if we handle everything correctly, darling."

She stood encircled by his warmth, happier than she had ever been, the fulfilment of his trust in her complete.

At dusk the following evening Mansoor drove the Ford truck away from Agadir and followed the back roads into Casablanca. On the edge of the city he stopped behind the mosque and pushed the revolver into his belt, left the vehicle and strode quietly away. Thirty minutes later he walked into the Rue Nabib and knocked on the door of number thirteen. The same dark-browed eyes scrutinised him through the top panel and the door swung open as the panel closed. Mansoor stepped inside. The servant turned, beckoning the arms dealer to follow him. They entered a large workroom at the end of a corridor and the light momentarily blinded Mansoor. The turbaned figure of Adnan Khalifa appeared, bowing stiffly from the waist, without taking his eyes from the face of Mansoor.

"I trust you have good reason to be armed in the house of Khalifa," he scowled.

Mansoor blinked in protest. "It was not my intention to give offence. I had to carry money through the city and did not want to be at a disadvantage."

Khalifa stared for a long moment, and nodded briefly.

"I accept your reason. Now, I have something to show you."

Mansoor looked at the scene in the workshop around him. Even at this late hour a small team of men were industriously working at assorted benches in the small armoury. Khalifa picked up a leather travelling case and placed it on a table in front of Mansoor.

"Open it," he commanded.

Mansoor opened the case nervously. Finding it completely empty, he looked enquiringly at the other man.

"A work of art, don't you think, my dear Achmet?" the turbaned Khalifa smiled confidently.

Mansoor picked up the case, weighing it in his hands, then smiled comprehendingly. "Truly, you are an artist in these matters, Adnan – and the explosive is built into the lining?"

Khalifa nodded confidently. "This is how it works. The Semtex is moulded into the frame, complete with a mercury tilt switch as the detonator. This can be activated from a distance electronically by this remote pressure box."

Khalifa held up his hand displaying a short aerial in a box with a red button easily covered by his palm. "The electric signal is only effective up to five kilometres so timing is important, but it also means it is possible to watch the results of your investment as it happens."

Khalifa picked up the case and banged it hard against the table causing Mansoor to flinch. The men working at the tables smiled gleefully at his discomfort.

"Is there anything else you are not sure of?" asked Khalifa.

"Yes, how many detonators are there around which can set off the explosive before I place it in position?"

Khalifa looked aggrieved. "You are indeed the most

cautious man I ever met, Achmet. Do you think I would keep the Semtex here if it could be detonated by another source?"

"I just like to be thorough. There is not much point in taking chances."

"Alas my friend, everything in life is a chance." Khalifa spread his hands philosophically. "It is by chance we are born and by chance we die."

Mansoor scowled, "Let us dispense with the quotations. I only wish to finalise our contract."

"So be it," Khalifa nodded, "then we shall have coffee and I wish you luck. I have the feeling you may need it."

The early morning street vendors outside the Chella Hotel awoke Suzanne. She watched through bleary eyes as Achmet Mansoor transferred the tightly packed banknotes from the briefcase into another case she had not seen before. He finally closed the lid with a flourish and locked it, pocketing the key and producing her a smile. They shared breakfast in their room and the girl spoke incessantly of their future plans. Mansoor listened, his mouth smiling but without hearing, his mind racing ahead to other affairs. Within a few days he would be rid of the girl completely. She would vanish in the bombing of the airliner to Israel leaving him with a new life and everything that money could buy.

They spent the day together exploring the old town, both happy but for totally different reasons. Mansoor bought the single plane ticket on the specific flight to Jerusalem, which had been ordered in the name of the Trading Company of Casablanca. During the afternoon, the girl, a mischievous glint in her eye, went shopping alone. Mansoor, guessing she had gone to buy him a present, used the opportunity to unpack the case obtained from Khalifa and fill it with newspapers, transferring the cash back to the original briefcase. She returned secretly happy with her purchase and it was at dinner that she placed a presentation gift box in his hand. He opened it curiously and took out a single gold wedding ring.

"I had it inscribed," she said. "Please wear it for me."

He looked at her trusting eyes and the inscription on the golden band. 'To Achmet from Suzanne Forever,' placing the ring ceremoniously on his finger. It felt like a chain confining him to this European woman. Anger rose in him as he raised a glass to her.

"To the future, Suzanne."

"To our future together," she corrected him.

Wolfe awoke instantly with the airport controller sitting on the side of his bed. Raschid Hirasch apologised quickly, "Excuse me, Monsieur, I did not mean to alarm you."

Wolfe swung his feet to the floor. "Is there a problem?"

"No, on the contrary, the news is good. I have just heard from Colonel Simeon on the Sahari border. He thought that you and Mademoiselle Danielle would like to know that there has been a complete rout of the enemy forces. If this had not been completed before the frontier was closed we would have had an impossible fight on our hands. As it happens the ruling military junta are claiming it was a breakaway element from their army which caused the trouble and are disclaiming responsibility."

Wolfe raised a triumphant fist. "Well, that is good news. There were times when I thought the battle was lost."

Hirasch chuckled. "From my short acquaintance with you, Monsieur, I don't think you would know when to accept defeat."

"And I don't know whether to accept that as a compliment or a reprimand," Wolfe replied.

"Assuredly a compliment. Perhaps you would like to inform Danielle of the news."

Wolfe stretched and stood up. "It's my pleasure, Raschid; she did as much as anyone. She will be very pleased."

The controller touched Wolfe's shoulder. "I hope you are still a winning team. Allah knows we can use some help."

Wolfe pushed his hair back thoughtfully. "Tell me, Raschid, I have seen some famous faces pass over the last twenty-four hours and I was not aware of them until they entered passport control."

"Yes, that is also a security precaution. We do not inform the media as it puts too great a strain on security. As this is an international airport we often have tycoons and movie stars who do not want to be recognised. As long as we use a *nom de plume* on the passenger list it works effectively. Our passport control is informed previously, of course."

Wolfe stared at the air controller. "I can spot an obvious loophole in that system, Raschid."

"I don't understand, where?"

"Well, this may work normally, but for a terrorist with a change of name, it's all the edge he would need to get aboard with his luggage or a bomb."

The controller smiled, "It would hardly be practical, Jack."

"Maybe not, but if his luggage was in the cargo hold and he did not take his seat, what would happen then?"

The understanding showed in the controller's expression. "We would take off without him."

"Plus one bomb in the hold?" said Wolfe.

Hirasch sucked in his breath, then strode to the door.

Wolfe, pausing only to splash water on his face, followed. He stopped at passport control and joined the queue of travellers filing past Danielle. She giggled as he tried to sneak past her.

"Just testing the system, Dany," he said. "Why did you let me sleep so long?"

"I thought you needed it, and I was not tired."

"But you have been awake all night."

"Well now I am tired so please don't shout at me."

Wolfe took her hand, "I have some news for you."

Her blue eyes blinked expectantly. "Tell me."

"Moroccan troops have regained control of the border. The military have just notified us."

"Oh Jack, I'm so pleased. It makes it all worthwhile. Did they find Rico Filila?"

"He wasn't mentioned. Maybe he will turn up eventually."

"Like the bad penny, eh Jack? Or perhaps his bones lie bleaching in the midday sun," she said dramatically.

"I think you read too many novels, Dany," Wolfe smiled. "Now go and get some sleep, immediately."

She clicked her heels together and threw her open hand upwards in a Fascist salute, "*Ja wohl, mien Fuhrer,*" she said, and turning quickly, strode through the immigration door.

The security men grinned, looking to Wolfe for a reaction. He shrugged his shoulders and tapping his head with his forefinger, settled down in the chair Danielle had just left.

The airline passengers were slowly filing through passport control, onto the tarmac outside the terminal building. Wolfe sipping mint tea was staring at the faces as they shuffled past. Danielle was unexpectedly beside him, her fingers tightening on his shoulder, spilling the hot liquid into the saucer.

"Jack, it's her."

"Where?" said Wolfe.

"At the end of the line. She has had her hair cut and is wearing shorts."

"Are you sure?"

"I shared a room with her for two years. I can't forget that figure."

Wolfe raised a finger to a plain-clothes security captain, indicating the end of the group. The man turned his back, speaking quietly into a hand-held transmitter. Seconds later a crisp female voice announced over the public address system, "Will Mr Socrates travelling on flight H36 to Jerusalem contact the information desk."

The tall man in shirt sleeves without luggage immediately folded his newspaper and dropped into the queue behind Suzanne Wolfe. Another casually rose from his seat, stretching his legs as he sauntered into line.

The uniformed girl at the departure gate apologetically closed the glass door, smiling sweetly at the travellers. "Can you wait just a little longer until the other passengers have taken their seats?"

The man behind Suzanne Wolfe grumbled and leaned against the wall as the progress halted.

Hirasch appeared carrying a clipboard. "Where is she?" he said softly.

"Near the end of the line," Wolfe said, "in front of your security men."

The controller ran a finger down the clipboard. "Suzanne Wolfe. She only booked in a short while ago."

"Where is the luggage now?" said Wolfe.

"Probably on the trolley waiting to be loaded."

"Then stop it quickly."

Hirasch spoke to the man beside him. "Stop it now but be careful we don't arouse any suspicions."

"Follow me," he said to Wolfe, "and, Danielle, keep out of sight."

Wolfe accompanied Hirasch briskly to the baggage area. Hirasch motioned the loading crew away from the motorised trolley piled with cases.

"Take every bag off the wagon and check it with the boarding receipts," he commanded the security staff.

Almost immediately one said, "It's here on the top."

"Right, now check all the others and then double check and bring that valise into the construction shed."

A slim young officer in a new boiler suit picked up the valise and strolled easily towards the building material store. He placed it on a heap of concrete blocks before feeling carefully around the seamed edges and the carrying handle.

"I hope he knows what he is doing," Wolfe said.

"He does. Sergeant Hussain is the best bomb disposal expert in Casablanca."

"Phew," said Wolfe. "I'm relieved to hear it."

The sergeant grimaced and taking a serrated knife from a tool roll pushed it gingerly into the lid of the valise, then gently cut away the outer cover. He removed the garments inside, inspecting them thoroughly then pulled out a smaller travelling case putting it down carefully on an adjacent bench.

"This could be it. Everyone leave," he ordered.

The security staff exchanged glances and shuffled to the door. "I'm staying," said Hirasch.

"I'll stay too," said Wolfe.

"You don't have to."

"I know that. I want to know what we are dealing with."

Hussain looked for confirmation from Hirasch.

"Carry on, Sergeant. Monsieur Wolfe is no stranger to risks."

"There is a distinct difference between taking a calculated risk and being foolhardy," Hussain said.

"But if you insist you can help. Just give me a few moments to settle myself."

Wolfe breathed heavily wondering if he had done the right thing in volunteering to stay.

Hussain knelt in front of the ordinary looking case.

"Right," the sergeant said. "First I shall slide back the catches," he fumbled for some seconds before releasing the case. "That's a good start – the thing is locked."

"What now?" said Hirasch.

"Cut through the lid again."

The serrated knife slowly slit open the leather valise and Hussain lifted one corner, peering inside.

"It is stuffed with newspaper. The lining is too thick – it seems to have a moulded unit.

Pretty standard kit for terrorists."

Wolfe blinking rapidly became aware of the perspiration coursing down his face. "Can it be defused?"

Hussain pondered. "Difficult to say. If it has a liquid detonator, no. If it has electric controls it could blow anytime."

"It does not seem much explosive for a bomb," Wolfe said.

"Perhaps not in normal circumstances, but enough to bring an airliner down."

"Then Mansoor must still be around," said Wolfe.

"He has to be, or someone to activate the signal."

"What is our next move?" said Hirasch.

"To have a controlled explosion here, put plenty of cement bags and blocks around it, if you want your bomber to think that everything is proceeding to plan."

"You have done well, Sergeant," Hirasch said. "If we leave this to you, can we carry on loading and allow the plane to leave?"

"And my niece?" queried Wolfe.

"She must go aboard as normal as she is most certainly being watched and something else you should know, the Israeli Defence Minister is also on the plane."

"Oh my God," Wolfe groaned.

The controller hurried to the doorway beckoning to his staff. "Carry on as normal, but stay vigilant. We have isolated the bomb, now we are looking for the bomber."

Hussain appeared at the controller's shoulder.

"You are looking for a detonator, probably hand held. It will be outside or at an opening where the signal is strongest and easily concealed. When the plane takes off you have one chance to find him. Look for signs of alarm or frustration."

Wolfe patted Hussain on the shoulder and returned to passport control to find Danielle watching Suzanne Wolfe walking across the tarmac to the waiting plane.

"She passed me, Jack. She was so close that I could have touched her, and she looked so happy. The poor girl – how could she be so stupid?"

"Search me," Wolfe said. "We have isolated the bomb, but it can still go off."

"Jack, she's waving to someone."

"You are right, Dany, she is waving towards the viewing balcony. Mansoor must be up there," Wolfe said, grabbing a hand phone from a security officer.

"Raschid can you hear me. Mansoor is on the spectator balcony," he said to Hirasch.

The answer crackled back, "How do you know?"

"We just saw the girl waving. It's got to be the place."

"Right, I'll put a cordon around it, there must be fifty people up there."

Wolfe stuck the transmitter in his pocket and ran to the first floor staircase leading to the balcony. Reaching the top he pushed open the swing door and walked indifferently out among the spectators, shading his eyes towards the runway. Small groups of children chattered amongst themselves accompanied by adults but there was no sign of a man alone.

Wolfe eased himself further into the crowd as the doors at both ends of the viewing area opened, allowing the entrance of more security men. The officers stood searching for a single movement that could reveal the identity of Mansoor, knowing that the hunt for the bomber could be over in just a few seconds.

The loaded plane taxied along the runway, then lifted abruptly, feathering over the palms at the end of the runway and gaining height rapidly. A tall dark tourist stood in the centre of a group of children. Slowly the man pulled a linen handkerchief from his pocket, holding it on the balcony rail. Wolfe's adrenalin surged through him as he spotted the unmistakable sign of a short aerial protruding from the cloth.

Wolfe motioned urgently to the security staff at the same time that Hirasch burst through the swing doors onto the viewing area. Mansoor swung round, confronting his pursuers, startling Wolfe with the malevolence in the dark eyes as he held up the detonating device in his hand.

"Shoot him now," roared Hirasch, stumbling through the crowd.

Mansoor deliberately pressed the button on the transmitting box. The muffled explosion from the construction shed blew out the windows causing the spectators on the balcony to duck urgently. Mansoor looked at the departing airliner in disbelief then threw the transmitter viciously into the face of Wolfe before vaulting cleanly over the balcony onto the concrete floor below. Wolfe staggered to the rail, stunned by the impact of the blow.

"Shoot him, don't let him get away," bellowed Hirasch, above the screaming and confusion of the milling spectators.

Wolfe's revolver was in his hand and he managed to trigger off a single round at the fleeing Mansoor before the Moroccan dived out of sight under the balcony and back into passport control.

Wolfe turned and ran for the stairs. Pistol shots rang out from passport control but the blow from the transmitter had clouded his vision, making him tumble headlong down the stairs. Regaining his feet he stumbled into the control area, appalled at the scene that greeted him. The uniformed girl on immigration rushed forward. "We tried to stop him, Monsieur, but he just fired at everyone."

"Where is he now?" Wolfe said, wiping his eyes hastily.

"He grabbed a small boy and ran off through the commercial area. We had no chance to follow with the gun pointed at the child."

"Anyone badly hurt?" said Wolfe.

The girl blinked rapidly and seemed unable to continue.

"Where's Mademoiselle Charni?" he asked suddenly alarmed.

It was the airport controller's hand that went to his arm and Wolfe knew instantly the news he feared.

"I think two are dead and two seriously wounded, Jack. Follow me over here," said Hirasch, pushing his way through the milling airport staff.

Danielle was laid on the floor, her head cradled by a young woman. There was sleepiness about her eyes and a trickle of blood at the corner of her mouth. One hand flapped weakly at the air. Wolfe took her palm gently and knelt beside her.

"Is that you, Jack?" she said quietly.

"Yes, I'm here, Dany," Wolfe answered, noticing the red bloodstain above her right breast spreading slowly outwards.

She shuddered and searched his face through her pain. "We did not have long together, Jack, but you said you loved me in the desert, do you remember?" she whispered.

He leaned over and kissed her gently on the lips, "I remember, I never told anyone that before."

The grip tightened on his hand. "You make me happy, Jack, I only wish..." her voice trailed off, eyes closing as the white-coated ambulance crew eased Wolfe away from Danielle, transferring her to a stretcher.

Wolfe could only stare, as the now silent form of the girl was carried hastily away, his frustration replaced with pain, then anger, as he walked blindly after her.

"Let the doctors take her, there is nothing you can do, Jack," Hirasch said, as gentle hands restrained him.

Wolfe put his hand to his mouth; Danielle's blood was on his fingers. A cold fury invaded his body startling the airport controller with his calmness.

"Where is she now?" he asked Hirasch.

"In the commercial section, surrounded. It is impossible for him to escape."

"But he has a hostage. Are you prepared to sacrifice the boy?"

"No, but we have men trained in negotiation for this kind of emergency."

"So you think Mansoor will give himself up?"

"I don't know what to think, nothing like this has happened before. We shall just hope Mansoor will see reason."

"Sorry. I don't share your optimism Raschid; this man has nothing to lose by finishing the boy. From the moment a hostage is taken it is better to think of him as finished or events can escalate if we give into threats. I don't think we should wait any longer."

Hirasch sighed wearily, " I have a duty to try to talk to him. I don't want any innocent lives on my conscience."

The radio in the air controller's hand crackled and Hirasch listened intently. "He has taken another hostage and they are making their way out, towards the light aircraft in the private area."

"So much for negotiation. Does he still have the boy?"

The controller nodded, "And the other hostage is a pilot."

Wolfe groaned in exasperation. "Where are the light aircraft?"

"This way," Hirasch set off at a run until they reached the large windows fronting the end of the commercial section.

"I see them," Wolfe pointed to the figures hurrying over the tarmac, the hapless pilot carrying the boy, with the pistol of Mansoor at his head.

"Oh for just one good shot with a rifle," moaned Wolfe.

"I fear it is too late for that. Once he is airborne I don't know how we will stop him," said Hirasch.

"Then track him on radar."

"We would do that anyway, but we are still powerless to do anything."

They watched helplessly as Mansoor clambered aboard the red Cessna, dragging the unwilling hostages after him. The single propeller spun into life and the light aircraft see-sawed its way bumpily down the tarmac.

"What is that?" said Wolfe, pointing to an adjacent hanger.

"You mean the helicopter? The army have them serviced here, but we don't have any pilots available."

"Yes we do," said Wolfe, pushing his way through the personnel door and running towards the hanger with the airport controller galloping along behind.

"You can't take that," gasped Hirasch. "We don't know what condition it's in."

Wolfe dragged open the panelled door of the Jetranger and leapt in, flipping the battery meter on the control board.

"Almost a full tank, trust the army to be thorough."

He jumped back to the tarmac and disconnected the restraining cable from the nose wheel. The airport controller barred his way to the helicopter door. "I can't let you take it, I don't have the authority and if anything happened there would be a hell of a row."

"Get out of my way, Raschid," Wolfe confronted the controller. "I mean it."

Hirasch only needed a few seconds to know the Englishman was near violence and he stepped backwards, pulling his revolver from its holster.

"Then you had better take this," he said, reversing the pistol and handing it butt first to Wolfe.

The madness died in Wolfe's eyes. "Thanks Raschid. I prefer you as a friend."

"Well go now, before I change my mind, because I already regret it. I shall be in the control tower. Get me on the open channel."

Wolfe levered himself into the flying seat, switching on the ignition. "See you when I return, Raschid."

"Don't count on it, I'll be lucky to have a job sweeping the leaves."

The single-engined Cessna climbed into the sky at a sharp angle, clearing the date palms at the perimeter of the airport.

"Why are you flying so low?" Mansoor jabbed his revolver into the ribs of the grim-faced pilot.

"We have not had clearance for take off. Do you want to hit a plane making a landing?" he answered.

"You will do as I say," commanded Mansoor, "or suffer the consequences."

"What will you do, shoot me? Will you fly the plane?" the pilot challenged.

"It makes little difference to me, but it does to him," Mansoor said, viciously jerking the youngster's arm.

The boy yelped in pain.

"Enough," the pilot said, "I shall take you wherever you want. Just leave the lad alone."

"Then we understand each other. If you challenge me, the boy gets if first, without warning." Mansoor put the pistol to the child's head.

"Where do you want to go?"

"How far can this thing fly with the fuel in the tank?"

The pilot shrugged, "I don't know, possibly two hundred kilometres at a guess."

"Well guess well my friend, your life depends on it and get rid of that," Mansoor said, smashing the radio panel with a single blow from his revolver.

The pilot's hands trembled on the control column but he smiled reassuringly at the tousle-haired boy wedged between them as the light aircraft gathering height, soared away above the roofs of Casablanca.

Wolfe brought the Jetranger to hover, checking the instruments on the panel before elevating the rudder and picking up speed into a climbing turn to the east. He stayed at five hundred feet keeping an eye peeled for approaching aircraft then pushed the machine forward until it achieved maximum cruising speed.

There was no sign of the Cessna and Wolfe, scanning the horizon, shoved on the headset and adjusted the radio. He was in contact with air traffic control immediately and asked to speak with Hirasch. The airport controller was still panting from his run across the airport to the tower but appeared very much in charge.

"We have picked up the Cessna on radar," he gasped, "but it keeps vanishing below our screen. There wasn't a sign of it at first. The pilot must have known we would track him; he is obviously being made to fly to orders."

"Can I go any higher?" Wolfe said, "I can't see anything if I am puddle-jumping."

"Affirmative," said Hirasch. "We have a state of emergency down here and you have clearance to twelve hundred feet. Stay on that heading and keep searching.

We will keep this frequency open. Let us know the minute you spot them and good luck my friend. We are all with you."

Wolfe lifted the Jetranger to twelve hundred feet and settled into his routine, checking compass direction, elevation and fuel levels while scanning the horizon for the light aircraft. It was only after his complete checklist that the events of the last hour weighed upon him. The picture uppermost in his thoughts was of the silent Danielle, the blood oozing from her breast. He found himself gritting his teeth in delayed anger. In the early days as a professional soldier he had been taught never to let vengeance cloud his vision, but it lost all meaning when it involved the pain of a loved one. It also made a man take unnecessary risks, but then life was not so important as to forget the rules of combat for safety. The city of Casablanca was soon on his starboard wing and he was becoming annoyed at not sighting the light aircraft somewhere in front.

He lifted the Jetranger to fifteen hundred feet and opened the channel to airport control.

"We have you on screen, but the Cessna keeps vanishing below our radar," said Hirasch.

"How far away am I?"

"Close, very close," answered the controller.

"And what is the situation at the airport?" Wolfe asked nervously.

"Everyone is coping, we are still in a state of shock but I expect your question was about the condition of the injured?"

"Just tell me the worst."

"I'm not sure, Jack, everything possible is being done and if I have any more information."

Wolfe swore viciously. "I have spotted them, hedge-hopping below me. At least I can't be seen from this angle."

"What are you going to do?"

"Apart from following, there is not much I can do until they land."

"Don't forget I need the hostages back – that is a greater priority than getting Mansoor."

There was a silence from the radio. Hirasch waited expectantly, "Do your hear me, Jack?"

"I hear you," responded Wolfe, "but don't expect me to reason with Mansoor. I intend to finish him given the slightest chance."

"But there is a small boy up there. Are you prepared to sacrifice two more innocent lives for revenge?"

"Something's happening," said Wolfe coldly. "I will get back to you."

He snapped down the transmit switch and taking off the headset laid it beside him.

The aircraft below was still on a south-east heading and Wolfe adjusted his speed to keep the Cessna in sight without betraying his own position. The ground beneath was gradually losing its fertile cover and after another fifteen minutes flying time the sharp grey shelves of the Atlas Range loomed high on the skyline.

Wolfe tapped the kerosene fuel gauge, which was showing below the halfway level. One hell of a place for a landing he thought as the first streaks of cirrus caused the temperature to become colder. He shivered painfully, aware of his lightweight clothing, and put on the headset and opened the channel to Casablanca.

The reception was faint and fragmented and Wolfe had difficulty making himself understood, but eventually the faint voice of the airport controller filtered through, "We have lost trace of you, Jack, can you give us a direction?"

"Sure, what is on the other side of the Atlas Mountains?"

The confused crackling in the headphones, "Algeria!"

"Well it looks as though Mansoor is going for it, because there is nowhere around here to land and he must be gauging his fuel."

"And yourself, how much kerosene have you left?"

"I dare not think about it. If I turned back now I should be all right."

"Is that your intention?"

"What do you think?" Wolfe said. "What is the latest on the casualties?"

"Repeat the question."

Wolfe started to speak slowly until there was a hissing sound from the transmitter, then total silence.

He took the head set off and threw it beside him in exasperation.

At the airport control tower Raschid Hirasch placed the intercom thoughtfully on the desk, turning to the attentive staff around him.

"That may be our last transmission from the Englishman but keep the frequency open. Listen for the unusual and stay alert. This crisis is far from over."

He turned and descended the steel stairway to passport control, pausing only to take a deep breath before pushing open the door and stepping through. A barrage of questions from all sides immediately besieged him. The police and the army were trying to calm the passengers and a government minister had just arrived.

Hirasch raised his hands in protest. "One thing at a

time. Everything is under control and your questions will be answered in due time."

"What of the injured?" he asked his captain of security.

The officer looked grave, "We lost another on the way to the hospital."

"Was it the girl?"

"No, it was one of the loading staff."

Hirasch sagged as the government minister approached extending his hand. The controller took it limply.

"I have to congratulate you, Raschid. You can be proud of your performance today."

Hirasch looked aghast. "How can I be congratulated after all of this?" he said, sweeping a hand at the bloodstains and debris from the shattered construction area. "We have three dead already, maybe four and the assassin has escaped with two hostages."

The government official frowned. "It's all a matter of degree Raschid. You have avoided an international disaster. There could have been two hundred dead including the Israeli Defence Minister and you have prevented the loss of an airliner. I think you are to be commended and I hear you have one of your pilots tracking the terrorist at this very moment."

"He is not one of my regular pilots," Hirasch said. "But it is true the bomber is being followed by one of our men."

"Then when the assassin is finally captured he will be brought to justice."

Hirasch shook his head. "I don't believe that to be the case. The man chasing him is not strong on compassion and his female companion was shot in the skirmish."

The minister smiled. "Good, that should save us trouble all round."

"Excuse me controller," it was one of the security men. "We have the parents of the kidnapped boy in the medical block. They want to know what you are going to do about it."

The minister took a step backwards and bowed. "I shall leave everything in your capable hands Raschid. My report will contain our appreciation of your capability."

He turned and walked briskly away to his waiting vehicle.

The white-coated nurses moving quietly around brought Danielle from unconsciousness. She squinted through half-closed eyes at the brightness, trying to focus on a single object while feeling a numbing paralysis holding her arm and chest in a deadening grip. She cried out at the realisation of her whereabouts as a gentle hand stroked her brow.

"Where am I?" she asked hesitantly.

"You are in the hospital in Casablanca," the nurse answered.

"Am I very ill?"

The nurse motioned a young doctor to the bedside.

"You must rest now. You have lost a lot of blood and will still be very weak."

Danielle felt the frustration rising angrily. "How do you expect me to rest until I know what has happened."

The doctor put his fingers around her pulse and looked at his watch. "How do you feel?"

"Like hell," the girl said.

There was almost a glint of humour in his eyes, as he pointed below her right shoulder. "We have removed a bullet a fraction away from your lung, there was severe rupturing of the blood vessels, causing massive haemorrhage. I would say you have been very lucky."

"Will I recover?"

"That depends on you and whether you can obey orders."

"How long have I been here?"

"This is your second day."

Danielle grimaced. "Can I have visitors?"

"For a few minutes only."

"Is Jack here?"

The doctor looked at the nurse enquiringly. "What does he look like?"

"European, light hair and soft grey eyes," Danielle said.

"There is no one like that but you do have a cousin who refuses to leave until she knows you are conscious."

"That will be Nabila."

The doctor nodded and the nurse hurried away, to return with the anxious woman. Nabila wiped her eyes when she saw her cousin helpless on the bed, then sat down abruptly beside her.

The young doctor waved a finger. "A few minutes remember and I don't want any trouble from you."

Danielle twitched her nostrils twice in response.

"We couldn't believe what had happened," said Nabila.

"It's on the radio and made the headlines in the newspapers."

"Have you seen Jack?" asked Danielle.

"No one has. After you were shot Mansoor took two hostages and escaped in a small plane, then Jack took an army helicopter and chased after him."

"Oh my God, did anyone try to stop him?"

"Well, I think at the time it would have been dangerous to try. He really was acting wildly by all events."

"Do we know anything more about them?"

"I am told the last transmission from Jack was from the base of the Atlas Mountains. After that there was no more contact."

Danielle lay quietly brooding; the dull throbbing in her shoulder confusing her logic, she hardly felt the small injection and the slow return to sleep.

# Chapter 10

The first signs of darkness were approaching as Wolfe lifted the Jetranger higher into the thinning atmosphere. The huge spired tops of the Atlas pinnacles soared perilously close, yet the awesome grandeur of the mountains was a fascinating scene. The tiny Cessna just a few hundred feet below was weaving and snaking around the approaching obstacles and Wolfe could only admire the undoubted skill of the pilot beneath him.

He tapped his fuel gauge again wondering why he always did that. He had one third of a tank left anyway, certainly not enough to return but he had made a choice and, right or wrong, there was no turning back. It was perhaps the same for the other pilot and although it may be a life-chancing game of bluff, the other man was not able to make his own decisions.

Wolfe straightened in his seat, pushing the stiffness in his shoulders away and feeling the intense cold on his body. He peered from his portside window, realising with agitation that the Cessna had vanished. Then the reason became obvious. The towering peaks of the High Atlas had gradually lost their stark immensity and the earth beneath was showing patchy areas of sand. The Cessna had reduced height drastically and Wolfe guessed the pilot must be looking for a safe landing area.

The darkness came quickly with the descent from the high horizon and Wolfe levelled the machine to eight hundred feet, keeping the light plane in view. The first signs of vegetation appeared at the edge of a cluster of date palms, the Cessna taking Wolfe by surprise with a 90-degree turn. He was sure he had been seen and he pulled the Jetranger higher in the hope of avoiding detection.

The propeller on the light aircraft below was feathering and Wolfe watched the frantic efforts of the pilot to keep the machine airborne. The small plane cruised to a good landing on an almost level patch of ground, the pilot holding his speed back until the very last moment. The wheels touched the soft sand for one hundred metres before sinking into the yielding earth and pitching the Cessna onto its nose.

The gathering gloom was making visibility difficult now, and there was no sign of movement from the stricken Cessna. It would obviously never be flown again but Wolfe could only guess at the state of its passengers.

He lowered the Jetranger to a bumpy landing five hundred metres away in a slight depression, cut the rotors and switched off the battery meter, unclipping his safety harness. The relief from concentrating made him slump forward on the control panel with fatigue. The lightening rays of the moon gave him a clearer view of the date palms in the direction of the Cessna yet as he peered blearily through the screen the wind started quickly. Just the first twisting flurry, then within seconds a whining storm of sand blocking all vision. Startled with the suddenness of the storm, Wolfe contemplated a dash towards the grounded Cessna but as the gale grew in intensity he reasoned that he could become lost within a few metres. If there were survivors in the light aircraft the possibility of a reprisal by Mansoor was equally out of the question and Wolfe stretched back in the confined cockpit resigned to an indefinite wait.

The wind in its surging onslaught rocked the Jetranger, heightening the claustrophobia he felt by the enforced isolation. Wolfe checked his watch for no reason: time did not seem to matter but at least he would know the length of his imprisonment. His wild aggression towards Mansoor had lifted yet a stubbornness to stop the Moroccan at any cost had replaced it. He tried to put the picture of Danielle from his mind, but it always returned to haunt him.

The moon flickered into view then disappeared again, yet after two hours of battering the Jetranger, there was a gradual lessening in the storm around him. He took the revolver the airport controller had given him and spun the chamber lining up a round under the hammer. It felt good in his hand. It was what he knew best. He pushed at the helicopter door and dropped to the ground, doubling low from the machine. The storm was still blowing its myriad sand needles into Wolfe's unprotected skin as he shielded his face on the crouching run towards the Cessna.

The pale outline of the scrubby date palms gave him a bearing on the wrecked machine. He covered the remaining two hundred metres, carefully dropping to the ground and snaking his way forwards as he neared the plane. The propeller was snapped off and buried in the sand, tail pointing into the sky, yet there was no sign of movement from the interior.

Wolfe wriggled forward until he could clearly see the

figure of the pilot hanging suspended in his safety harness with one leg doubled beneath him and the young Moroccan boy pressed face downwards and silent against the front screen. Wolfe took an uneasy look around before leaping to his feet and opening the cockpit door.

"Where is he?" Wolfe shouted above the gale.

"Gone, he left as the storm started."

"Which way did he go?"

"How would I know, hanging upside down like a trussed chicken?"

"Can you move?" said Wolfe.

"No, my right ankle is broken. It hurt at first, but now I can't feel anything."

"How about the boy?"

"He has been like that since we crashed."

"Right, I am going to get you out," Wolfe said, levering himself under the pilot. "When I lift, unclip your safety harness."

The man groaned with pain from the fractured limb as he fell across Wolfe and was pulled to the ground outside. The wind had ceased its unbearable surging and the yellow moonlight was showing again as Wolfe turned his attention to the boy. He was a small, curly-haired youngster about eight years of age, his eyes closed, and had heavy bruising to the side of his face. Wolfe lifted him gently from the plane, then felt his limbs for breakages.

"How is he?" the pilot asked through gritted teeth.

"Not sure, looks like concussion to me. I will get him back to the chopper then return for you."

"You were unlucky," the pilot said. "We had no idea you were following until our fuel ran out. It was on landing that we saw you. I had given up hope until then."

The boy was limp in Wolfe's arms as he carried him back to the Jetranger and laid him carefully on the floor, before doubling back to the Cessna. The man on the ground was almost insensible and his breathing was shallow. His ankle was twisted at an unusual angle and Wolfe removed the pilot's footwear with difficulty. It looked a serious fracture but there was nothing suitable for a splint. Wolfe ran across to the scrappy palms nearby and pulled off one of the lower branches, stripping off its leaves.

The man opened his eyes as Wolfe returned.

"Put this in your mouth," Wolfe said, handing him a fibrous twig from the palm. "It may hurt a bit when I set your ankle."

"Be quick as you can," the pilot said.

Wolfe placed one hand under the leg, and then pulled the twisted foot straight. There was no sound from the man on the ground. He had passed out.

"Just as well," Wolfe thought, as he ripped his own shirt into bandages and set about tying the broken limb to the splint.

With difficulty Wolfe managed to lever the insensible pilot onto his shoulders and stagger back to the Jetranger. He collapsed to a kneeling position as the man finally stirred.

"How do you feel now?" panted Wolfe, laying the man down.

The pilot eyed his lower leg. "The pain is less, but don't expect me to run anywhere."

The boy whimpered from inside the Jetranger. Wolfe climbed inside and held the youngster in his arms.

"His name is Ali and he is a plucky little lad," the pilot said. "I am Saddam."

"Call me Wolfe."

"Tell me what happened after he snatched the boy."

The pilot pulled himself upwards using the helicopter stanchions for support, standing on one leg. "He said he would shoot the boy if he did not find a pilot. I volunteered."

"Then what happened?"

"He grabbed some supplies and we flew here. I told him we had not enough fuel to fly over the Atlas, but with a gun pointing at my head I did not think I could win the argument."

"Did he hurt the boy?"

"No, that's the strange thing. He seemed really protective when we were over the mountains. He held the lad like a father would."

"Where do you think we are?" said Wolfe.

"Perhaps Algeria, it is hard to say."

Wolfe helped the pilot into the passenger seat. "Well, we shall stay here until first light and then try and spot Mansoor from the air."

Saddam looked at Wolfe incredulously. "You mean you don't intend to fly us back?"

"Yes, after I finish Mansoor."

"But we don't have any jurisdiction outside of Morocco. If we were to find him, there is nothing we could do."

Wolfe's face tightened. "Sorry you feel like that, but I have chased this man across the country and breaking the law doesn't mean much."

"So you will put the life of the boy in danger?" Saddam's voice was rising. "It is clear you have no regard for your own skin but how will we survive if something happens to you?"

"Nothing is going to happen to me," said Wolfe doggedly.

"You can't be sure of that," Saddam shouted back. "You

are concerned only with vengeance. You are as vicious as the man you seek."

Wolfe stared back in surprise as the boy cried out again.

"You know I am right," Saddam said. "Do you want the death of a child on your conscience?"

Wolfe felt the resolve drain away, leaving a total emptiness. He stretched out a hand to the lad's tousled hair.

"I don't even know if we have enough kerosene to get halfway back."

"Well we can't stay here forever talking about it."

Wolfe looked back towards the grounded Cessna and the trackless land beyond. Mansoor was out there somewhere and he wouldn't be expecting pursuit. This would be the best opportunity to follow and complete the action, but at what cost to the already weakened couple with him? He turned and levered himself into the flying seat.

"Strap yourself in Saddam, this could be very bumpy. We shall head for home. Just how far we will get is anyone's guess."

The rotor rocked into action as the Jetranger hovered briefly before making a looping turn away into the night sky.

# Chapter 11

The flight to Israel had been routine and uneventful. Suzanne Wolfe gazed thoughtfully from the starboard window drinking a glass of red wine after her inboard meal. She felt good and was looking forward to her arrival in the new country. The laconic passenger at her side had not spoken during the entire journey but had buried his head in the newspaper without comment.

The safety belt warning light appeared overhead and she pushed the small table back into the upright position, as the engines changed sound on the long downwards angle approaching the airport. The dusk was closing rapidly as the plane cleared the approach lights and touched down. The girl was mildly disappointed that her first sight of Jerusalem should be in darkness but as the airliner taxied towards the main terminal the feeling of well-being returned.

The stewardess, after thanking everyone for flying Air Maroc, stood attentively at the gangway exit as the passengers gathered hand luggage from the compartments overhead, and began to wander down the aisle. Suzanne stretched and made to stand up. A hand was placed firmly upon hers. "Please remain where you are Mademoiselle until the plane is empty."

She stared speechlessly at the man who had travelled beside her from Casablanca. "Is something wrong?"

"Captain Malik, airport police," he said, producing a card with his photograph and credentials.

She fell back into her seat, the shock of the unexpected command driving away her excitement.

"The problem is, Mademoiselle, you are not allowed to depart, and will return with us to Morocco," the chief officer said.

"But that's ridiculous, I have done nothing wrong," she protested.

Captain Malik raised a warning hand. "You move in dangerous circles Mademoiselle and will be handed over to the authorities when we get back to Casablanca. I would advise you not to be difficult, it will only make it worse for you."

There was an undeniable threat in his tone and Suzanne shivered at the warning.

The man beside her rose. "Can we have a seat in the rear of the plane, Captain? It will be quieter for the young lady back there."

The pilot nodded. "Just keep her out of my sight. The sooner she is off this plane the happier we will be."

Malik took Suzanne by the arm. "You will surrender your passport to me now."

Suzanne gulped. "Am I under arrest?"

"Unfortunately yes."

"On what charge?"

The man looked sad. "I don't need a charge Mademoiselle. This is not Europe – I can hold you indefinitely on suspicion."

"For what reason?" she persisted.

Malik sighed and shrugged slowly. "Conspiracy to bomb an airliner, attempted assassination of a government minister, transportation of prohibited materials, association with known criminals. Shall I continue?"

The last question was lost on Suzanne as she dropped speechless back into her seat.

The Jetranger climbed high into the Western sky, Wolfe levelled the machine and opened the throttle into cruising speed. Above the diminishing dust clouds the night was clear, but the jagged crests of the High Atlas reappeared all too soon and Wolfe had to use full concentration to avoid the rapid approach of the thrusting pinnacles. He tried the radio again without success, resigning himself to the possibility of returning by compass only.

Saddam, strapped in the rear seat with the boy cradled in his arms, said little, not wishing to disturb the man focused on the helicopter controls. The Moroccan pilot had been unprepared for the change of attitude in Wolfe from the remorseless pursuer to the thoughtful pilot. The tousled head in Saddam's arms twitched and the boy blinked rapidly without moving from the pilot's grasp.

"Where are we?" he said croakily.

Saddam stroked his brow. "We are going back to your family."

"My head hurts."

"Well you have had a nasty bump but it will get better now."

"I'm hungry," the lad said.

Wolfe smiled with relief.

"Good," said Saddam. "There can't be much wrong if you want some food."

The youngster closed his eyes again and settled back into Saddam's arms. "I am beginning to feel better about this," the Moroccan pilot said. "I had the definite feeling at one point that we were done for but no…" The engine coughed briefly.

"I hope you didn't speak too soon," Wolfe grimaced. "This chopper was at Casablanca for servicing."

"How much fuel do we have?"

"Difficult to say, less than one hundred kilometres."

"Try the headset."

"It's useless," Wolfe said, "but you can give it a go if you think it will help."

Saddam eased the sleeping boy into the rear seat, and put on the headset. The engine jolted once more.

"Don't like the sound of that," the Moroccan pilot said. "What do you think it is?"

"Fuel lines or electrics probably. Whatever it is I shall have to reduce height."

"Reduce height over this?"

"Not much of a choice is it?" Wolfe looked sideways at the Moroccan pilot as the Jetranger dipped towards the towering bluffs. "Unfortunately this is not a glider but it would not help much if it was."

The radio crackled and the Moroccan pilot fumbled with the tuning control.

"Can you raise them Saddam?"

"There's a lot of static but I can just about hear."

Wolfe pulled the Jetranger abruptly higher weaving an irregular pattern through the mountain range. The engine misfired again, then settled back into rhythm as the Moroccan pilot spoke urgently into his transmitter.

"Have you made contact?" Wolfe asked.

Saddam nodded. "They should soon have us on radar," he said, as the motor spluttered again.

"About now would be a good time."

The engine on the Jetranger stalled completely.

For a few heart-sinking seconds, the only sound was the violent threshing of the rotor blades above. Saddam swore before reaching out to the child and holding him tight in his arms. Wolfe sat gripping the control levers, the realisation of his worst nightmares only too imminent. The vivid memory of a spiralling descent into the jungle, the bone-shattering impact and the tearing of metal flashed across his senses as the blood pumped wildly into his veins.

"Are we going to make it?" Saddam shouted.

Wolfe wrestled with the controls. "Get a 'May Day' out and make it quick – we only have a few seconds."

He pushed the nose of the Jetranger downwards as the spinning blades slowly decreased speed. The Moroccan pilot spoke urgently into the intercom, Wolfe fighting the controls as the ground swept towards them.

"Brace yourselves," Wolfe shouted, as a few metres from impact he flipped off the battery and snapped all switches closed. The labouring helicopter bounced to a bruising crash landing, flinging its occupants violently about. The Moroccan pilot yelled in pain as the youngster slipped from his grasp.

Wolfe pulled himself upwards from his broken harness. "Let's get out of this tin can before anything blows."

Saddam squinted through swelling eyes. "You made it. That was a bit of fancy flying."

"Did you get any response to the 'May Day'?"

"Maybe, but I don't know how they will find us out here."

Wolfe kicked open the buckled Jetranger door and leapt

to the ground holding the young boy. Saddam, hampered by his splintered leg, fell as he clambered awkwardly from the cockpit, knocking Wolfe to the ground. The two men lay gasping under a night sky, staring at the barren landscape around them.

The swirling wind finally ceased its choking assault. Achmet Mansoor rested gratefully, his back to the clouded moon in angry silence. The last few hours had seen the total ruin of his plans. By ruthlessness and sheer luck he had managed to escape capture at the airport and only the timely arrival of the sandstorm gave him the chance to flee from his pursuer. He had been face to face with Jack Wolfe for a few seconds, yet the image of the face and the remorseless expression told him that this had to be the man piloting the helicopter that followed him from Casablanca to Algeria. The same unrelenting renegade that hounded him across the Sahari border, disobeying all laws, as he did himself.

He had been surprised to see the helicopter lift away into the night sky and fly west, convinced the machine would return, and he strained his ears for the sound of an engine. This man Wolfe was an infuriating character, not to be under-estimated, but then, neither was Achmet Mansoor. In different circumstances they could perhaps have become allies. They both gambled against long odds and were both totally committed to winning yet Jack Wolfe stood on the opposite side to him. The grudging respect Mansoor felt for the man was overshadowed by anger and fear. The only freedom he would ever have would be when the Englishman was silenced forever.

The barren plain of the Algerian land held no threat to Mansoor. He had been raised in the desert; he knew its secrets and could use its caprice to his advantage. The only certainty was, he would have to get back to Casablanca. Payment for the bombing was under the seat in the jeep at the airport. It had been a cruel mistake leaving the vehicle unattended, but now, because of the intervention of the Englishman, he was stranded alone with the daunting prospect of the High Atlas Range between him and what was rightfully his.

The resentment surged again and the question uppermost in his mind was, how had he been traced so easily? He shielded his eyes with his hands. Some three kilometres away in the light from the moon was an unmistakable line of palms. Where there were dates in the wilderness, there would be men. It took two hours of clambering over the uneven terrain to reach them, ever attentive to the sound of an engine.

As the dawn hours lightened into day he reached the trees and stood on a high dune looking down at the track below. This had to be more than chance. After his headlong flight across country and evading capture by sheer determination, fate had placed him within walking distance of an established trading route.

"We are not finished yet, Jack Wolfe," he said bitterly.

The Moroccan pilot awoke with the dawn, his teeth chattering in the cold and the boy Ali curled up in the crook of his arm. Saddam focused his twitching eyes on the figure of Wolfe a short distance away with his hands inside the engine compartment.

"Can it be fixed?"

"Sure, if I had a replacement and a box of spanners."

"Then we can't take off again?"

Wolfe looked gently at the sleeping boy. "Doesn't look like it. We wouldn't get far if we could. We shall have to hope your 'May Day' gave Casablanca our position before we went down."

"But they could be searching for days."

"That's true but they will only be looking for us in daylight. If we have not been found by morning tomorrow I am going to walk out of here carrying the boy."

"Well I won't be walking far," said Saddam.

"That's why I must leave you. This way we will have two chances and I don't like the idea of hanging around too long anyway."

The Moroccan nodded. "It's good reasoning. It will double our chances but I don't envy your walk."

"Neither do I, but we can do better than that. We will make our own signal beacon."

Saddam looked around, "With what? There isn't a blade of grass for miles."

Wolfe banged the fuel tank. "We still have some kerosene left, enough to blow the machine up. It should give us a good blaze for a while."

The pilot looked aghast. "That's a bit drastic, isn't it?"

"Well I never was a company man," Wolfe said. "The only problem is what to light it with."

The Moroccan pilot fumbled in his pocket and produced a small book of matches. "Will this help?"

Wolfe grinned in relief. "Saddam, you are a magician and they say that smoking can kill you! Now, I want you and Ali at least one hundred metres away. I will make a short fuse and stay under the helicopter. We don't want the thing to ignite after our bird has flown away and we may only get one opportunity."

The pilot grimaced. "You could blow yourself up with the dammed helicopter."

"Not if I am careful."

"Now that I have yet to see. I haven't noticed anything cautious about you."

Wolfe stooped and picked up the sleeping boy.

"Let's get you both away from here before you talk me out of it."

The youngster awoke as he carried him to the shelter of a rock formation then he returned for the pilot, staggering with his weight. The earth was brightening with morning sunlight and a slight breeze caused Wolfe to shudder with the welcome warmth. The exertion from carrying Saddam was exhausting Wolfe and the lack of food and sleep added to his lack of concentration. He almost fell to the ground as he lowered the pilot to the rocks.

"Stay in the cover, it could get hot during the day. At the first sign of anything moving, fire this into the air," he handed the pilot the Smith & Wesson revolver.

"I have not fired a pistol before. What do I do?"

Wolfe smiled in surprise, "Just push off the safety catch like this and pull the trigger. Careful where you point it."

The Moroccan took the weapon in his forefinger and thumb looking at it with distaste. "Not the kind of tool I like to have around."

Wolfe went back to the Jetranger and stripped off the remains of his shirt, tying it into a long fuse, then unscrewed the fuel tank cap and thoroughly soaked the cloth, leaving it hanging a metre out. He crawled under the shaded side of the helicopter, waving to the two figures one hundred metres away. They waved back as he rested, the thirst making his mouth dry. He popped a pebble into his mouth to suck on, an old trick but effective. The increasing warmth was causing drowsiness and he adopted the cross-legged sitting position enabling him to rest without completely sleeping. He tried to work through the events at the airport, fearful of the outcome. If he lost Danielle, surely he would feel something, emptiness or a loss, not just the physical exhaustion of the moment.

The sun reached its height too soon. The two figures of Saddam and Ali had vanished into the shadow of the rocks. A trickle of perspiration ran into Wolfe's eye and he brushed it away with the back of his hand. The enforced sitting position was causing his legs to cramp and he stretched his body out, watching the mountainous horizon through the faint heat shimmer. The youngster must be feeling the strain now. The following day he would walk out carrying the boy. The weariness covered him like a cloak, his eyes twitching to stay open.

It was the boy who heard it first. The low hum of a single-engined plane, flying a thousand feet overhead. Ali pulled urgently on the Moroccan pilot's arm, pointing at the approaching aircraft. Saddam screwed up his eyes then yelled frantically at Wolfe. There was no movement from the figure flattened under the helicopter. The pilot screamed again at Wolfe's inaction.

"Damn you, Wolfe, damn you," he grabbed the boy. "Run quickly Ali. Monsieur Wolfe has fallen asleep. Wake him up now."

The youngster rushed towards the helicopter, tripping in his haste, and Saddam watched in dismay as the plane slowly approached.

Wolfe awoke instantly as the boy rushed into his arms.

"Monsieur Jack, the plane is passing us by."

Wolfe was on his feet fumbling for the box of matches, knowing well that the fuse was too long to alert the aircraft in the time left before it disappeared.

"Run, Ali, run as quick as you can," he shouted, pushing the youngster away.

The boy spun around and ran headlong back to Saddam.

Wolfe lit the fuse, shielding the match until the flame rippled along the cloth then deliberately pushed it into the kerosene tank before twisting away. He was six metres from the Jetranger when the blast hit him squarely from behind, the explosion somersaulting him into the air as the heat scorched his skin. The stricken helicopter danced briefly before vanishing in a ball of flame as the metal wrenched apart.

Saddam dragged himself painfully over to Wolfe, lying spread-eagled and face downwards on the ground. Wolfe opened one eye and spat sand from his teeth, "Why didn't you fire the bloody gun?"

The Moroccan pilot grinned in relief. "I forgot about it, everything happened so quickly."

Wolfe rocked back to a kneeling position and turned to look at the burning Jetranger. "Do you think they saw us?"

The boy was leaping about waving his arms. "The plane is turning back."

Saddam peered at the circling aircraft. "It must have worked. I am sure he has spotted us."

Wolfe stood up, and then swayed back to the ground. The Moroccan pilot flopped beside him. "Stay down my friend. You will have concussion and your back is very burned. With any luck, help will be on its way."

The blood was rushing through Wolfe's temples and he had difficulty focusing as Saddam cradled his head. The dusk would soon arrive and another night without being found would leave them all in desperate trouble.

The hours dragged by and there was no sign of rescue. A delirium invaded Wolfe's mind and the shimmering haze played strange tricks with his vision. The threshing of wings and confused images appeared unexpectedly as the two giant birds swept menacingly down towards them. Wolfe shielded his face as the hawk-like shadows descended, the violent threshing of their rotors drowning his cries and then the boy was shouting excitedly, "The helicopters are here."

In the central police station in Casablanca, Suzanne Wolfe sat alone in a stark, white-washed cell. The sun had long since set and the solitary light bulb above her cast a feeble glow around the sparsely furnished room. The only possessions she had been allowed to keep were the clothes she was wearing when arrested. Her luggage had been thoroughly searched before her eyes. The initial embarrassment was replaced with profound shock at her involvement with the situation and the possible consequences.

During the middle of the day she had been formally charged and was held pending further enquiries. For the last eight hours she had received a non-stop verbal battering from a team of trained investigators. She had vehemently denied the documented evidence against Achmet Mansoor until it became increasingly obvious that she was implicated in the plot to sabotage the airliner.

The officers leading the inquiry recognised the obvious signs of distress followed by the fixed expression and a refusal to communicate and knew if they pursued the troubled girl much further she could possibly go into deep shock, making their efforts to obtain further information difficult.

Her hesitation to believe that the arms dealer had made her the dupe in his plans and the indignation of the charges against them had eventually been replaced by dismay at the calculated way he had rewarded her loyalty to him.

Her inquisitors had left, looking a trifle less aggressive than at the start of her questioning and she stared, unseeing, at the wall in front of her. The girl's hopes and dreams had come to an abrupt halt with the rejection of her love for Mansoor. She was alone, in desperate trouble and unable to accept the truth. She started to cry softly.

The quiet man sitting outside the locked cell door waited a few moments, then rose and walked along the passage to the main office. The group of interrogators discussing the proceedings looked up as he entered. "I think she is ready to talk now."

"Do you really think she is innocent?" one man asked.

The quiet man shrugged. "They say love is blind! In my experience it is also foolish."

"Do you need any help?"

"No, I would prefer to do this alone. She needs help now and I shall play the part of confidante. I may be able to find out more this way."

"Do you think she will betray Mansoor?"

The quiet man nodded. "Love and hate are easily reversed, especially if a woman is rejected."

"Then we shall leave you both together Ashock."

The quiet man nodded, then turned purposely back along the corridor.

There was a silence from the cell as the policeman made a noisy entrance, grinding the key awkwardly in the lock to give the girl time to compose herself. She was slumped forward with her face buried in her hands. The quiet man sat on the bunk beside her without speaking, then gently put a hand on her shoulder.

Suzanne looked up sharply through puffed eyes at the concerned face of the man with her. "Am I in a lot of trouble?"

"More than you know," sighed the policeman.

"I can't believe this has happened. It was only yesterday I was starting a new life with the man I loved and now I find he has tried to kill me and I am involved in all kinds of treachery." The words came in a torrent.

The man beside her nodded agreement. "You have been cruelly deceived, but you must be careful not to become further involved or it could be the end for you."

Suzanne's eyes were riveted on the policeman. "What can I do?"

The man smiled sympathetically. "My name is Ashock. The other officers were hard with you today because they believe you played a part in this planned assassination. If you confide in me there may be a chance that I can save you."

"Do you think I am guilty?"

"I think you are guilty of letting love cloud your common sense and that this man has duped you unmercifully. I do not think you knew you were carrying explosives onto the airliner; there would be little future in that."

"I didn't. I knew nothing," protested the girl.

"Then let us start at the beginning. You must tell me all you remember if I am to help, because I take no pleasure in sending a pretty girl like you to prison for the rest of her life."

"No! No! I would sooner kill myself."

The policeman patted her shoulder again, and opened

his notebook. "Well, let's hope it will be over soon. May I call you Suzanne? If we are trusting each other, we should be friends."

The night had fallen as the two army helicopters returned to Casablanca Airport. Wolfe covered in a blanket, lay behind the pilot on the flight back, fighting the nausea and ache in his back and shoulders. As the Sikorsky touched down and its rotors stopped spinning he struggled upwards to see from the port window the grinning face of the airport controller in a small group awaiting them. The soldiers helped Wolfe to the ground as Hirasch grabbed his hand and pumped it furiously. "I never thought we would see you again," the controller announced.

"You nearly didn't and I'm afraid I sabotaged your helicopter."

Hirasch pulled a face. "That counts for nothing against bringing back the hostages."

Wolfe raised a smile. "Good, because I had a feeling you were going to make me pay for it."

"We have the young boy's parents in the medical centre. They want to speak with you. They need to congratulate you on getting back safely."

"Oh no," groaned Wolfe. "Spare me from that. Can you just tell them I am too sick to be bothered just now?"

"But they only want to give you their blessing."

"Yes, I understand that. Tell them thanks and that their son is incredibly brave. Without his help we would not have been seen by the search party."

"That I will gladly do, Jack, but there is someone here who will not leave until he has spoken with you."

Hirasch took Wolfe's arm pushing him towards the terminal building.

"Take it slowly, Raschid. I feel like I have been barbecued," Wolfe grunted.

Inside the terminal the Moroccan pilot was sat upright on a stretchered trolley with medical staff in attendance. Saddam's eyes glistened as Wolfe approached.

"Call yourself a flyer? You didn't look so chirpy when you nose-dived your Cessna into the sand."

Saddam grinned in return. "Yes, two planes in two days – we must claim that as a record."

The last Wolfe saw of the Moroccan pilot was when he was wheeled away.

Hirasch spoke, "And I have news for you, Jack. You will be pleased to hear that Mademoiselle Danielle is out of danger and making steady progress."

Wolfe released his pent up breath and swayed against the wall. He had not dared to ask the question and the longer he delayed only served to convince him that his worst fears would be confirmed. The comfort and fatigue surged through him.

"Where is she?"

"In the hospital, not far from here, which is where you will be very shortly."

Wolfe did not disagree and allowed himself to be supported into a waiting ambulance accompanied by two nurses and the airport controller. As the vehicle sped away from the terminal he remained silent, resting, until they stopped at the hospital on the outskirts of the town. A porter opened the rear door, helping Wolfe to get out.

"It's straight to the emergency ward for you," one of the nurses said.

"I think not," said Wolfe resolutely.

The girl was startled and looked to the airport controller for guidance.

"Do you know where Mademoiselle Charni is?" Hirasch asked.

"Well yes, we brought her here."

"Then take us there now and afterwards you can have Monsieur Wolfe all to yourselves."

The nurse arched her eyebrows but looked pacified.

"Oh yes, I understand."

She took his arm and Wolfe dragged wearily along the dimly-lit passages until they entered a small room. He stood blinking in the sudden light.

Danielle was resting upright on the bed, her arm in a sling. She looked pale beneath her matt complexion, her dark hair curling loose at her shoulders, as the blue eyes scrutinised his face. "I never gave up believing that you would return, Jack," she whispered.

The airport controller pulled at the nurse's belt with a knowing smile then closed the door quietly behind them.

The next morning was cloudy. Wolfe, refreshed after a night's sleep, was woken by a doctor, to check his condition.

"Why do the medical profession always wake their patients to ask how they feel?" Wolfe said.

The doctor smiled. "I think perhaps you are already improving Monsieur although this bruising on your shoulders needs to be tended. I will change the dressing on these other wounds and then you can see the two visitors waiting for you."

"Who would that be?"

"Only the police I'm afraid. We have a room at their disposal next door. If you feel well enough to come with me I will take you."

Wolfe stood and struggled into the shirt and jeans provided for him.

"All right, let's see what they want."

In the adjoining room were two men Wolfe had never seen before and the airport controller.

"Good morning Jack, I hope you slept well." He turned to the other men, "May I introduce Monsieur Wolfe? This is Captain Ashock from the Serious Crimes Department."

Wolfe nodded – the two policemen remained seated.

The directness in the gaze of Ashock made Wolfe instantly uneasy of the quiet man confronting him. It was the trademark of the trained interrogator and Wolfe knew from past experience that this was a person without conscience in the pursuit of justice. Ashock flipped through a notebook and stared at it during an uncomfortable silence. Wolfe, always careful in the presence of policemen, had not expected the 'waiting game' yet knew it was part of the treatment to make him nervous. He smiled to himself and relaxed into a chair.

Ashock noticing the unaffected manner said. "There are some people who regard you as a courageous man, Monsieur. Personally I am not one to make snap decisions and now I think you have been extremely lucky."

Hirasch was about to speak until Ashock silenced him with a raised hand. "Indeed had it not been for the involvement of your niece and supply of arms by your own brother, none of these regrettable incidents would have happened."

"You cannot blame Monsieur Wolfe for any of that," the controller intervened vigorously.

"I did not suggest it," Ashock continued, "but I have interviewed Suzanne Wolfe at length and perhaps your involvement is more than you have told us."

Wolfe felt his anger rising and checked it with difficulty. Ashock's stare was unblinking as Wolfe leaned forward until his face was a foot away from the policeman.

"You may have great success in frightening young girls, but if you expect to trace Achmet Mansoor you can start by not threatening me."

Ashock folded his arms defensively. "Then you still wish to help us?"

"You don't give me much choice, do you?"

"Why do you say that?"

Wolfe paused, "Because, if I am interpreting you correctly, you are about to say that if I don't co-operate my niece may never leave custody again."

The policeman's aide shifted uncomfortably on his seat as Ashock dropped his gaze.

"You are a shrewd man Monsieur Wolfe, but I would not have put it so bluntly."

"Then how would you put it?"

Ashock sniffed. "We still do not have a witness who can positively identify Mansoor except Saddam the pilot or Mademoiselle Charni. As they are both hospitalised you are still the only one we can rely on."

"So if I can trap Mansoor, you will give me a deal and release my niece?"

Ashock lips curled. "If you are instrumental in the arrest of the bomber we may look favourably upon the release of the girl."

Wolfe stood up. "That's not an answer. Find him yourself."

The policeman was clearly startled. Years of negotiation and applying pressure were not working.

"Then you will leave your niece to her fate?" he blustered.

"She made her choice long ago. I don't work under threat," Wolfe said.

The man beside Ashock stood up. "I am sure the captain did not mean to offend you Monsieur. He is doing his best to bring this butcher to justice."

Wolfe scowled. "Well, he won't have much success if blackmail is his method."

The airport manager intervened. "Just one moment. This is all getting out of control. I was under the impression that we were here to enlist the help of Monsieur Wolfe and not penalise him."

Ashock wilted visibly. "It was not my intention to…" Wolfe stopped him with a gesture. He was enjoying watching the man squirm. "Are you offering me an apology?"

"If we could start over again, Monsieur?"

"Good," said Wolfe. "Now these are my terms. I am prepared to continue the search for Mansoor, but I want a free hand and I also want my niece out of custody right away."

Ashock sighed, "She will have to remain in Casablanca and will not be allowed her passport until the assassin is found."

"But what makes you so confident that you could catch him when our own police have failed?" Hirasch asked.

"Because I have a personal interest. Mansoor has got to return to Morocco. Somewhere I shall pick up his trail and my methods of extracting information from my niece will be easier than yours."

Ashock almost smiled. "Revenge is sweet, Monsieur Wolfe."

"Let's just say it's better to shoot a mad dog."

"Where would you be prepared to shelter your niece and give us access to her movements?" Ashock said

"Mademoiselle Charni has a cousin in Casablanca. I will ask if she can stay there."

The two policemen nodded approval. "We agree. I think this concludes our business for the moment. We will take our leave now but need to be informed of every development."

The two officers left with the briefest of farewells, leaving Hirasch staring after them.

"I never thought they would be so co-operative, Jack and it surprises me they are letting your niece go, but why did you not object to her surveillance?"

"Well I reckoned I had pushed them far enough. They are policemen and will promise me anything until I find Mansoor, by which time they can change the rules."

"Do you think they would do that?"

Wolfe laughed sarcastically. "They are the law, they do as they like."

Achmet Mansoor had no time to lose. The light aircraft had crash-landed within kilometres of an established trading route in the foothills of the High Atlas. The wide-eyed camel drovers completely believed his story that he was the pilot of the stricken Cessna and they had given him every help at their disposal to return to Morocco.

It was imperative that he move quickly. His money reserves and evidence to convict him were in Casablanca. There was a trail across the mountain, a difficult and little-used track, and it should take at least ten days of hard travelling to retrace his flight. The unsuspecting drovers supplied him with two camels fully believing they were helping an unfortunate traveller and it was with feelings of pride and regret that they bade the wily Mansoor goodbye.

He knew he was finished as a tool of the Liberation Bureau and the Arab leader Gaddafi. He would be a marked man, yet he had the money for the bombing. Although it had been unsuccessful, he was not about to relinquish anything. He dug his heels viciously into the flanks of the leading camel, pulling hard on the halter of the following animal.

If the Moroccan authorities were waiting, they would not expect him to cross the mountains for three weeks by which time he would be in hiding. His credibility with the girl Suzanne was finished; her fate was no longer his concern. He would have liked to even the score with the Englishman, but the chances were highly improbable. The man was a devil, unyielding and completely without mercy. If a confrontation were ever to arise again, it would be without compassion that Mansoor would strike the deathblow.

The early rising sun was sending long shadows from the High Atlas scurrying across the sand. He snarled at his mount, urging it towards the mountain range. It was going to be a hard ride back.

Danielle was waiting in her hospital room when Wolfe entered. She was wearing her purple kaftan with gold trim, her hair loose to her shoulders. Wolfe smiled approval. "How do you manage to look so good with your arm in a sling?"

She laughed, "It wasn't easy, but you look distracted, Jack. What did the police have to say?"

Wolfe kissed her on both cheeks. "Not much I don't suppose. If I am capable of catching Mansoor, Suzanne goes free. If I don't she can be imprisoned indefinitely."

The girl caught her breath. "But that's unfair, they must know Suzanne is innocent. How much do they expect from you? And how do they think you can find him?"

Wolfe was thoughtful. "Perhaps I won't have to look for him. Mansoor left too quickly to finish his business here.

I have a distinct feeling he will need to get back. I think Suzanne will give us a clue because she knows more about his whereabouts than she realises, but we don't want her to mislead us again. It was nearly the end of us last time."

"But she is still in prison."

"Not for long. She is in our custody, but under house arrest if she can stay with Nabila. Can it be arranged with your cousin?"

Danielle beamed. "Oh yes, I'm sure it will be all right, but Suzanne must be dreadfully upset, Jack."

"I expect she is. The only thing bothering me is that Nabila's house will be watched twenty-four hours a day."

"Is that a problem?"

Wolfe pulled the girl close, smoothing the silken hair away from her neck. "Is that your favourite kaftan?"

"I wear it a lot, why do you ask?"

"Do you still wear the veil?"

"Sometimes, when I feel like it."

"Good!" said Wolfe. "I should like you to wear it more often."

She pulled away from him examining his face intently. "You're up to something."

"Perhaps. Do as I ask, it will make things easier. If I tell you why, it may not work."

"Oh poof," her French accent and the set of her mouth made him smile. "How can you say that, Jack? I am already involved."

"Do you feel well enough to leave, Dany?"

"Surely, Nabila will be pleased to help and it will be wonderful to see Suzanne again."

"Then let's get out of here now. Hospitals give me the creeps."

The key rattled noisily in the cell door. Suzanne Wolfe looked up at the appearance of the policeman.

"Can you follow me?" Ashock said quietly.

She stood and shivered in the coolness of the white-washed chamber. Although she felt caged, the fear of the future made her cling to the sanctuary of the stark walls and she followed her interrogator into the main office with trepidation. The strong sunlight from the latticed windows dazzled her and she did not immediately notice Wolfe and Danielle standing anxiously waiting.

"You have been temporarily released into the custody of your friends," Ashock said, "and are still under house arrest as we need to interview you further. You must stay at the address nominated, and give us every possible help. Do you understand all I am saying to you, Suzanne?"

She nodded dumbly, unable to believe the change in her circumstances.

"Then go now and keep in mind your friends are responsible for you."

Her feet hardly touched the ground as she was propelled between Wolfe and Danielle outside into the tree-lined boulevard with the flowering bougainvillea climbing the red stone walls. She threw her arms around Danielle's neck, her shoulders heaving with relief.

Wolfe stood back mildly surprised at the show of emotion until Suzanne turned to him. "I am terribly ashamed, Jack. I just wanted to die."

Wolfe blew out his cheeks, "You nearly did, along with a few hundred more, but we are not out of the woods yet by a long shot."

"Will I have to go back to prison?"

"Not if I find Mansoor."

"But I still think I love him, Jack."

"Oh my God," Wolfe exploded. "The man tried to kill you."

"I know. I just can't help it."

Danielle took the girl's arm. "Let's walk for a while. I think we need some time to settle down."

Wolfe was angry with his niece but also annoyed with his assumption that Suzanne would now want to repay Mansoor for his treachery. He stamped alongside Danielle in silence until they reached the Crazy Dolphin Restaurant at the edge of the souk. Once inside his mood of vexation passed as he listened to Suzanne recount the history of her misfortunes.

"You have been cruelly deceived Suzanne, all men are tricksters," Danielle said, scowling at Wolfe, emphasising the bond between the two women. He remained quiet in agreement with Danielle's subtlety, as Suzanne relaxed and continued to describe her time with Mansoor.

Wolfe prompted a question. "There's one thing I should like to know. What has Mansoor done with the money he showed you, Suzanne?"

The girl looked blank. "I don't know – it's in his house probably. He did not keep money in banks."

"But he did not have time to go to Marrakech if he was taking you to the airport. What was the name of the hotel he stayed at when he rang you?"

"I think it was the Chella." She was becoming agitated.

Wolfe patted her hand. "Don't worry about it. You are back with friends – enough for today."

They arrived later at the house of Nabila who welcomed Suzanne generously, giving her the room Wolfe had previously occupied. The genuine warmth of the family had a soothing effect on the girl and she readily accepted Nabila's suggestion that she should rest.

Wolfe sat in the white-walled garden, deep in thought, until Danielle sat beside him.

"Do you think Mansoor will return, Jack?"

"He has to, if he wants his money."

"If you can find it before he gets back, you can set a trap for him?"

"That's the plan, Dany."

"Where do you begin to look?"

Wolfe tapped the tabletop. "I have to anticipate his thoughts. Mansoor obviously doesn't trust anyone with his takings so he must have hidden it. It can't be very far away because he did not expect the reception at the airport and he certainly wasn't carrying anything."

"How can I be useful?"

"You can do something. Every morning at the same time I want you to walk to the market. You must wear your purple kaftan and veil but keep your arm in the sling. Remove the veil as you come back."

Danielle's eyebrows came together. "Is this one of your jokes?"

He shook his head. "I'm deadly serious. Just behave normally and don't return for at least a couple of hours."

"Are you going to tell me why?"

He stood and pulled her to him, the jasmine and her scented hair fragrant in his nostrils. He ignored her question and kissed her upturned mouth for a long time until interrupted by Nabila carrying a coffee-laden tray.

Danielle looked troubled. "I fear for you, Jack. Are you still wearing the hand of Fatima?" she searched at his chest for the silver amulet.

"Of course, I am never without it."

"It has already kept you from harm. Do not underestimate the power of the talisman," she said seriously.

He nodded submissively. "I have to leave soon, there is much to be done."

"But you are sick, Jack. If anyone needs rest it is you."

"Plenty of time for that, when this is over."

Nabila handed a steaming cup to Wolfe. "Never argue with an obstinate man, Danielle. You will only be wasting your time."

Mansoor's house in Marrakech was deserted. Wolfe, forcing the door, searched every corner diligently. It was an unusual experience to have a free hand and the full co-operation of the law although he notified Captain Ashock of his intentions. There was much evidence of an opulent lifestyle, yet a complete absence of documents or contracts of any kind. It was obviously not the headquarters of the man he was chasing, more probably a temporary home of the Moroccan arms dealer.

After an hour of thorough investigation of the walled garden, Wolfe wearily climbed into his hired Volvo to continue the journey as closely as possible to that described by his niece. The night breeze from the Agadir coastline was cooling the air when Wolfe found the Chella Hotel. The concierge asked no questions when asked for a specific room. It was the same that Mansoor and Suzanne had shared the night before the aborted bombing.

Wolfe sat on the verandah in the twilight considering the incongruity of the situation, trying to analyse the reasoning of the arms dealer who occupied this space only a few nights before. The man had to be without feeling to spend the night together whilst planning the death of the person who loved him. A diligent search of the room proved fruitless and the concierge assured him nothing had been left or deposited.

Wolfe decided to retrace Mansoor's movements approximately the same time the following day and head for the airport at Casablanca. It seemed Mansoor must have been carrying the money when he left the Chella Hotel.

The night closed quickly and Wolfe retired to the bed lying in a confused sleep with the old nightmares and the plummeting descent of his helicopter at the forefront of his dreams. He awoke abruptly, the perspiration clouding his eyes and sat bolt upright in the recognition of an unanswered question. He looked at his watch. It was not yet midnight.

The telephone shrilled eerily in the house at Casablanca. Nabila picked it up.

"It's Jack. I want to speak with Suzanne."

The girl took the receiver nervously.

"Sorry to ring so late," Wolfe said. "Tell me, how did you and Mansoor arrive at the airport?"

"We drove there in an old army jeep."

"Now think carefully, did you stop for any reason?"

"No, we didn't have time. We went directly there."

"And you left the jeep in the car park?"

"Yes."

"Thank you, that's all I need to know. Say goodnight for me," Wolfe replied as he put the phone gently back on its stand.

# Chapter 12

The security patrols around Casablanca Airport were more in evidence than Wolfe had expected. Next morning many of the staff, recognising him, waved greetings. He drove slowly between the neatly terraced rows of cars parked in the waiting areas without seeing any sign of the jeep he was looking for. It was inconceivable that Mansoor had returned already, but there was a chance he had contacted an accomplice to remove the vehicle. If that were the case, the trail would end here. Then he spotted it, an old American jeep with its bonnet showing from inside a corrugated sheet compound. He reversed his Volvo into the yard to be approached by a smiling security guard.

"How long has that jeep been there?" Wolfe asked.

"A couple of days now, Monsieur Wolfe. It was causing an obstruction and no one removed it after twenty-four hours so we brought it in here with the tow truck."

"Has anyone asked about it?"

"Not yet, Monsieur."

"Would you ask the airport manager to come here immediately?"

The only visible places of concealment on the vehicle were the toolboxes, under the front seats. Wolfe tilted the passenger seat forward apprehensively, expecting a tell tale sound from a booby trap device. Reason dictated this to be the obvious hiding place and yet the sight of the leather briefcase inside was more than Wolfe could have hoped for. He slid the catches to one side finding the case unlocked. The neat bundles of bank notes tightly packed together caused Wolfe to stiffen with surprise as the airport controller hurried into the compound.

Hirasch grabbed the windscreen for support. "What is that?"

"Blood money, Raschid. The stuff people get killed for."

"It makes me feel dishonest just looking at it," the controller said. "How much do you think is there? I won't feel happy until we hand it over to the police."

"Only one problem with that," said Wolfe. "We are not handing it over to anyone."

Hirasch looked astounded. "You don't mean to keep it?"

"No, but this is the bait that will bring Mansoor back."

"Then you think he will return? We must be ready for him. I will have marksmen alerted. We can't let him escape again."

Wolfe put a restraining hand on the controller's shoulder.

"Now just slow down, Raschid. That may be what Mansoor would expect. If I were in his place, I would find it easier to send an unsuspecting man to drive the jeep away. The sensible thing to do is to return the vehicle to its original position and leave everything as it was. We must appear to know nothing of the money and follow the jeep, providing of course, that I am guessing correctly."

"Then we don't inform the police?"

Wolfe shook his head. "They gave me a free hand. Mansoor can smell the law ten kilometres away. We can work better alone, but I still need your help."

"You've got it, Jack."

"Well now, it's the waiting game again. There's nothing we can do until he makes a move. There are a dozen different ways to Casablanca but the longer he waits, the more chance he has of having his loot discovered."

Hirasch nodded vigorously.

"I want two of your best men to know about this and they must understand absolute secrecy."

"No need to put temptation around too much, eh?" said Wolfe. "Now, I have much to do so I shall leave you to move the jeep and have it guarded without being seen. I think it will be ten days before we can expect Mansoor to return. I have something important to sort out."

The controller looked puzzled. "But what can be more important than catching our man? I thought you needed to be here at the finish."

"Well this is a separate matter, Raschid. Within a week I should be back and what you don't know, you won't worry about."

"As you wish, Jack. I only hope you are right."

Wolfe sighed. "I hope so too."

It was early morning when Wolfe stopped his Volvo outside the white-walled house of Danielle's cousin. Although the family were not about, the rich smell of ground coffee greeted him, and the ever-cheerful Nabila quietly summoned Danielle. She appeared in a white robe with embroidered babouche on her feet, hair tousled from the early awakening. She traced the curls away from her brow with a slender finger.

"Well, how did it go, Jack?"

"Better than expected, but how do you feel?"

"I walked to the market twice wearing the veil, with my arm in a sling. Are you going to tell me why?"

Wolfe grimaced. "I'm surprised you are still an invalid. Did you wear the same purple kaftan?"

"Of course, just as you asked."

"Has there been anyone watching you?"

She laughed, "Oh, the police you mean? Yes, they are in the old Volkswagen parked at the end of the street. One of them followed me the first time, trying to look inconspicuous, so I walked a long way to wear him out but ended up tiring myself out. He did not bother the second time."

Wolfe grinned, "How's your shoulder?"

"Oh much better," she said, settling into the wicker chair on the verandah, "but tell me your news."

Wolfe described in detail the happenings of the last few days, from the search of Mansoor's house in Marrakech to the overnight stay at the Chella Hotel in Agadir and the tracing of the jeep, leading to the discovery of the money under the seat.

She listened in silence until he finished, her blue eyes widening at every detail.

"I just can't believe he would leave the money like that. What did you do with it, Jack?"

"I left it where it was. It is the only bait that will bring him into the open and the price we have to pay for Suzanne's freedom."

"But if you trap Mansoor the police have an agreement with us to release Suzanne."

Wolfe eyed the Volkswagen at the end of the road thoughtfully.

"I'm not taking any chances that they will change their mind. When I can find a fishing boat I shall take Suzanne out of here myself."

"*Mon Dieu*," she lapsed into startled French. "How will that be possible when we are being watched? She will be seen immediately."

"That's what I am gambling on. Tomorrow morning would be a good time. She will be wearing a purple kaftan and veil."

Danielle shook with silent laughter, "And of course with her arm in a sling, what a lovely touch."

Nabila handed Wolfe a steaming coffee cup, which he balanced precariously on one knee.

"Well, Dany, the police are not watching you. In the afternoon you can walk out again. They will think they missed your return. I don't believe they would include that on a report and if I am lucky enough to grab Mansoor, they will not implicate us any further. Anyway it's the best chance we have."

He turned to Danielle's cousin, "Do you have a jeleba with a hood that I can borrow Nabila?"

"Surely, I have some nice ones."

"The older the better. I don't want to be conspicuous and must leave pretty soon."

"Then come and change in my room," Nabila said.

"No, I just want it rolled up. I shall carry it."

"This is all very mysterious. I shall get you one right away."

"Are you coming back today, Jack?" Danielle said.

"With any luck I should not be too long."

He finished his coffee slowly, then rolled the jeleba into a small bundle and pushed it under his arm.

The iron gate squeaked shut, as he turned into the dusty street and strolled in the direction of the Volkswagen car, one hundred metres away. The man in the driving seat studied Wolfe carefully before engaging his passenger in earnest conversation. Wolfe walked slowly past without glancing at the vehicle, apparently oblivious to the watchers. At the corner of the street he paused, deciding which way to take, and looked back at the Volkswagen. It contained one man.

Wolfe continued walking towards the market, pausing occasionally for signs of pursuit, but without success. If he was being trailed the man was adept at his trade. His own training in evasion tactics made him appreciate the skill of hiding with little cover and moving without being seen. If the man was not behind he could have anticipated Wolfe's direction and moved ahead using another street to get in front.

He reached the outskirts of the market. Early morning street vendors noisily bartered their goods and the man had still not shown his hand. Wolfe had that uneasy feeling that comes from a lifetime of caution. He was still being stalked. There was a simple way to prove it – make a dash for it, but that would only alert his pursuer.

Wolfe stopped at a corner bar with a view of the souk and ordered a mint tea, slowly sipping the fragrant liquid from the glass. A solitary figure with his back to Wolfe stared intently into a window across the street. Why he should be so interested in an empty window was perplexing. Wolfe chuckled. It did however have a mirror-like refection of the bar Wolfe was in. He finished his tea then went to the services at the rear and closed the door behind him. Hurriedly donning the jeleba and pulling the hood over his head, he walked out as a trio of merchants, in similar garb, decided to leave. Wolfe tagged on the rear of the group as they turned and walked towards the medina. As he disappeared among the market stalls he looked round to see the solitary man still peering into the window reflection.

The port of Casablanca had once been a flourishing centre for trade of all kinds. Since the construction of the International Airport most ships were principally concerned with industry. The once-busy fishing fleet was limited to a handful of small boats, scraping a meagre living from the ever-depleting fish stocks on the coast.

Wolfe sauntered between the rotting carcasses of ancient hulks watching the grizzled old men repairing their nets until he found what he was looking for, an unhappy young man, coiling ropes on the deck of a recently-painted lugger.

"How was the catch?"

The young fisherman looked up at Wolfe's enquiry.

"What catch, Monsieur? The further we go, the less we find."

Wolfe frowned in sympathy. "It must be a problem. Would you hire your boat for two days?"

The young man sniffed. "I do not smuggle, Monsieur."

Wolfe laughed aloud. "I assure you, it is purely a pleasure trip. My sister and I like sailing. We may choose to visit the mainland." He indicated the coast of Spain, shadowy on the horizon.

"There is a ferry every day," the fisherman said.

"I know that," countered Wolfe, "but we can't please ourselves on the ferry. What would you say to 1,500 dirham for the two days?"

The man blinked. This was more than he would have asked. He looked at his empty nets hanging to dry in the breeze.

"My name is Yousef, Monsieur," he said leaping onto the jetty and extending his hand.

"Good," said Wolfe cheerfully. "I will see you tomorrow. Let's hope the weather is good."

"And what name do you have, Monsieur?"

"My name. Oh yes. Call me Achmet, Achmet Mansoor."

There was a family party that night in the house of Nabila. The young children were particularly noisy and the cheery mood conveyed itself to the adults, forcing them to join in the frolics of the youngsters. Suzanne Wolfe came in for special treatment and had not a moment to herself. Wolfe watched, remembering with nostalgia that it was a few brief years ago that he had seen her teasing him in the same adolescent way.

Nabila and Danielle smiled happily at the little group. What the next few days would bring was uncertain, but one thing was certain in Danielle's mind and that was the overwhelming feelings she felt for the Englishman and the trust she felt in his judgement. Jack had not made any declaration as to their future but she decided it made little difference. No other man had made her feel that way: at least for a short time she had known happiness. She reached out and took his hand and the softness in his glance was only for her.

"Do you think it will work?" Nabila asked apprehensively.

"In a few moments we shall find out," said Wolfe.

"This is the time every morning that Danielle has been walking to the market. By now our nosey friends in the Volkswagen will be expecting the same routine. Does everyone know what to do?"

The three women nodded vigorously.

"I have been rehearsing all night long, I hardly slept at all," said Suzanne.

Danielle took a deep breath and adjusted the veil beneath her eyes. "Let's do it then."

Wolfe left the villa and walked into the road carrying clothes and a small valise, which he threw into the rear seat of the Volvo. The women followed him out and he kissed Nabila and Suzanne on the proffered cheeks before turning to Danielle. She lowered her veil and he took her in his arms and kissed her fully on the mouth, momentarily lost in the closeness of their bodies and the fullness of her lips. He released her reluctantly, still holding her hands, the scent of jasmine lingering.

"They couldn't fail to notice that," Nabila whispered.

Wolfe chuckled and climbed into the vehicle, then drove slowly to the corner of the street on the route to Marrakech. The women paused in conversation, then returned to the villa.

Fifteen minutes later a familiar figure in a purple kaftan and veil strolled leisurely past the Volkswagen parked in the road outside. Suzanne could hear the pounding of her heart as she held the gaze of the two men under her mascara-darkened eyebrows and was prepared for the sound of a voice calling her until she reached the corner and discovered the occupants had not moved.

She moved casually towards the open market, pausing only to prod the produce and examine the assorted pottery. She almost began to enjoy the game and purchased a bunch of camellias from a stall, carrying them in the crook of her arm. She wandered across the cobbled square and paused at the open carved doors of the Exposition Centre. It was gloomy inside and the girl walked quickly through the sheaves of hanging carpets and wooden artefacts until she reached a door at the end of the building. She pushed hard to open it and staggered into the sunlight outside. The bedraggled figure squatting against the wall in the faded jeleba stood up.

"What kept you?" said Wolfe.

"I'm sorry, Jack. I was trying to behave normally. I don't think I was followed."

"Where did you leave the vehicle?" she asked

Wolfe grinned, "Outside Police Headquarters. It should not be noticed there – and leave the flowers, the trail stops here. Now follow me Suzanne, but not closely, until we reach the harbour."

Wolfe took a direct route, walking quickly with his niece following behind and arrived at the jetty. He greeted the waiting fisherman as Suzanne accompanied him on board. The boatman nodded to the veiled figure and cranked the amidships engine into life. Wolfe motioned the girl into the deck cabin and engaged the fisherman in conversation until they cleared the breakwater.

"Where to, Captain?" the fisherman asked amiably, clearly relieved of the burdening responsibility of the fishing.

Wolfe flicked his hand towards Gibraltar. "Onwards Yousef, towards the sun."

The man spun the wheel starboard, steering the small vessel into the rolling breakers of the shipping lane.

Suzanne looked back at the rapidly disappearing coastline with a feeling of relief. Her liaison with Achmet Mansoor and the penalties it could have caused paled into insignificance as the diesel-engined vessel chugged steadily away. Soon they were among the shipping lane, and a feeling of elation grew as the Spanish coast and the thrusting Rock of Gibraltar showed strongly on the approaching skyline. She discarded the purple kaftan and wiped the heavy mascara from her face before stepping back onto the pine decking.

Yousef stood open-mouthed at the appearance of the blonde girl in a T-shirt and shorts, suspecting he had not been told everything. The hard-muscled man beside him did not look the type to argue with. The fisherman indicated the heavy outline of ancient rock, "Gibraltar, Monsieur."

"Good," Wolfe said. "This is where we get out."

The small vessel negotiated the harbour and steered slowly among the moored pleasure craft until it reached the jetty. Wolfe pulled out a wallet and counted out the dirham as the young man's eyes gleamed in anticipation. "If I can be of further service, Monsieur?"

Wolfe nodded. "Thank you. Achmet Mansoor always pays his debts to his friends."

"What was that all about?" Suzanne asked.

"Oh, someone helped you to leave Morocco. With any luck the boatman should remember his name."

As the small vessel left the quayside they climbed the stone steps against a high wall of flowering hibiscus, surveying the grey outline of the African coast opposite.

"I can't believe I am really here, Jack."

Wolfe put a protective arm around her shoulders. "Your problems are not over yet, Suzanne and quite honestly I don't want to be around when you meet your father again."

She looked suddenly glum. "I know. Was he terribly annoyed?"

"We all have our weaknesses, Suzanne. You were your father's. Everything he ever did was with you in mind."

"But I never wanted it. He was never there when I really needed him."

"I think he realises that now, but he wanted you back so desperately he begged me to find you, and that didn't come easily to your father."

Suzanne plucked a hibiscus flower and smoothed the petals. "I suppose not, but now I have separated you from Danielle."

Wolfe smiled. "If I had not been looking for you I wouldn't have found her."

She looked shyly at him. "Why did you never settle down? Daddy used to say you were wild and frightened of responsibility."

Wolfe sniffed. "Daddy was right, but I'm not frightened for myself. How could I expect anyone to share the life I had. People get hurt around me."

She pushed the hibiscus flower into his shirt front.

"You over-estimate yourself, Uncle Jack – and you don't understand women."

Wolfe sighed, "I won't disagree with that. I have no ambition to make anyone a young widow."

"But you will see Dany again? She is my greatest friend and together you are terrific."

She watched the hard set of his mouth and the colour rise in his cheeks. "Let's stop talking and get into town. I still have a contract to finish."

She took his arm and walked the mile and a half until they reached the main street with the souvenir shops and the traditional English shopping arcade. Suzanne listened to the familiar voices and watched the uniformed soldiers on parade as they came to the Rock Hotel. Wolfe booked a room overlooking the rear gardens then picked up the phone and dialled. It was Nabila who answered the shrilling tone.

"The pigeon is on the rock," said Wolfe distinctly, then replaced the receiver.

Wolfe dialled again and it was some time before he got through.

"Where the bloody hell are you?" The startled voice of George Wolfe in his Jersey retreat was annoyingly sharp. "I haven't heard anything from you since God knows when and now you just ring me without so much as…"

Wolfe cut him short. "Just listen a moment," and he handed the phone to Suzanne Wolfe.

"It's me, Daddy."

There was a confused silence at the end of the line then Suzanne said, "I have been very stupid and I don't know if you can ever forgive me, but will you come and get me, Daddy?"

Wolfe looked across the gardens at the darkening clouds gathering from the east, without hearing the sudden intense conversation beside him. Somewhere over there on the Moroccan mainland was a desperate man, perhaps waiting to settle a score and regain compensation for the way Wolfe had persecuted him? What could Mansoor expect to find on his return and how would he handle it?"

Suzanne was oblivious to it all; the only thing, which interested her, was the sound of her father's excited voice.

Wolfe paused a moment, then quietly left the room. Leaving the hotel he took the cobbled pathway back towards the port.

Nabila turned and embraced Danielle. "It was Jack. They have reached Gibraltar safely. Now you must carry out your part of the bargain."

Danielle pouted, "It is very hard for me to leave, Nabila.

How do I know if I will ever see him again? And waiting for news alone in Tangier is going to be awful for me."

Nabila kept a comforting arm around her cousin's shoulder. "You silly girl, he asked you to go home for your own good. He does not need to be fettered now, especially with work to do and he is blaming himself that you were injured."

"I know that," said Danielle, "but it doesn't make it any easier." She looked suddenly very vulnerable and young and her blue eyes were moist with concern. "Do you think when this madness is over he will come back to me, Nabila?"

The older woman frowned. "It is not over. He loves you more than he realises and if he comes to Tangier, it is for one reason only."

Danielle stood up. "Then I shall go back home. Whatever happens now it is for Jack to decide."

The foothills of the High Atlas Range were strewn with sharp flints and Achmet Mansoor picked his way carefully around the razor-like outcrops of jagged stone. One lame dromedary had already been abandoned a hundred kilometres behind in the vastness of the mountains and he was not risking the same thing with the second camel. In these conditions he had little choice but to walk ahead leading the animal. Although the trail had been well defined Mansoor had pushed through the darkened hours, causing him frequently to lose the track. His anger at retracing his steps was vented on the unfortunate animal and yet for all his misfortune he made steady progress and was now only two days travelling distance from the city of Casablanca.

The Moroccan arms dealer had spent hours brooding

over his ill-luck and the consequences following his humiliation at the airport. What was driving him onwards was the hope that his money, recklessly left in the jeep, had not been discovered. If it were intact perhaps there was still some salvation. If it had been found, then the Englishman and his woman would suffer.

It would take careful planning and split-second timing to recover the money. This man Wolfe was an assassin and had perhaps set a trap. Mansoor felt a nervous chill at the prospect of confrontation but the thought of the rewards urged him on.

The daily ferry to Casablanca had been on time. Wolfe mingled with the voyagers on the return trip in the warmth of the spring day. The ship turned slowly into the harbour and docked at the newly-built jetty, lowering the companionways as the engines topped turning. A group of embarkation offices stood casually watching the leaving passengers with passing interest. In front of Wolfe a burdened Moroccan housewife was awkwardly manoeuvring her three children towards the companionway.

"Permit me, Madame," Wolfe said, sweeping the youngest child onto his shoulders.

The woman accepted his offer gratefully, following him closely to the jetty as the child began to wail. Wolfe ambled past the waiting customs officers receiving nothing more than a sympathetic look in his direction until they were clear of the officials. Once outside the dock area he gave the child back to its mother and walked the half-mile to the police station, recovering his Volvo still parked outside.

The short drive to Casablanca Airport brought him to the controller's office as the rays of the late sun were slanting across the rooftops. Always Raschid Hirasch greeted Wolfe warmly, genuinely pleased to see the Englishman again. "You have been busy, Monsieur Wolfe?" It was more of a statement than a question.

"You know me too well, Raschid," Wolfe replied, "and our preparations?"

"I have done as you asked. The jeep is back where Mansoor originally left it and is watched by two security staff continuously. We have kept a low profile as you suggested but are ready with marksmen if we can identify the right man."

"I returned as quickly as I could," said Wolfe. "I hope this time luck will be on our side."

"It would have been a simple matter to put a tracer on the vehicle," Hirasch said. "We could have followed it without problems."

"Too obvious, Raschid. Anyone who can produce an explosive timing device would easily find a bug and we know what a slippery customer Mansoor is."

The airport controller nodded reluctantly. "So now we have to wait. But for how long?"

"Ah that's the million dollar question. We know the longer Mansoor leaves the money, the higher the chance of it being discovered. I don't think it will be long before he makes his move."

"You are assuming that Mansoor has returned?"

Wolfe twitched his shoulders. "Well, of course we cannot be sure of anything, but I have an uneasy feeling in the small of my back that trouble is not far away."

He looked across the cargo area towards the passenger car park. "Where are our men?"

Hirasch extended a finger. "The man vigorously sweeping

the car park is Sergeant Muselain."

Wolfe grinned, "He is making too good a job – road sweepers don't normally work as hard."

"Perhaps he is hoping for a permanent appointment," Hirasch laughed.

"How about security after darkness?"

"The gate attendant is Salim, a dedicated policeman."

"I have met a few of them recently," said Wolfe sarcastically. "Are they armed?"

"Of course, but are under orders only to shoot if fired upon."

"And there is only one exit from the airport?"

"Just the one, Jack."

"Then I shall position myself there and I need radio contact at all times."

"That is easily arranged, but you can't stay there twenty-four hours a day."

"That's maybe true, but tell me this. If you were Mansoor, when would you recover the jeep?"

The airport controller looked thoughtful. "There would be a better chance at night."

"I agree. I shall spend the nights at the exit road and Sergeant Muselain will sweep the car park during the day."

"Do you think we have covered it all?"

"As much as possible," Wolfe said, "but you can't anticipate everything."

"What shall we do right now?"

"If it's all the same to you, Raschid," Wolfe stretched his arms and yawned, "I would like to get some sleep."

The controller looked startled. "I don't think I can sleep again until this is over," he said.

*

The panelled door opened silently and Achmet Mansoor stepped inside. He was exhausted from his journey over the High Atlas but waited until dusk before venturing to the neighbourhood of Adnan Khalifa. The dark-browed servant who had admitted him on previous visits met him. Adnan Khalifa appeared bowing courteously but his manner was brusque.

"You're a wanted man, Achmet. You cannot be welcome in the house of Khalifa."

Mansoor was astounded at the dismissal. He opened his mouth in protest but was stopped by an upraised palm. "You are too dangerous and death follows you like a hungry dog. The chances you take are not worth the payment," Khalifa said.

Mansoor struggled with his anger. "You were not so quick to get rid of me when I paid double the price for your poor workmanship."

Khalifa's stare remained fixed. "One contract does not form a brotherhood and you have failed in your venture. In my business, anonymity is essential for survival."

"Then you are refusing to negotiate?"

Khalifa hesitated, "I did not say that."

Mansoor understood now. The crafty Moroccan had caught him like a fish on a line, slowly winding him in, making further help expensive. He choked back his frustration. He was not in a good bargaining position and did not have any choice but to play Khalifa's game. Contracts had been broken before.

"I need three men to help me recover my possessions," Mansoor said. "They must be prepared to use a knife or gun if necessary."

"How long will you need them and when?"

"One week maximum, maybe less."

"It can be arranged. Do you want to know the fee, Achmet?"

Mansoor nodded. It was clear the man had always intended to give assistance and the game he played was to increase the value.

Khalifa looked grave. "The price will be 8,000 dirham."

Mansoor nearly smiled. The price of thuggery was far less than expected.

"You drive a hard bargain, Adnan," he growled.

"Then it is a contract? The men will be available at nightfall tomorrow."

"Where can I contact you?" said Khalifa.

Mansoor felt a surge of unease urging wariness. "I will contact you," he answered, turning towards the panelled door.

Khalifa bowed stiffly. "May Allah reward you."

The dark-browed servant closed the door behind Mansoor and turned smiling to Khalifa. "It would appear that Achmet is going to lead us to his money."

Khalifa placed his hands on the other man's shoulders.

"I have to agree Omar. Our friend Mansoor is not the type to leave his wealth in banks and that is why I must send you and two others to relieve him of it."

Omar chuckled. "If he knew we were brothers, perhaps he would not be so trusting. If we recover his money what then?"

Khalifa shrugged. "He asked for men who were prepared to use knives or guns. The choice is yours brother."

On the outskirts of Casablanca, a collection of ramshackle buildings known as the 'Bidonville' house emigrant workers.

Achmet Mansoor walked briskly towards the area, secure in the knowledge that he would be safe among the anonymous ragbag of vagrants who lived in the village. With difficulty he resisted the urge to make his way to the airport and check his vehicle was intact. Nothing could be achieved without a plan and it was clear a diversion would have to be prepared. After days of deprivation crossing the High Atlas it would be stupid to blunder into failure at the last hurdle. Perhaps it would be easy. With luck this time tomorrow he would have regained his money, then life could begin again.

He drifted towards the cluster of fires burning openly in the shantytown, keeping the unfortunate groups of the homeless warm. As he approached a feeling of danger checked his footsteps. It was the fear of the unknown and the chance of capture the following day.

Mansoor warmed his hands at the fire, oblivious to the hapless creatures around him. He could wait another twenty-four hours. Tomorrow he would be a powerful man again with all the possessions that money could buy. Yet the doubts prevailed.

Tapping on the Volvo window awoke Wolfe. The bearded face of the security guard grinned down at him.

"You can go to bed now, Monsieur," Salim said.

Wolfe winced at the cramp in his legs and rubbed his hands vigorously together for warmth. "How many nights is this?" he asked.

"This is your fourth in the Hotel Volvo," Salim taunted him.

Wolfe tried unsuccessfully not to smile. "I have stayed in better places."

The radio crackled in the security man's pocket "Yes!

Salim reporting for duty," he said into the receiver.

Wolfe stretched, and then closed the Volvo door behind him. "I am going for some breakfast. Don't forget – the slightest thing." He patted the transmitter at his breast pocket. "I want to know right away."

"You really think he will come, Monsieur?"

Wolfe nodded. "I am convinced of it."

He trudged wearily towards the staff cafeteria to find the airport controller patiently awaiting him.

"You look exhausted, Jack."

"Yes, I feel a bit weak, another night in that dammed car and I shall be cracking up. Maybe it's a good idea to change the rota."

"You did say we should not establish patterns," said Hirasch.

"I agree, patterns can be broken," Wolfe nodded. "Any developments overnight?"

The controller poured Wolfe a coffee. "Yes, there was. We had a request from Libyan Airlines for landing clearance for a small jet aircraft. Shortly after touch down, a car arrived and three men were taken aboard in handcuffs. Their papers were in order and they were military personnel without uniform. Part of the Liberation Bureau from Tripoli. Anyway they left without protest. Rumour has it, there has been an attempted coup in Libya, but tales around here are often exaggerated."

Wolfe studied for a moment, "Do you think it should concern us?"

Hirasch clicked his tongue, "I think not. Justice is swift in Libya, but I feel sorry for an adversary of Colonel Gaddafi."

"I know what you mean," Wolfe said.

The coffee was bitter, sharpening his wits, pushing away

the last vestiges of sleep. The airport controller stayed for some minutes, leaving Wolfe laid back in a chair deep in thought. He would have liked to contact Danielle again. She must be back in Tangier now. The vision of her young face danced before his eyes. He pushed it from his mind, it was not the time. When it is over he said, that is what he should stick to. He placed the coffee cup on the table and stood up. There was still some checking to do.

It was a long day. The constant demand on his time was causing Wolfe extreme frustration. He recognised the weakness in himself. It was at times like this when the body was physically low that danger signs would be overlooked. Part of the boredom was his shortage of adequate rest. The evening approached, the shadows disguising the buildings, always the preparation time for the hard night.

He was startled by the radio message from the gatehouse car park. "There is someone checking around the jeep," Salim said.

Wolfe was immediately alert, "Describe him."

There was a pause, "Short, built like a gorilla. He just walked around the vehicle and pretended to drop something. My guess is that he is checking underneath."

"It doesn't sound like Mansoor," said Wolfe. "Is he alone?"

"Hard to say. Why doesn't he just take the briefcase from under the seat?"

"Because he doesn't know it is there. Mansoor is not taking any chance of being double-crossed by his own men."

"There's only one problem." Salim said. "He is walking away. Maybe I have made a mistake."

Alarm bells were ringing in Wolfe's brain. "Don't you

believe it. Mansoor is back, I can feel it."

"Do I follow him?" Salim asked.

"No! This is probably a way of testing us. We have to follow the money, it's the only way to get to Mansoor."

"Where are you now?" Salim said.

"Making my way to the Volvo, I need to be ahead if the jeep moves."

He walked unhurriedly back to the vehicle, pulling his faded jeleba around him, patting the re-assuring weight of the heavy revolver at his waistband. It was calculating of Mansoor not to take unnecessary chances. He was cunning like a fox, but his luck must run out somewhere. Wolfe reached the Volvo to find Salim anxiously waiting by the perimeter wall.

"Sergeant Muselain had just arrived when I radioed," Salim said. "I decided to wait with you. If anything happens he will let us know."

"Get in the driving seat, you know the town better than me," Wolfe commanded.

"Then you think it will happen soon?"

Wolf nodded, "Time is not on Mansoor's side."

The security guard sat gripping the wheel, staring intently into the dusk.

"Relax! It could be a long night," Wolfe advised.

Salim grimaced at his nervousness, relaxing his grip, "I hate this, it's making me jumpy."

"I know," Wolfe agreed, "but we are in ambush and that is our advantage. Mansoor is not sure of anything and is taking it very slow. He has a lot to lose and we have nothing."

The first stars began to show in the early night sky and the time dragged by. Salim kept in regular contact with Muselain watching the jeep, but there did not appear to be much happening in the parking area.

"I don't think he will come," Salim announced. "I think we were mistaken. It could have been anyone looking at the jeep."

"Perhaps you are right, but it's too late now to take chances," Wolfe said.

Salim peered through the Volvo window at the faint red glow on the commercial side of the airport and the sudden blossoming of flames.

"My God, something's on fire," he exclaimed. "I must notify control."

He pulled at his radio and Wolfe checked him, "Leave it, I want our channel open at all times."

"But it's my duty to…"

Wolfe interrupted. "It's your duty to take orders. If this is a diversion we want no part of it. Let's do the job we are here for."

Salim looked confused and sat in silence until the first fire siren howled through the night and a posse of airport vehicles sped towards the fire.

Wolfe's radio engaged.

"The jeep is moving," Muselain said urgently.

Salim switched on the Volvo ignition and revved the engine into life.

"Gently does it," Wolfe said. "We are not chasing him, only following at a distance."

They waited almost five minutes and Wolfe was beginning to have doubts about the exit from the airport, until the open jeep with one man drove slowly past the Volvo and turned right at the entrance. It was impossible to distinguish the driver's features yet Wolfe was convinced he was not following Achmet Mansoor.

"OK. Keep him in sight and don't switch our lights on," ordered Wolfe.

"Suppose someone piles into us?"

"Just do it," said Wolfe testily.

The vehicle to the front of the Volvo drove steadily for six kilometres, before taking a quiet road to the outskirts of the town. If the driver had any indication of being followed, it was not apparent to the men in the trailing Volvo.

"I don't think he knows he is being followed," Salim said.

"Anyway, where are we now?" Wolfe asked.

"This is the Bidonville, or shantytown to you. Not the best of districts but we could lose him if we are not careful."

Wolfe spoke into his radio telling Muselain of his location and the jeep slowed to a walking pace among the piles of rotting garbage littering the alleys.

"Keep him in sight," Wolfe grunted as the vehicle made a sharp turn and appeared to vanish abruptly.

Salim nodded and arrived at the spot the jeep had disappeared to see it bouncing crazily down a long flight of old stone steps towards the jetty at the mouth of the harbour.

"Very clever," Salim said. "We have no chance of following him down there."

"Well, he is not going to drive back either," Wolfe answered. "We shall have to leave the motor and chase him on foot. There is nowhere to go unless there is a boat waiting." He jumped from the Volvo and sought the cover of the shadows with the security guard close behind him.

The jeep reached the collection of huts built precariously on the old wooden pier and drove slowly until it stopped at the end vanishing in the gloom. Wolfe calculated the distance. "About three hundred metres, but not much to hide behind," he said.

"I don't like this, we are an easy target. If we go down there it is a perfect place for an ambush," Salim muttered.

Wolfe glanced at the security man. He was showing clear signs of alarm. If he was hesitant at this time it could be exactly what Mansoor was banking on.

"Cover me," Wolfe said, and ducked away before Salim could object.

He made the weaving run to the bottom of the steps and gained the jetty, slippery with age-old slime, and skidded to a halt behind a collection of discarded diesel drums. He waited listening for sounds of discovery then, as the moon faded behind a reef of clouds, continued swiftly along the rotting pier.

At the first gunshot Wolfe dived to the decking, then a succession of reports and he realised the bullets were not aimed in his direction. In the last cabin on the pier a door swung open and from the dim light of an oil lantern he saw a figure stagger backwards, collide with the jeep and pitch headlong into the sea. Wolfe covered the remaining distance at a run, launching himself through the open doorway into the dimly-lit area inside.

Between the heaps of old fish netting and tackle, a vicious fight was taking place. A bearded man lay awkwardly in one corner, vainly trying to staunch the blood from a neat hole above his ear, as his eyes glazed into lifelessness. The immediate ferocity was between a stocky dark-browed Moroccan and the tall figure of Achmet Mansoor.

Beneath the thrashing bodies was a leather briefcase, its bundles of paper currency spilling onto the floor. As Wolfe watched in detached fascination the taller man twisted his body and pulled his stocky opponent towards him like an embrace as he thrust a short-bladed knife deep into his chest. They stood locked together glaring into each other's eyes until the shorter man suddenly frothed blood over the shoulder of Mansoor. The arms dealer released his hold, retaining his grip on the knife as the man fell to a kneeling position then pitched onto his face.

Mansoor moved like a man in a dream, apparently oblivious to the revolver in Wolfe's hand and levelled at him. He slowly gathered the blood-stained bundles of money together, pushing them haphazardly into the briefcase, then sighed and looked Wolfe full in the face. "It does not have to end like this," he said.

Wolfe had to admire the audacity of the man. With the odds stacked against him, he was still trying to negotiate, and his refusal to admit defeat could only be marvelled at.

"Too late, Achmet," Wolfe spat the name like a curse.

"Then you will have to shoot because I am not being taken alive," he said, rising to his feet.

Wolfe lifted the revolver a few inches from the arms dealer's head and thumbed back the hammer. "I never had any intention of letting you live," he said.

In the few moments that Mansoor stared down the dark barrel of the gun, the realisation of his cold-blooded execution showed on his face. The devil and eternity were seconds away.

Salim burst through the doorway as Wolfe briefly turned and failed to see the desperate lunge from Mansoor's knife as it slashed across his ribs. His revolver exploded immediately as the arms dealer threw himself backwards, extinguishing the single light from the oil lantern. Salim yelled an obscenity and fired furiously where Mansoor had been, missing Wolfe by inches. It was Wolfe's turn to curse and his revolver fell from his hand as the impact of the knife blow maddened him in pain.

The briefcase hit Salim squarely in the face as Mansoor hurled himself from the darkness at the security guard framed in the doorway. Salim went backwards, collapsing to the decking as Mansoor collided with him. Wolfe staggered to his feet after a vain scramble to find his revolver. It was unbelievable but Mansoor was escaping again. Wolfe heard the man's foot-steps pounding away across the pier as he leapt over the groaning shape of Salim and then the unmistakable sound of an outboard motor being engaged. He ran towards the chattering engine clearing the end of the jetty.

The small boat was at least three metres away when Wolfe crashed down into it. The suddenness of the plunge rocked the tiny craft, as Mansoor turned round in disbelief groping again for the knife at his belt. Wolfe kicked the man full in the crotch and then grappled with the arms dealer, desperately holding onto his wrists as he head-butted the shrieking Moroccan into submission. Without warning the small boat turned over completely, trapping the struggling men underneath.

A wild suffocation seized Wolfe as the inky blackness closed over him yet he gripped the throat of his threshing enemy even harder, feeling his desperation in the struggle, time losing all meaning. The rushing noise in his head, the spuming bubbles and the increasing pressure on his chest, then the relaxing pleasure as he breathed inwards, submitting to the blackness around him.

\*

The police launch idled slowly to and fro across the entrance to the harbour as the morning sun tipped the waves in gold. The steel grappling hooks retrieved nothing and the search was becoming clearly useless as the current flowed steadily into the Atlantic Ocean. The patient figures of the airport security guards stared silently at the scene, busy with their own thoughts.

A limousine halted and a bandaged Salim saluted the airport controller.

Hirasch shaded his eyes towards the sunlight. "Found anything?"

Salim shook his head. "I think it's all over. We have searched all night. The chances of us finding anything else are pretty remote. Apart from a few bundles of money there is no trace."

Hirasch sniffed. "Then that is probably the end of Mansoor. He was an evil man but I have a feeling he was sorry for Suzanne Wolfe. He even managed to take the girl to Gibraltar under the noses of the police. We traced the fisherman who took them but Mansoor wasn't to know that she would be released if Wolfe had captured him."

"Yes, there is something very strange about it all," Salim added.

"And how about Wolfe?" the controller asked.

Salim managed a smile. "A tenacious bastard that one. He tried to strangle me as I pulled him from the water. I swear he was unconscious at the time."

"Where is he now?"

"Being stitched together I expect. He lost a lot of blood and was pretty weak when they carried him to the ambulance but that didn't stop him from yelling at me for bursting in when he had Mansoor cornered."

Hirasch turned to leave. "I will go to the hospital and see if there is anything we can do. Do you have any messages for him?"

The security man grinned, "Yes, tell him he didn't do too bad, for an Englishman."

The evening sun was yielding unexpected warmth and causing a saffron reflection from the sea, a unique natural phenomenon of the springtime in Tangier. Pausing to admire the phosphorescent glow in the luminous sky, Danielle felt a sense of wonder at the softness of the ribboned clouds.

She had returned home three weeks previously and recovered slowly from her injury, but the old pleasure normally experienced by homecoming had been strangely dulled. The girl had been welcomed and feted by her friends and yet there was an undeniable emptiness in her life. She suppressed the wave of melancholia as her eyes misted without reason.

That day she had met with her old confidante Ravel Boidoin at the French Embassy and had excused herself hurriedly, taking the busy route home through the Grande Socco. It was always the same, bustling, ringing with the sound of motor klaxons, the traffic in a frenzy of disarray and the shrewd street vendors cajoling and wheedling their goods into the baskets of thrifty customers. Najib, the snake charmer who had entertained on the same spot since Danielle's grandmother's day, gave her a solemn wink as she wandered through the Magreb Arch in the Kasbah towards home. A small street urchin watched her pass with a look of wide-eyed innocence, and started after her with a small flower, which he pressed shyly into her hand. She thanked him and placed the bloom high up in her dark hair, seeing instant pleasure in the smile of the youngster.

There was something unusual about this evening, a feeling of expectancy coming from the curious eyes watching her. Without realising, her footsteps quickened and as she reached the villa the girl opened the ornamental gate with an unusual feeling of awareness. Yousef, the old man who tended the garden, bowed as he always did, yet there was a decisiveness in the way he inclined his grey head. She climbed the short flight of stone steps in puzzlement and stared transfixed at the silver amulet dangling from the brass door handle. The hand of Fatima shimmered in the softening light. Its appearance confused her and, with growing nervousness, she pushed open the door, peering into the darkened interior. The room was empty and the disappearing sunlight was only just visible on the railed balcony. There was a movement, then silence again as the girl hovered towards the sound.

The sleeping man only stirred as Danielle took the flowered bouquet from the relaxed fingers, breathing in its fragrance. She sat quietly beside him until the saffron of the evening slowly surrendered to the night.